Robert Bruce

A Voice from the Australian Bush

Robert Bruce

A Voice from the Australian Bush

ISBN/EAN: 9783337312152

Printed in Europe, USA, Canada, Australia, Japan

Cover: Foto ©Andreas Hilbeck / pixelio.de

More available books at **www.hansebooks.com**

A VOICE

FROM THE

AUSTRALIAN BUSH.

BY

ROBERT BRUCE,

WALLELBERDINA, S.A.

WITH THREE PLATES.

ADELAIDE :

FREARSON & BRO., PRINTERS AND PUBLISHERS, KING WILLIAM-ST.

1877.

PREFACE.

HAVING, at different times of my life, so far forgotten myself as to perpetrate rhymes on various subjects, I, like others afflicted with the same incurable malady, became desirous that I should not be the only sufferer, so, inflicted a small edition on my friends, the people of South Australia ; and the critics of the said Province having been very merciful, (I was going to say *just* and merciful) and the public most easy to please, why, the book sold, and I (being reinforced by a friend who understands punctuation, and is a severe, though kindly critic) furbished up some of the old poems, and made some new ones, and I now offer the same to be properly cut up by the critics, if it will give them any satisfaction to do so ; and, thereafter to be perused with all sorts of sensations, by more unsophisticated readers who desire to see things described as they are, and to understand what they read.

As what is pleasant and nutritious pabulum to one, is poison to another, I have ranged from " the sublime to the ridiculous," so as to have a plum for all who investigate my pudding.

In justice to my critical friend, I must here observe that several pieces occupy pages in this book which he wished left out, but I think, if they draw off the venom from a crabbed critic or two, they will have served a good purpose, and I shall be recompensed accordingly.

R. BRUCE.

WALLELBERDINA,
   May 6th, 1877.

LIST OF PLATES.

No.   Page.

1.—THE LAST VOYAGE OF THE LONDON—*(Frontispiece.)*

2.—THE DINGO HUNT   82

3.—BURNING OF THE COSPATRICK   121

THE LAST VOYAGE OF THE LONDON.

List to that capstan song, and with me view
The gallant steamship, which her active crew
Haul from the crowded dock, whose gates, thrown wide,
Permit her egress to the Thames' dark tide.
Slowly she glides, her ev'ry motion scann'd
By crowds of gazers gather'd on the land ;
And by the harbour-master who, alert,
Can well his brief authority assert,
And order all—the ready tars obey
His short, sharp mandates, which brook no delay.
Out to mid-stream the good ship grandly glides ;
Swings with the tide, and there in safety rides.

Now, with colossal force, the prison'd steam
Drives the vast vessel o'er the deep, dark stream.
Proudly she moves, while from the crowded strand,
Loud cheers resound for her, and for her band
Of emigrants who, from the decks, reply
With fainter shouts and kerchiefs waved on high ;
And many tear-dimm'd eyes are strain'd to keep
In view some friend, who tempts the stormy deep ;
Buoy'd by the hope that, in that southern land,
Wealth may repay the labour of his hand ;
That smiling fields and new found friends, in part,
May fill the void occasion'd in his heart
By this rude sev'rance of those social ties
Which men hold lightly ; but perversely prize
When they are sunder'd by stern strokes of fate
That, all too often, vex this mortal state.

With steady skill the quartermaster steers
The ship down stream, amid the crowded tiers
Of merchantmen, whose lofty hamper shows
Like a dense forest with incumbent snows
Piled on its branches, for the wind-worn sails,
(Bleach'd by exposure to unnumber'd gales),
Now trimly folded by the gallant tars,
Gleam, like bright snow-wreaths, on the taper spars :
These, nicely-balanced on each lofty mast,
Full oft have bravely borne them to the blast.

Onwards she steams, while many a vessel's crew
Crowd to the sides the stately ship to view),—

B

Her size, her spars, her graceful lines they praise,
And tell, with confidence, the tale of days
Her trip will occupy ; but not one word
Of evil augury is to be heard,
For all that skill, and all that wealth can do,
Has been expended on the ship they view.
Well-found, well-mann'd, and with a master-mind
To guide her motions, waves or stormy wind
Against her prestige, and her perfect state,
Seem to weigh nothing in the scales of fate.
But men are blind ; and what may her befall
Is known to Him, and Him alone whose call
Can wake the hurricane, and with it heap,
In awful waves, the bosom of the deep.
Then on, brave ship ! and ye who in her sail
Trust, in your hearts, the Ruler of the gale.

Gravesend is gain'd—the engines stopp'd—and now
The anchor plunges from her lofty bow ;
While, from the deck where it in folds has lain,
Out through the hawse-pipe surges forth the chain ;
And o'er the waves loud rolls a sullen roar,
In growling thunder, to the distant shore.
Now to and fro the busy wherries glide,
Urged by strong oarsmen, o'er the brackish tide,
To bring more emigrants, or to convey
Some from the ship, who, e'er they sail away
(Perhaps for ever) from their native shore,
Take this last chance to visit it once more ;
For very dear, unto a Briton's heart,
Is England's soil when from it he must part.

The grimy stokers, down below, once more
Heap high the fuel, and the red flames roar
Within the furnaces, and quickly raise
The toiling giant of these modern days,
Which, bred from water, by consuming fires
Within its prison fuming fierce perspires,
Ready to drive, with vast untiring force,
The noble vessel on her trackless course.
Forth from her funnel floats, in volumes vast,
The rolling smoke upon the chilly blast,
Which, through the shrouds, with mournful moaning sighs,
As if sad spirits, with prophetic eyes,
Lament above that gallant craft, which they
Presage to Ocean as its destined prey !

The ship is clear'd—the anchor is aweigh,
And lingering friends no longer can delay
Their last farewell ; yet still, with wish to cheer,
They force the smile and check the rising tear ;
Exchange long clinging pressure of the hand,
Then gain their boats and row towards the land ;
Though still their eyes, fix'd on the vessel's deck,
Mark the lov'd face, till it becomes a speck
Soon lost to view, for 'neath full head of steam,
With hissing prow, the LONDON cleaves the stream,
Her broad red ensign gleaming darkly through
The smoky cloud, which almost hides from view
The long black hull ; tho' still distinct and clear,
Above it shows her taut and lofty gear.
That, too, with distance, disappears, and then
Naught, save the smoke, remains to gazer's ken.

The Nore is reach'd, but night is falling fast ;
And, from the Downs, the bitter, biting blast
Sweeps thro' the rigging ; while the seamen's eyes
Mark the wild scud that 'neath the black clouds flies,
Like evil harbinger of angry strife,
Which, in the elements, will soon be rife,
And warning gives to those who, on the deep,
'Midst rocks and shoals, their anxious vigils keep.
And so the captain, versed in nature's signs,
All thought of progress, for the time, resigns ;
At least till Phœbus, o'er the narrow sea
Shall shed his light, or winds become more free.

His will express'd the skilful pilot hears,
And for safe anchorage, the vessel steers ;
While toiling engines their vast labours stay,
And sullen rest, when, with fast failing way,
The ship sweeps on till, at a given word,
A rattling roar and heavy plunge are heard,
And once again amid the waves, which glide
With fretful splash along her dark strong side,
She anchor'd lies ; while, in a fleecy cloud,
The steam pours forth with clamours fierce and loud,
At once, with liberty, to lose its might,
And with the mists to swell the dews of night.

Four bells are struck, the evening's watch is set,
While, in the cabin, passengers have met
At the long tables, tempting cheer to try,
Which in profusion gladdens ev'ry eye ;

For, 'neath the swinging lamps' soft mellow light,
Bright comfort reigns, and scares the dreary night.

When now the voyagers retire to rest,
What novel fancies agitate each breast!
For all is strange, and, though they feel no fear,
Strange uncouth noises from outside they hear—
The wind's shrill whistle thro' each pendant block ;
And, 'gainst the side, the constant splashing shock
Of dashing waves, which, fast succeeding, roll
O'er deep, dark channel and o'er sandy shoal ;
While sounding strokes, upon the ship's large bell,
The flight of time unto the wakeful tell ;
And on the deck, above their heads, with slow
And measured tread, parading to and fro,
The watch is heard, whose duty 'tis to keep
A keen look-out upon the trackless deep—
To note huge dusky forms come driving past,
With spreading sails before the chilly blast.
Full in their front a lantern, gleaming bright,
Marks their advance, while phosphorescent light
Glimmers like glowworms 'mid the yeasty flakes
Of dancing foam which gather in their wakes.
Swiftly they dash ! For *them* the wind is free,
Their port near gain'd ; the fatal, stormy sea,
Its rocks and shoals, its fierce tornado blast,
And wild lee shores are now but dangers past.
Blithe are their crews, and ready to obey
The pilot's orders ; for another day
Of servitude their slavish duty ends ;
Then hey ! for home ! for sweethearts, wives, and friends !

The Sabbath dawns—the winter's sun once more,
With feeble beams, illumines sea and shore ;
But still, adverse, above the foam-fleck'd waves
The gale sweeps on, and through the rigging raves.
Still, overhead, the low scud swiftly flies,
And all betoken, to a seaman's eyes,
A time of trouble, with dread dangers fraught,
To those who needs must leave their friendly port.
The adverse signs the careful pilot notes,
And, with regret, another day devotes
To dull delay ; then, with the new-born year,
He will to sea his gallant vessel steer.
But now, with cable straining to the tide,
And England's banner floating free and wide
From her high peak, the London, in her might,
Anchor'd remains, to all a noble sight.

The hours glide by—night falls—is past—and now,
With early dawn, the anchor at her bow
Is safely catted ; and, with prow of speed,
She dashes on like some high-mettled steed
That needs no spur, but, with collected force,
Champs his steel bit, and swiftly takes the course ;
So, like a thing of life, she seems to glide,
And, all majestic, cleaves the flashing tide.
Ramsgate and Margate fast recede from view,
Then Dover's famous cliff, of chalky hue,
(With its green brow, and ancient castle's walls),
Which long has braved stern time and gusty squalls.
Next, Goodwin Sands, (so oft the greedy grave
Of gallant vessels and their seamen brave),
Are safely passed ; and, o'er the dark green tide,
The Isle of Wight looms grandly in its pride,
While glancing sails of vessels homeward bound
Hover, like sea birds, o'er the waves around.
But soon again the fast-increasing wind
With fury raves, and drives the ship to find
Shelter in famed St. Helen's Roads till free
It should become, and less disturb'd the sea.

Now Night on ling'ring pinions takes her flight,
When with the early, cold grey morning light
They weigh the anchor, and the ship, again,
Urged by her engines, ploughs the restless main.
The curling billows seem to own her sway,
While 'neath her bows, engaged in glancing play,
The porpoises before her swiftly glide,
And, in succession, leap above the tide
Close to the prow ; confusedly they dash,
The sparkling waters from their bodies flash.
Amused, the passengers their antics view,
But, to the hardy, weather-beaten crew,
Their sprightly gambols tell a certain tale
Of rising waves, and fast increasing gale.

Onward she glides, and soon the Needle Rocks,
Which have, for ages, braved the tempests' shocks,
Are safely passed, and to the open main
The London steams, but to be foiled again ;
For, toiling hard, thro' adverse seas she ploughs,
Which, in fierce billows, thunder at her bows.
Wild wails the wind amongst the rigging high,
While with hoarse cries the wheeling seagulls fly
Toward the land, where now, with ceaseless roar,
The boiling breakers whiten all the shore.

The pilot, warned by all these portents drear,
Now for Spithead designs the ship to steer.
She slowly wears, then, like a startled steed,
Upon her course flies with redoubled speed.
The wind, now free, seems shorn of half its might,
The crested waves scarce catch her in her flight.
From side to side her taper spars incline,
With graceful sweep, toward the flashing brine ;
While far astern, in long extended line,
White seething foam-flakes on the waters shine.
Swiftly the outlines of the coast appear
To change in form—cliffs rise and disappear ;
For, urg'd to speed by wedded steam and sail,
She skims the waves, and near outstrips the gale.

When now the sunset gun upon the shore
Sends pealing forth its booming sullen roar,
The London gains the harbour, where the pride
Of England's fleets has long adorn'd the tide ;
But night advancing spreads her mantle o'er
The lofty shipping and the busy shore ;
Then soon again the London on the deep
Is safely moor'd, and those within her sleep.

When two dull, cheerless winter-days are fled,
And Phœbus' beams again are coldly shed,
Forth steams the vessel, bound once more to fight
With wind's wild fury, and with ocean's might.
Onward all day and through the night she flies,
Till morn's grey twilight fills the eastern skies ;
Then through the fog, which curling floats around,
Dimly appears the mouth of Plymouth Sound ;
While a trim cutter, dashing o'er the sea,
Comes sweeping out, and brings to on her lee,
Where, bounding gaily on the billows high,
She seems perfection to a seaman's eye.
Her lofty sails gleam in the morning light,
Her copper sheathing glitters red and bright ;
Broad is her beam, a press of sail to stand
When, on a wind, she beats out from the land—
Knife-like her bows to cleave the heaving brine,
Her long, straight floor all steeply doth incline
Toward the bends, so that no angle may
Gather dead water, and impede her way.
Her sharp, clean run allows the parted tide
Beneath her quarters easily to glide,
And meet again almost devoid of spray,

As when lithe dolphins thro' the ocean play,
Urged by broad tails in curving lines they glide,
And leave no ripple in the azure tide.

Now from the davits at her stern behold
A dingey launch'd, mann'd by two pilots bold.
Their brawny arms the bending paddles ply ;
Through driving spray the shallop seems to fly !
Now, in the trough—now, on the summit green
Of some huge billow is the dingey seen.
But ah ! a thrill of pain invades each breast,
For a vast wave, with overhanging crest,
Whirls the light boat high on its heaving side,
Then overturns it in the raging tide !
" Lower the lifeboat !" Captain Martin cries.
Swift to the call each eager seaman flies !
With nimble hands the gear they overhaul,
The sheaves revolve—they ease away each fall,
Then ship their oars of tough and pliant ash,
The rowlocks rattle, and the oar-blades flash.
" Pull ! with a will !" the ardent steersman cries,
The strong ash buckles, and the lifeboat flies !
But all too slow to save one seaman brave ;
The raging sea must now become his grave !
Swift through his brain, with speed of lightning, gleam
The past and present like a vivid dream.
One cry he gives for mercy on his soul—
One thought to home—and then the billows roll,
With sullen fury, o'er that manly form,
Which oft has braved them in the fiercest storm ;
Invading torrents force its spirit's flight,
And seal its senses in an endless night.

But on, brave fellows ! if ye yet would save
A brother seaman from a wat'ry grave ;
For still the waves he battles for his life,
Nor yields to fear in the unequal strife.
A floating oar tenaciously he grasps ;
The brine near chokes him when for breath he gasps,
As wave on wave o'er him with fury pour,
While in his ears resounds their angry roar.
The driving spray stings like a knotted scourge,
The greedy waters round him fiercely surge ;
Cold's icy fingers grapple at his heart,
And Death, above him, seems to poise his dart.

Courage ! brave pilot ! for one moment more,
With stern resolve, clutch fast that buoyant oar !

For see, high on the fast advancing wave
The lifeboat flies to save thee from the grave.
Bowman, prepare his sinking form to seize ;
Oarsmen, your labours for one moment ease ;
Steersman, be skilful, and be cool withal,
For one false move, e'en yet, would ruin all ;
Back-water, hard ! for now you almost graze
The worn-out man, whom brawny arms soon raise
From out the deep, and tenderly bestow
Beneath the thwarts, upon the floor below.
Then, with faint hope, the other man to save,
They row around, and peer into each wave ;
But vain their search ; his troubles now are pass'd—
His grave, the deep ! his dirge, the howling blast !

But when all fruitless would be longer stay,
The gallant tars reluctantly obey
Their captain's signal to return on board
With him, whose life they hardly have restored,
Whom now they question thus about the dead :—
" Will helpless orphans want for daily bread ?
" Will loving wife list for *his* step in vain,
" Who ne'er shall cheer her longing sight again ?
" Had he a mother ? or an aged sire ?
" His name ? his age ? his country ?" they enquire.
To which the rescued man replies.   But now
The London's side, with long-extended row
Of anxious faces peering o'er the rail,
Looms overhead, and screens them from the gale.
Beneath the falls once more they quickly glide,
And nimble seamen scramble up the side,
Save those who hook the tackles, and prepare
The boat to steady as she mounts in air,
For steam, resistless, gives the needful strain,
And to the davits soon she swings again.

With hollow splash the screw the water spurns,
Which, white with foam, around her rudder churns ;
Her hissing prow points in toward the land,
Which, right before her, parts on either hand,
Leaving a passage for the sea's salt tide
To enter in, and 'midst tall hills to hide ;
While, from the shore, toward the south, appears
A massive pier, the work of many years ;
Built of huge stones, and based on solid rocks,
It bears, unshaken, Ocean's fiercest shocks.
In clouds of foam the baffled waves recoil,

And, at its base, in whirling eddies boil.
High on its end a lighthouse rears its form,
To guide the seaman, flying from the storm,
To the safe anchorage where often meet,
In peaceful times, the ships of England's fleet.
And thither now the London holds her way
With graceful sweep, and anchors in the bay.

Swiftly toward the stately steamer's side
The restless shore boats skim across the tide,
To bring those passengers who view'd with dread
The channel passage, with fell dangers spread,
When wint'ry gales with sullen fury roar,
And breakers thunder on the wild lee shore ;
And those who, loth to leave their friends, delay
The painful parting to the latest day.

But see ! " Blue Peter " flies—more coals are stored—
The ship is clear'd—the captain comes on board,
And all is ready (fatal Friday pass'd)
To brave once more the billow and the blast.

Now Phœbus setting, his brief duty ends,
And dusky night o'er all the scene descends,
Blotting the battery upon the height,
The busy dockyard, and the beach from sight ;
While, in their stead, unnumber'd lights appear
Along the shore, and on the shipping near,
Whose constant flames like glowing planets shine,
Their beams reflecting on the heaving brine ;
While, brighter far than other lights around,
The sea-wall beacon flashes o'er the Sound,
A certain guide unto those seamen's sight
Who seek to gain, or leave, the port by night.

Meanwhile within the London's cabins shine
The swinging lamps in long extended line
Above the passengers, now met around
The social board, with smiling plenty crown'd.
On snowy cloths the varied dishes steam,
And sparkling wines in polish'd crystal gleam ;
Comfort and elegance combine to cheer
The outward bound, and banish thoughts of fear.
Onward she steams, and in her rigging raves
The rising blast ; while huge white-crested waves
Beat at her bows as if to stop her way—
She ploughs thro' all 'mid show'rs of sparkling spray.

Now from the vision of the favour'd few
Exempt from sickness, fast recedes from view
The cloud-like streak—last glimpse of England's shore,
That much-lov'd land they ne'er may visit more !
Anon, 'tis lost, for Ocean's wide expanse,
Dotted with sails, is all that meets the glance ;
While, on the forecastle, the crew begin
To get the ponderous, crooked anchors in,
So that the hawsepipes may be plugg'd to stay
The hurtful ingress of the brine and spray.
Spare spars are lash'd, the litter of the port
Is quickly clear'd, and ropes are all haul'd taut ;
Then ends are coil'd upon the pins around,
And the brave ship is fairly outward bound.

The day wanes quickly, and the winter's night
In turn is banish'd by the God of light,
And Sabbath dawns, but not in peace, for o'er
The watr'y waste, wind's gusty forces roar ;
And, urged by these, huge billows swelling rise,
Like foam-crown'd giants, to insult the skies,
Or on the ship (which onward hardly ploughs)
To fiercely bound, and break above her bows ;
Or aft the mainmast, with dread shock and din,
O'er futile bulwarks rush impetuous in.

Woolley and Draper, pious men and true,—
Of sects diverse, but with one end in view,—
Expound the Word to passengers and crew ;
And, void of bigotry, unite to keep
The Sabbath sacred on the mighty deep.
With equal fervour either good man glows,
And each with love and kindness overflows.
No paltry envy lurks within their hearts,
They preach their faith, and act true Christians' parts.

Another night has slowly passed away,
And Monday dawns, a wild and stormy day,—
For mountain-waves, impell'd by raging blast,
Come rushing on before each other fast
Against the ship, and o'er her plunging bow,
And rolling waist, in heavy masses flow ;
Though still the voyagers, secure and warm
Within their cabins, do but hear the storm ;
And the bold sailors very little reck
The wet discomfort of the slipp'ry deck.

To stop the engines Martin gives command ;
And in the rigging swarms a nimble band
Of gallant tars to loose each trim-stow'd sail,
Which, sheeted home, stands stiffly to the gale.
With lessen'd motion soon the ship careers,
But from her course a spreading angle steers,
While the vex'd passengers, confined below,
Suffer from landsmen's ever-dreaded foe.
Sick near to death, small pity do they find ;
The stewards deaf !—their loving friends inclin'd
To leave their patients to imagin'd care,
And mount the poop to breathe the bracing air.

The noontide past, the gale, with lessen'd force,
Sweeps o'er the ocean in its viewless course ;
And though the waves are monstrous as before,
Their foam-crown'd heads break with diminish'd roar ;
While warm, though scatter'd, sunbeams fleeting past,
A cheerful glint upon the waters cast ;
And Hope, to sanguine bosoms, now foretells
A pleasant passage o'er the ocean's swells.

Now Sol sinks coldly in the cheerless west,
And darksome Night broods o'er each billow's crest ;
Yet, like a phantom thing with gleaming eyes,
The ship glides on beneath the gloomy skies,
Until, compell'd before Aurora's face,
The sullen power withdraws with creeping pace ;
When with fresh fury roars the angry blast,
And rolling waves, from ocean's surface cast
Their mighty forms, whence flies, like winter rain,
The biting spray across the troubled main.
Yet onward still, with black and gleaming bows,
The gallant London thro' their masses ploughs,
Whose foam-crown'd crests, like headlong torrents, dash
Upon her deck with never ceasing splash,
Then, through the scuppers, forceful spout again,
In briny torrents, to the parent main.

But now a billow, of gigantic size,
Full on the ship like some huge monster flies,
And, all resistless, fiercely rends away
A buoyant lifeboat, to its might a prey,
This, with sad hearts the tempest-beaten crew
Watch, till astern it disappears from view.
But soon, alas, fresh dangers, thick and fast,
Come crowding on, each greater than the last ;

For as " two bells " proclaim Time's steady flight,
The ship is hoisted to a giddy height ;
Then headlong down into the trough she dives,
And in the sea her flying-jibboom drives.
Above her head the whirling waters fly,
While, high in air, her stern invades the sky.
As stricken whale, with tail erected, darts
To 'scape its foes, and ease its burning smarts
(Down, down it dives ! then seeks again the air,
Death-dealing lance-thrusts helplessly to bear),
So that vast vessel, in that awful gale,
Impetuous plunges, and the boldest quail ;
For with a roar the raging flood assails
Her buried head, and tears away its sails ;
Masts, yards, and cordage in one ruin lie
About the deck, or down to leeward fly ;
Though still aloft, the huge fore-topmast swings
Held by its rigging, while beside it hangs,
The wrench'd-off royalmast, which joins the foe,
Sweeps with the ship, and deals out blow on blow.
The shatter'd jibboom, shorn of taper sail,
Drags in the water and assists the gale,
While the main-royalmast is also torn
From its high stand, and of its hamper shorn.
Thus, by one stroke of Ocean's angry tide,
The ship drives on despoil'd of half her pride.

But, all undaunted, strive her hardy crew
The trailing wreckage from the ship to hew ;
Yet, fruitlessly, unnumber'd strokes they try,
From iron ropes their axes glancing fly ;
For like tough canes that bow before the blast
To rise directly its full force has pass'd,
They hang in loops, and, swinging to and fro,
Evade the edge, and disappoint each blow ;
While wave on wave, upon her cumber'd deck,
Incessant pour, and seem to claim the wreck ;
With rage increasing raves the awful storm
As night descends, and veils each seaman's form.

Slowly drag on the dreary hours of night,
And those below begin to yield to fright ;
And prayers arise from many who, till now,
Had quite forgot their stubborn knees to bow.
For, though the lamps still brightly burn within,
Loudly resounds the tempest's dreadful din ;
While to and fro upon the slipp'ry deck

The waters dash, suggesting thoughts of wreck—
Of black despair—of painful death—and *then*
Of prayer to God—for thus it is with men !—
They eat, they drink, they sleep while all is well,
Of heaven they think not, and they fear not hell !
But danger comes—destruction hovers near—
Then, grov'ling low, they rave a useless prayer !

But not so all ; some trustful spirits now,
With steady faith, before their Maker bow,
Or strive to cheer the sinking hearts of those
Whose terror points unnumber'd coming woes ;
Whose ears drink in and magnify each sound ;
Who see destruction hov'ring all around ;
In vain regret, who moaning pass the night,
And, all-impatient, wait for morning light.

Meanwhile the captain, true as temper'd steel,
Seeks not repose, but, station'd at the wheel,
Scans his ship's course, exposed to every blast
That sweeps the sea, and bows each groaning mast.
Out in the darkness, with keen, anxious sight,
He looks for squalls of more than common might,
Or giant seas which, high above the rest,
Come rolling down with fiercely foaming crest ;
Marks with what force they fall upon the deck,
Cumber'd with casks, with coals, and broken wreck ;
And, in his mind, weighs all the chances o'er
Of ever reaching far Australia's shore.
Shall he keep on, and dare the awful force
Of wind and wave which now oppose his course ?
Or shall he turn and seek to make his way
Back to the port where she so lately lay,
There to repair all damages, and wait
Till winds and waves their fury should abate ?

To this last view his notions most incline ;
He calls brave Harris, that he may combine
The judgment of his second with his own ;
And thus begins, with low and anxious tone :—
" You see the state our noble craft is in ;
" You hear the tempest's fast increasing din ;
" You see those seas which, with increasing roar,
" Upon our decks their mighty volumes pour ;
" Say, then, shall we the ocean still engage,
" And struggle on against its awful rage ?
" Or turn again, and, homeward-bound once more,

" Seek some safe harbour by Old England's shore,
" Where our lost spars may be with speed replaced,
" And all the damage of the storm effaced ?"

The careful seaman in his mind revolves
Each chance and danger either course involves,
Which, quickly done, he with his chief agrees
That it were wise to leave the angry seas
For some safe port, where they might renovate
Their crippled spars, and for fair weather wait.
But, e'er they try to wear the ship, they go
To scan the chart, and work her course, below,
With nicest care—her speed for days now past—
Likewise her course, and leeway from it lost.
This figured up, and marked upon the map,
They both consider (maugre fresh mishap)
In Plymouth Sound, before two days are o'er,
Their noble craft shall safely ride once more.

Now, as " six bells " send forth their measured sound
Into the tumult rioting around,
To raise full steam the captain gives command.
The sooty stokers, in a willing band,
With iron rakes turn the caked cinders o'er,
And useless refuse from each furnace draw,
Then heap fresh coals, until the blinding heat
Flies fiercely forth, and urges swift retreat.
The doors are slamm'd upon the rising blaze,
Which, with loud crackle, on the fuel plays ;
High mounts the steam, and, with Titanic sway,
Propels the London on her storm-vex'd way.

Sharply the helmsmen whirl the polish'd wheel ;
The ship sweeps round with heavy pitch and reel ;
While, flutt'ring fiercely in the raging blast,
Her mizen-staysails rise from mast to mast.
Loud o'er the din the seamen's cries resound,
As the huge yards come sweeping slowly round
To meet the wind, which, from the icy north,
Rushes along, terrific in its wrath,
Across her path, as once more, bound for home,
The vessel staggers in a sea of foam.

Now, o'er the waves which heap the troubled main,
The young day dawns in sullen gloom again ;
While the fierce gale, with still increasing wrath,
Assails the London on her fated path.

But though her hamper is in partial wreck,
And waves enormous roll upon her deck,
Her hull, yet proof against the forceful tide,
Contains no water in its dark inside.
Still unimpair'd, and shining to the view,
Her willing engines swiftly whirl the screw ;
Onward she drives, while in her rigging swarm
The nimble seamen, careless of the storm,
With axe and knife intent to cut away
All useless wreck, or hamper slack to stay.
Seamen and officers alike engage
To make all snug despite the tempest's rage ;
Then set the staysails to each lofty mast,
Now made secure to stand against the blast.

Meanwhile, o'erhead, the driving clouds divide,
And scatter'd sunbeams gild the steamer's side ;
While on the poop, with instrument in hand,
The gallant Harris and his chieftain stand,
And through stain'd lenses note the sun's slow race,
Till of his course he gains the highest place,
Which makes the noon ; they tell the time and go
Down the companion to the deck below
To certify their place upon the deep,
And work the course their vessel now must keep,
To gain their port, full seventy leagues away ;
For, labouring in Biscay's dreaded bay,
The London tosses in a cloud of spray.

As evening falls the wind, increasing still,
Howls, as if urged by fell demoniac will !
While awful waves their baleful forms uprear,
And like dread Genii of the storm appear,
From out the gloom, in never ceasing throng,
They seem to glide, then, ruthless, rush along
Toward the ship, which steering N.N. East,
Still struggles on like some poor hunted beast,
Which, spent with toil, betakes it to the flood,
When hounds dash after, thirsting for its blood :—
Swimming around they glory in its pangs,
And rend its flesh with sharp, white, tearing fangs.—
So, girt with waves which rave in wrath around,
The ship drives on, to sure destruction bound.

And now black Night its darkest robe extends
O'er all the scene, and sky with ocean blends
In one dread chaos, whence, with wild shrill wail,

The squalls terrific still the ship assail,
Which, under staysails, wallows in the sea,
While fear-struck passengers bow low the knee,
And mutter prayers, the while they scarcely know
What words they are which from their white lips flow.
But pious Draper, in his trumpet tones,
Bids them to cease their troubled tears and moans,
Exhorting all in humble faith to fly
To Him who looks with ever-watchful eye
Upon His servants, and, with mighty arm,
Can, if He will it, save from every harm.

Thus they below ; while overhead the crew,
With doubts increasing, their position view ;
For now two staysails, with a deaden'd roar,
Burst from their bolt-ropes, and are seen no more.
In whirling shreds to leeward they are blown ;
The masts relieved, reel backward with a groan ;
While on her deck the raging billows beat,
And the drench'd crew to shelter'd nooks retreat
To 'scape the bitter blast and waves, which fly
O'er every part, and leave no corner dry.

But now a billow, vaster than the rest,
With curling head, and fiercely foaming crest,
Swoops on two boats stow'd on the starboard side,
And in small fragments strews them on the tide.
A cutter that, a buoyant lifeboat this,
Their loss adds largely to the great distress.
But for regret no time the storm allows,
Which ev'ry instant to fresh fury grows,
Till at " two bells," in the first watch of night,
The hurricane is nearly at its height ;
For in vast chasms is the ocean riven,
And to their depths the hapless ship is driven,
Involv'd in foam which gleams with ghastly light,
And swells the horror of the awful night ;
Then upward heav'd, upon stupendous wave,
As if ejected from a yawning grave,
She meets the blast that, with a deaf'ning roar,
Rends all her sails, and seems to howl for more.

Meanwhile brave Martin, to his duty true,
With great example animates the crew.
Now here—now there—his manly accents sound
O'er strife of elements which roar around ;
And, when the sails are from the vessel torn,

By telegraph his will below is borne
To loose the might of fuming steam again,
And with its aid to stem the wind-scourg'd main.
Onwards she drives, but soon remorseless fate
Hurls fresh disasters of a crushing weight
On the doom'd ship which, girt with terrors round,
Battles the billows of the vast profound.

For as five strokes upon the ship's large bell
The march of time proclaim with measured swell,
O'er the port gangway, with prodigious weight,
A huge wave falls, and seals the vessel's fate !
For thro' the engine hatch of teak and brass,
With iron gratings o'er its thick plate glass,
The waters burst with terrifying crash,
And thro' the breech resistless torrents dash,
Hurling two seaman to the lower deck,
Where waves, usurping, herald coming wreck ;
While, of the late strong hatch, now naught remains
Save splinter'd wood, bent bars, and shatter'd panes !
For, as an avalanche, down Alpine steeps
From icy glacier, with fell fury sweeps,
Trees, rocks, and chalets, in one ruin hurl'd,
Are borne before it to the lower world,
Grim desolation marks it as it flies,
And sullen thunders shake the earth and skies,—
So, with like fury, fell that sea on board,
Burst in the hatch, and thro' the chasm roar'd.

Swift to the place the mate and captain fly,
And shout for help—the ready crew reply.
With spars and sails the torrent they would stay !
The sea sweeps each impediment away !
Tarpaulins, blankets, mattrasses they bring,
And booms and ladders o'er the opening fling !
Yet 'tis in vain such barricades they heap,
For, all implacable, the raging deep
Its billows hurls, as if in scorn of those
Poor puny mortals who its might oppose.
They strive in vain ! the waters bear away
Their frail devices to retard its way.
Men, sails, and spars it dashes to and fro,
And, thro' the rift, descends in tons below.

Brave Jones and Greenhill by their engines stand,
While stokers huddle in a frighten'd band,
Watching the waters, with dilated eyes,

c

As the cold waves around their bodies rise ;
While, in their ears, resounds the hollow roar
Of mighty seas which down the hatchway pour.

Meanwhile, on deck, brave Martin and his crew
Do all that merely mortal men can do.
Some work the pumps—the passengers assist ;
Heroic Brooke and Woolley swell the list ;
With soft white hands, but with undaunted hearts,
Through that dread night they act strong heroes' parts,
And, by example, greatly animate
The faint of heart to fight against the fate
That clamours for them from the howling gale,
And from each sea which dashes o'er the rail.

Now, as the hours to midnight near approach,
The rising waters on the fires encroach.
First hiss the bars ; and, in a moment more,
The vanquish'd flames expire with splutt'ring roar.
Thick, noisome vapours all below assail,
And gallant Greenhill must convey the tale,
Fraught with distress, to his commander, who,
Calm and collected, animates the crew
To vast exertions, when their worn-out frames,
And sinking hearts for rest put forth their claims.
True to his trust he labours here and there,
All things directs, and battles with despair !

With unmov'd face heroic Martin hears
The dreadful news, that Greenhill to him bears ;
Of fires put out—of engines which no more
Will pump the ship, or urge her to the shore.
He thinks a moment ; then, unto his band
Of British seamen, give the loud command
To loose the huge maintopsail ; at the word
That splendid crew, by danger undeterr'd,
Scale the bleak rigging and, despite the gale,
Undo the buntlines, and set free the sail,
Which flutters fiercely in the passing squall,
As brawny arms upon its halyard haul.
Up the smooth mast the huge yard slowly creeps—
Hoarse is the cry that time for haulage keeps ;
But soon the rope yields nothing to the hands,
And, to the blast, the sail like armour stands.
It stands not long, for, with a dread report—
As when a shell, exploding in a fort,
Ignites the magazine, and hurls on high

The blazing ruins to the startled sky—
It bursts in twain ! then, in long ragged shreds,
Streams on the gale above the seamen's heads,
Who, for an instant, their endeavours stay,
And, breathless, watch it as it flies away
Into the darkness of the murky night ;
Then turn, once more, to wage unequal fight
With raging ocean, which but mocks their pain,
And seems to rave and surge with deep disdain.
Well may the captain say, amidst his cares,
" My gallant fellows, we may say our prayers !"
For, through the hatchway, wave succeeding wave
Resistless pours, and sinks her in her grave.

'Tis twelve o'clock—of night the solemn noon—
And all who can meet in the large saloon
To pray to Him who now alone hath power
To show them mercy in this dreadful hour,
And save their lives, if such should be His will,
For, to the waves, He sayeth, " Peace, be still !"
And they obey Him ; who of old hath said,
" Have faith in Me, and be ye not afraid."
Also to those, by pain and grief oppress'd,
" Come unto Me, and I will give you rest."
To Him they pray ; while Draper's accents sound
Like words of life to those who kneel around.
Strong in his faith, by trouble undismay'd,
He sees, past Death, bright Paradise display'd,
With gates wide open to receive the band
He fain would pilot to that better land,
Where death is not, and where no pain or strife
Can enter in to mar Eternal Life.

Oh ! faith most wonderful ! to thee is given
To lift from terror to glad thoughts of heaven
The souls of men ; though dreadful death be near,
They who the words of consolation hear,
Forget their anguish of despair, and find
A peaceful calm pervading every mind.
Scales seem to fall from off their eyes—they see
A parted passage through the raging sea
To peace for ever ! now, no more they hear
The ocean's roar with sickly qualms of fear,
But calmly wait their near approaching fate,
And humbly hope a bright eternal state.

These thus employed ; upon the sea-drench'd deck,
The seamen toil to save the sinking wreck.

Nerv'd by despair they work the pumps in vain,
The inside waters on them swiftly gain.
Still, on the hatchway, gallant fellows strive
To fasten sails, which briny torrents drive
Down through the aperture, while to and fro
Themselves are driven by the ebb and flow
Of the vast seas, which breaking o'er the rail,
Relentlessly the weary men assail.—
So shaggy wolves, on Russia's dreary plains,
Made bold and fierce by hunger's gnawing pains,
With dismal howls some traveller attack ;
His madden'd horses foam along the track ;
In vain the driver his red scourge applies,
Death in his soul, and horror in his eyes,
They can no more, for, closing all around,
The brutes dash in and drag them to the ground ;
Then awful cries of agony ascend,
As countless fangs the hapless victims rend ;
Wolves heaped on wolves above their bodies rise,
And fiercely wrangle for the bloody prize !—
So raging waves around the London rave,
To wreck destruction on her seamen brave.

Now, from the noontide of that fatal night,
Into the past, four hours have wing'd their flight,
When a huge sea, with overwhelming force,
Thro' the poop windows takes its ruthless course,
Driving the shutters of the dead lights back,
And spreading ruin on its onward track.
Tons of salt water thro' the cabins flow,
And penetrate unto the decks below,
Flooding the place where Draper still consoles,
And preaches mercy to repentant souls.
" Father," he prays, " may those who round me bow
" In deed and truth become converted now,
" And humbly bend beneath Thy chastening rod,
" Nor dread Thy call, ' prepare to meet thy God !'
" Faith over fear the victory has won,—
" Father,' we answer—' Lord, Thy will be done !' "

Meanwhile the carpenter, the ports to bar,
Shores up the shutters with a strong spare spar,
The which, sustain'd by main deck post, may foil
The ocean's fury for a little while.
A brief success ! for, in the engine room,
The waters rise, and hurry on her doom.
Deeper she sinks, and soon the sea once more

Drives in the ports, despite the strutting shore ;
Then hurls its billows, wave on wave, within,
With tenfold fury, and with splashing din.

But as brave soldiers, in a fortress pent,
Beset by foes upon their death intent,
Still, with stern valour, fight for fame and life,
And falter not in the ensanguin'd strife ;
So, with like brave bravery, the seamen toil
Amid the waves which round them surge and boil ;
Prompt to obey their officers' commands,
They struggle on in two unflinching bands.
One, with the captain, strives, with efforts vast,
To bar the hatch, courageous to the last ;
But all their struggles are of no avail,
Their best devices, and their labours fail.
For the dread cohorts of the ocean leap
Into the hold, to swell the volumes deep
Of fatal floods, which in it darkly flow,
Forcing their prey to wreck-strewn shades below ;
And the brave captain owns with bitter pain
No cheering hope can in his breast remain.

But still he cries (when he regains the deck)
To those who would the deadly leakage check,
" Put down your buckets, men, and strive, with me,
" To bar the hatchway to the raging sea ;
" Which, could we do, perhaps we yet may save
" Ourselves and vessel from an ocean's grave."
They answer to his call ! again ! again !
Unheeding hunger, weariness, and pain.
With valiant hearts strive hard, but strive in vain ;
For the wild waves their labours all confound,
Beating their bodies on the wreck around ;
Death, for his victims, with impatience craves,
Shrieks in the blast, and rides the rolling waves.

Thus they.   The others work the pumps and bale,
With half-nude forms exposed to biting gale.
Woolley and Wilson, Grant, and others toil
To wrest from ocean its expected spoil.
There too is Brooke, who, on the mimic stage,
Has oft affected Hope, Fear, Joy, and Rage ;
But now, all fearless on the stage of life,
No weakness shows amid the tempest's strife
Which round him roars.   He sees huge waves descend
Upon the ship, as if at once to end

The painful struggle ; sees the sails all torn
In ragged shreds, and on the tempest borne ;
Sees fellow-shipmates driven o'er the side
To meet their death beneath the cruel tide ;
And knows the ship (now brimful of her foe)
May, any instant, to the bottom go ;
Yet, with brave heart, and mighty, iron will,
Remains undaunted and collected still.

With naked feet and head to tempest bare,
He seems all present, aiding here and there ;
Now from the cabin striving hard to bale
The rising floods which threat its inmates pale ;
Then at the pumps is he a host indeed
To give relief to those who rest most need.
He seeks no rest, but still toils bravely on,
Till all may see that no more can be done ;
Then stands aside ; and soon his musing brain
Rolls back the tide of his past life again ;
His home, his friends, his joys and troubles past,
Throng to its call, before him thick and fast ;
His happy childhood, his maturer years,
Triumphs—reverses—mingled hopes and fears
By turns excite th' emotions of his heart,
But, from his eyes, can cause no tears to start.
So hours drag on ; and still he silent stands,
His thoughtful visage resting on his hands,
As, leaning o'er the half companion door,
He views the scene, and hears the tempest roar,
Calmly awaiting till his soul shall be,
By rushing waters, from his frame set free ;
And in his last grand character appears—
A man superior to human fears !
Then ye, who honour valour good and true,
Weep, as ye bid heroic Brooke adieu !

Now, once again, unto their longing eyes,
The dawn gleams coldly from the eastern skies,
But brings no comfort, on its wings of light,
To scare the terrors of the bygone night.
For, like foul vultures flocking to the slain
On fatal desert or ensanguin'd plain,
Dangers unnumber'd harpy-wing'd appear,
Dread harbingers of dissolution near ;
And hover round, the last faint hope to scare
From human hearts, fast yielding to despair.
For in the sea, now level with the deck,

Labours the ship, a helpless, sinking wreck ;
Waves rolling o'er her in their ruthless course,
As, in a battle, rush the charging horse !
Full of dark seething brine ; she scarcely floats ;
And now 'tis death ! or rescue by the boats !

Vain hope, indeed ! for four alone remain,—
The rest are swallow'd in the raging main ;
But these are plugg'd, and soon a scanty load
Of bread and water in their depths bestow'd.
Then, first the starboard pinnace they design
To heave aloft, and to the sea consign.
This, built of iron, will with safety bear
Full fifty men, if launch'd with skill and care.
Six seamen enter as the rail she leaves,
And swings above the angry leaping waves,
Towards which she glides, but far too swiftly, for
The foaming billows o'er the gunwale pour ;
Headlong she dives, and, vanishing from view,
Leaves in the water her unlucky crew ;
But waves, o'er-ravenous, disgorge the men,
Bruis'd, and half-drown'd, upon the deck again,
Which, scarcely safer than the greedy wave,
Is still a respite from a wat'ry grave.

Now the spent crew and passengers refrain
From painful toils they feel to be in vain,
And to the chief saloon at once descend,
As if in company their lives to end.
Then the brave captain, with a solemn air,
Bids them at once for painful death prepare ;
The awful warning they in silence hear,
For no loud outcries testify their fear ;
But to the place where Draper prays aloud
They move, a pallid, but collected crowd.

Here, hapless mothers o'er their offspring weep,
So soon to perish in the raging deep !
While they, with piteous accents, beg to know
Why yield their parents to such hopeless woe ?
There, men and women, crouching low, are seen
To search their Bibles, as if thence to glean
Assuring hope from passages, wherein
Pardon is promised to repented sin.
But when brave Martin presently appears,
All eyes throw on him, thro' their welling tears,
Enquiring glances ;—he at once replies

To that mute question from imploring eyes.
" Ladies, no hope remains for us I fear ;
" Nought save a miracle can interfere
" To save our lives !"   A voice is heard to say
(It is the preacher's), " Come then, let us pray."
And solemnly to heav'n ascends once more
The voice of prayer amidst the tempest's roar.

The hours drag on their weary, leaden flight,
And Sol once more attains his midday height ;
Still, in the ship, the deadly fluid gains,
And the wild sea is level with her chains ;
Round her vast stern the greedy waters swirl,
And mighty billows o'er her bulwarks curl,
When mate and captain once more make a stand,
And seek to animate a gallant band
Of mariners, to make one effort more
To launch a boat wherein to gain the shore.
King, Grant, and Daniels aid with willing hands,
And brave young Angel by his engine stands,*
Ready to hoist her o'er the vessel's side,
And drop her lightly on the seething tide.
Warn'd by mishap, three men alone descend
Within the boat ; from off the side to fend
Their small frail ark, which seems as if 'twould be
At once engulph'd within the raging sea.
But, like a cork upon the ocean cast,
(Her sides too low to catch the mighty blast),
She rises buoyantly, on billows high,
From horrid depths, as if to scale the sky.
But so unsafe she seems that very few
Seek to augment the number of her crew ;
But, in pale groups, cling on the sea-lash'd deck,
And wait destruction with the sinking wreck.

To Greenhill, now, brave Martin gives command
To leave the ship, and head the hardy band ;
Who, nimbly springing o'er a chasm wide,
Gains the light cutter from the vessel's side.
An awful leap ! but desperation lends
A stern resolve, that far mere strength transcends.
For nerves and sinews, in the human kind,
Are urg'd and govern'd by the mighty mind.
" Go," Martin says, " the cutter is *your* care,
" And, though not likely, may in safety bear
" You through the tempest ;—as for me, I stay

---

* Donkey-engine on deck.

" My evil fortune's hard demands to pay ;
" For, with my passengers, in death I'll sleep
" Far in the soundings of the mighty deep !"

Meanwhile, below, the pious Draper still
Exhorts compliance with the Heavenly will.
" Prepare," he cries, " prepare at once to meet
" The Great Creator at the Judgment Seat !
" Your hour is near.   Repent ! repent ! before
" The fatal floods annihilation pour
" In wrath upon you !   There is now no hope,
" Saith our good captain, with the storm to cope.
" Yet, to the penitent, the hope remains
" Of life, for ever, where Jehovah reigns !"

The faithful wife beside her husband stands
With quiet eyes, and meekly folded hands.
Buoy'd by her faith she sees the waves encroach,
And falters not at dreadful Death's approach ;
But, with true kindness in her woman's heart,
Can feel for those who in the boat depart.
" Take this," she says unto a seaman bold,
(And gives her rug) " 'twill shield you from the cold."
And when he urges, " Madam you will need
" It for yourself," she answers, " Take no heed
" Or care for me ; a few short moments more,
" And all my pain and trouble will be o'er."
Oh, noble woman ! pious, good, and true !
Death must be blind to seize on such as you !

Now earthly numbers all too meanly sound
The praise of him who, by his duty bound,
Stands with his wife and children, hand in hand,
A loving, lovely, undivided band !
He, though the water, on the leeward side,
Rolls in a deep and fast increasing tide,
Firmly withstands the efforts which a friend
With words persuasive makes, his soul to bend.
" No !" he replies, when urged the boat to gain,
" My promise made, with these I will remain.
" Words cannot shake the purpose of my heart ;
" For, as thro' life, in death we will not part !
" But help the children to this side with me,
" Where, for a time, the greedy rushing sea
" Cannot assail them.   Now give me your hand—
" Good-bye, dear Jack ! and should you reach the land,
" Seek out my friends, and tell them Hickman died
" With a clear conscience by his lov'd one's side."

No more is said, for Wilson hastes away,
(Man's strongest instinct eager to obey!)
And hails the boat; but now its crew declare
That it another passenger will bear.
"Go, bring a lady," is the seaman's cry,
And Wilson stays not to give back reply,
But, in wild haste, seeks eagerly in vain
For one, alas! he ne'er will see again.
And, as the moments all too swiftly fly,
He asks a maiden, who is standing nigh,
"Will she for life cast in with them her lot?"
She looks compliance, though she answers not.
With willing arm he bears her to the rail,
When, horror struck, she shrinks from sea and gale,
And cries, "Oh, no! I cannot make that leap."
This seals her fate; for Wilson o'er the deep
Springs to the boat, and leaves her to the fate
She now, perforce, must with the others wait.

But Mrs. Owen would attempt to save
Herself and infant from an ocean grave
On board the cutter. This brave Martin hears
Her tell young Edwards; and (mov'd e'en to tears)
He begs she will not needlessly expose
Herself and infant to protracted woes.
No chance, he owns, *his* vessel has to float,
But drunken men may be on board the boat,
Who, all unruly, would soon cause to fill
The craft, converted into a screaming hell!
She listens sadly to his warning voice,
And with the ship remains her mournful choice.

Now the young middy looks with longing eyes,
And for admission to the crew applies.
They answer, "Yes;" he leaps the chasm o'er,
And the foil'd billows for him vainly roar.
Then Jones, the last man from the fated bark,
Bounds from her bulwarks to the tossing ark.
"Come! captain, come!" the eager seamen call;
But death approaching cannot him appal;
For, to their offers, he replies, "No! no!
"Here, at my post, down with the ship I'll go!
"That none, with truth, shall, in the future, say
"He, scared by danger, did his trust betray!
"My passengers, my all, remain,—and I,
"A British seaman, at my post will die!
"Your course is Nor.-Nor.-East to Brest, and, here

" Catch you this compass, by its aid to steer,
" With God's good blessing, safely to the land.—
" Good-bye ! Good-bye !" Then, waving high his hand,
A last farewell he signals to the band ;
And on his ship, now level with the sea,
Calmly awaits till all engulph'd shall be.

But, as the boat deserts the sinking wreck,
A woman's voice comes shrieking from her deck ;
And o'er its rail a livid face appears,
The starting eyes exhausted of all tears.
Wildly the men she with her arms would stay,
Her soul to anguish and despair a prey ;
Then shrieks the offer, through the tempest's din,
" A thousand guineas if you take me in !"
But no response comes back against the blast,
The fatal die, for life or death, is cast !
Not all the wealth of all the world could stay
Those seamen stern !—for life they pull away.

Soon from the boat the members of its crew
The last dread struggles of the London view.
For high in air ascends her giant bows,
As, o'er her stern, the rolling billows close ;
While from below the air, till now close pent,
Through bursting decks gives its fell fury vent,
Driving the people, with terrific force,
Toward the prow in its resistless course.
Down ! Down ! she plunges, and vast whirlpools sweep
Round awful vortex in the riven deep ;
Whence, madly shrill, a wild, heartrending cry
Pierces the tempest to the frowning sky !
Then rav'ning ocean, rushing on its prey,
Hides its sad victims from the face of day.
They sink for ever ! and the sullen blast
Raves a hoarse requiem as it hurtles past !

THE CALL OF DEATH.

1

O THOU, to whom both young and old,
The cringing slave, the freeman bold,
 Resign their breath :
At whose dread call must pass away
The spirit from its house of clay—
 Thy name is Death !

2.

The ailing infant wildly press'd
Unto its anguish'd mother's breast,
 At thy request
To its Creator yields its life,
Escaping sorrow, sin, and strife,
 And findeth rest.

3.

The agèd man with silver hair,
Weighed down by weary years of care,
 His blear'd eyes dim :
A weak resistance makes in vain
To thee, when from his life of pain
 Thou callest him.

4.

The king upon his couch of state
Must yield him tamely to his fate
 When thou dost call ;
For bishop's prayer or army's might
Avail him nothing in thy sight,
 Thou king of all !

5.

The beggar on his bed of straw,
Spread on the mouldy cellar floor,
 Can not prevail
On thee to lengthen out the span
Allotted to him as a man
 By whining tale.

6.

The lawyer, like the common thief,
Is summoned from existence brief
 By writ of thine,—
To answer for his moral flaws,
And plead his soul's eternal cause,
 In courts divine.

7.

No legal quibble can avail,
No human law 'gainst thee prevail,—
    He must away,
And wait (with those whom for a fee
In earthly court defended he)
    The judgment day.

8.

The soldier in the battle's din,
Eager a crown of fame to win,
    By foeman's hand
Goes down beneath war's horrid wave,
And sinks into a blood-stain'd grave,
    At thy command.

9.

The sailor, calm when tempests lower,
And resolute e'en in the hour
    He meets with thee :
Storm toss'd upon the coast is cast,
And midst fierce breakers breathes his last,
    At thy decree.

10.

The widow's only darling son,
Whose toil alone her bread has won,
    No pity gains ;
For stalking grimly on your prey,
You force his fainting soul away
    With racking pains.

11.

The prodigal, who all his life,
At home has been the cause of strife,
    And now away
Against his parent's just command,—
Must quit his wanton comrade band,
    And thee obey.

12.

The faithful brother, bold and strong,
Who to his only brother clung
    With single heart,
All helpless on the level plain,
Thrown from his quiet horse was slain
    Swift by thy dart.

13.

The sneaking coward, who afraid
Of e'en the shade himself has made,

And danger shirks ;
Altho' he double like a hare,
Must fall at last into the snare
   Thy fell hand works.

14.

The miser old thou dost surprise
At midnight, when with greedy eyes
   He counts his gold ;
Than thee, he fears the parting more
From it, that yellow shining store,
   So often told ;

15.

The lucre gain'd in many lands,
He clutches in his skinny hands,
   Till his last grasp ;
But what no tale of misery
Or want could gain, is torn by thee
   From his close grasp.

16.

At thy approach the infidel,
Who oft has laugh'd at heav'n and hell,
   Now with despair
Beseeches thee with sighs and tears
To grant him yet a few more years ;
   Ah ! fruitless prayer !

17.

His time is come, he must away—
Whither ? ah ! whither, who shall say ?
   He will be tried
By *Him* who gave a soul to man,
And in whose sight no mortal can
   Be justified.

18.

The dying Christian calmly waits
Thy call, and thro' thy frowning gates
   Can glory see ;
And longing for the joys above,
Where all is painless peace and love,
   He fears not thee !

19.

Tho' *thou* canst claim the mortal frame,
Thou canst not interfere with fame :
   For tho' all die,
A good man's name is ever dear,
And lives with his descendants here
   In memory.

20.

Then let us all improve each day
Of sojourn here, that when away
   We too must hie :
Like Christians we may meet our end,
And bid each sorrow-stricken friend
   A calm good-bye.

THE BUSHMAN'S REVERIE.

1.

PLEASANT it is of home to muse,
   When from it far away ;
Of woodland walks we used to choose,
Where oaks and elms and sombre yews
Lent their cool shade to joyous crews
   Of children at their play.

2.

Often I lie at close of day
   Upon my sheepskin bed,
When memories both sad and gay
Of bygone times, long pass'd away,
My fancy's magic call obey,
   And are before me spread.

3.

I seem to see each face again
   Well-known to me of yore :
The cripple's, with its look of pain ;
The merchant's, shrewd and keen for gain ;
And fellow-schoolmates, who would fain
   Dispense with bookish lore.

4.

And scenes in which each took a share
   Are brought back to my mind :
The gay and festive village fair,
With happy rustics gather'd there,
Who for the time devoid of care
   Such pleasure seem'd to find.

5.

In viewing certain learned pigs,
 Which seem'd strange things to know ;
Or gaping at the merry rigs
Of harlequins with supple legs,
In particoloured tights, and wigs,
 Before some strolling show.

6.

I see them crowding up to pay
 The small admission fee,
Eager to view the wretched play—
(" George Barnwell " mostly, by the way,
Was the one acted in my day—
 A doleful tragedy).

7.

The boys who purchased gingerbread,
 And swing-boats swung in then,
How many of them now are dead !
Others, by fickle fortune led,
In wild bush lands their life-paths tread—
 Time-sobered, bearded men.

8.

The merry girls are matrons staid,
 And care is on each brow ;
To me they seem as when we play'd
Together in each copse and glade,
Or by the stream for cowslips stray'd ;
 'Tis so I see them now.

9.

And she on whom I used to look
 With lover-like regard,
Who paddled with me in the brook,
And in my sport such interest took—
She slumbers in a quiet nook
 Within the old churchyard.

10.

But still her form and features, aye,
 Her very smile I see,
In dreams by night, in thoughts by day,
As when we sported in the hay,
Or sought for violets in May ;
 Ah ! pleasant memory !

11.

The skylark singing merrily
 I seem to hear again,

As almost past the ken of eye
He mounted toward the glowing sky,
And sang his wild sweet melody,
    Unconscious of all pain.

12.

I see again the village green
    Upon a cricket day ;
When, grouped wherever trees would screen,
The village folk with happy mien,
Watch'd well the match ; a homely scene,
    Yet picturesque and gay.

13.

I hear them raise the cheering shout,
    Delighted one and all,
When old Tom Sewell, hale and stout,
So neatly caught some batsman out,
Or Sherman put the stumps to rout
    With well-delivered ball.

14.

I see the church, with carvings queer
    Beside each window tall,—
The heads of storied saint and seer,
And one with lengthy ass-like ear,
With crooked horn and horrid lear,—
    The enemy of all !

15.

I see its massive tower high,
    Its grey and buttress'd wall ;
Its green graveyard where thousands lie,
Hidden for aye from mortal eye,
Waiting the summons from the sky,   .
    Of quick and dead the call.

16.

The Sabbath bells—remember'd well—
    I seem to hear again :
As when with clear resounding swell
They summoned those who near did dwell
To come, and hear the pastor tell
    Of Him who suffer'd pain

17.

And ignominy, so that He
    Might all lost nations save ;
And how He walk'd upon the sea,
And always succor'd misery,
Until He died on Calvary,
    And was laid in the grave.

D

18.

And how in silent death he lay,
    Then woke to life again :
Exemplifying how that they
Who on this earth the Lord obey,
From death awake, to speed away
    To life devoid of pain.

19.

And then the chimes ; so soft and clear
    Their music seems to fall
Again upon my list'ning ear,
As when they knell'd the dying year,
And seem'd to welcome, without fear,
    The conqueror of all,

20.

In person of the ruddy heir,
    That Phœnix-like arose
From off the snow-encumber'd bier
Of the decrepit worn-out year
That had just closed his short career
    Of mingled joys and woes.

21.

And wedding bells with seeming glee
    Engage in tuneful strife ;
While village rustics flock to see
The couple who now vow to be
Partners in joy or misery
    While they shall be in life.

22.

I hear again the tolling bell
    With measured solemn boom
Float o'er each verdant hill and dell,
Casting on some a pensive spell,—
To others sounding as a knell
    Of their own earthly doom.

23.

And oft I seem to hear again
    The corncrake's pleasant cry
Proceeding from the waving grain,
As when in some green shady lane
I've often waited long in vain
    The pretty bird to spy.

24.

The slimy snail at dewy eve
    Across the pathway crawls,

As tired farm men slowly leave
The standing grain, and surly grieve,—
From toil to gain a short reprieve
    Within their cottage walls.

25.

The timid hare steals to the crop,
    And frogs begin to croak,
While from the copse wild rabbits hop,
And gay cock pheasants cry " cock-op,"
When flying to the spreading top
    Of some low sturdy oak.

26.

Then night's shades veil each fertile dell
    So late with sunshine bright ;
And on the ear with soothing spell
Falls the clear notes of philomel,
While some adjacent village bell
    Proclaims the hour of night.

27.

But now mosquitoes fiercely sing
    Upon my startled ear ;
With grating discord does it ring,
As lightning down with venom'd sting
They cause my vision to take wing,
    And from me disappear.

CHRISTMAS, 1876.

HAIL, much-lov'd Christmas ! hail, thou festive time !
    So dear to Christians, spread o'er all the earth.
In icy region, and in burning clime,
    Hearts glow with gladness, and with harmless mirth,
    And men's bright angels hover near each hearth.
Care flies, with Sorrow, for a little space,
    Even from those who from their very birth
Have known privation, and the carking race
Of all the haunting ills of poor man's dwelling place.

Now glow with light the mansions of the great,
    And music floats upon the evening air ;
Blithe are the measures, as with hearts elate,
    Whirl in the dance each animated pair,
      Youths gay and stalwart link'd with maidens fair.
Jocund the laughter at the merry jest
    Flashing from tongues which wines of vintage rare
Loosen right glibly ; while they warm the breast
Of even pompous age beneath its costly vest!

Hark to the fiddle in that lowly cot !
    List to those voices in a chorus blent !
Say, do their owners envy grandeur's lot ?
    Now that their hearts on harmony are bent,
      And all their thoughts to happiness are lent ?
No ! for to-night they own the jolly sway
    Of pleasant Christmas, to us mortals sent
To crown with joy each year, and drive away
The troubles of this life, at least for one short day.

Here, in Australia, may this Christmas be
    A sunny stepping-stone in life's wide stream ;
A resting-place of fragrant memory ;
    A page of history, from whence shall gleam
      Fair illustration for Old Age's dream ;
Fresh to remain, a picture bright and clear,
    For future converse aye a cheerful theme.
And now I'll bid you all, my readers dear,
A pleasant Christmas Day, also a blithe New Year.

A BUSHMAN'S ADDRESS TO THE MORNING STAR.

1.

Hail, morning star ! thou fairest gem
In night's refulgent diadem !
    I hail thee with delight,
When, just before the dawn's first gleam,
Like spirit's eye you softly beam
    All beautiful and bright.

2.

Though constellations, hung on high
To grace the glowing midnight sky,

Like heav'nly jewels shine,—
Not they, nor meteoric flame,
Nor even Phœbe's self, can claim
Such loveliness as thine !

3.

Through winter's night my vigils drear
I keep, among the saltbush sere,
In lonely solitude,
Where nought is heard save curlew's cry,
Or dingo's howl ; while, hobbled nigh,
My horses crop their food.

4.

Time, like an endless phantom vast,
Glides noiselessly into the past,
And sleep deserts mine eyes ;
When thoughts and scenes of bygone days
Crowd thickly o'er me as I gaze
Into the starlit skies.

5.

Stars slowly set ; but still the night
Waves not her sable wings in flight
Before the God of Day,
Till in pure radiance you rise
To herald, in the eastern skies,
Aurora's first faint ray.

6.

No longer lonely do I feel,
For o'er my senses seems to steal
A train of musing fair ;
When ah ! what luxury for me !
My mind, like soaring lark, is free
Awhile from earthly care.

7.

Then hail ! all hail ! thou planet bright !
So dear to lonely bushman's sight !
No star can vie with thee,
When, like some guardian seraph fair
Watching the world from upper air,
You seem to smile on me.

8.

But now an all-pervading light
Gilds old Mount Arden's craggy height,
Announcing Phœbus near ;
The stars have vanish'd one by one,
And thou, thy cheering mission done,
Must also disappear.

THE DINGOES.

A TALE.

One cold and cheerless night in May,
When clouds obscured the milky way,
Two Dingoes—quite a pretty pair—
Went prowling round in search of fare,
Resolved to kill, if not to eat,
All helpless creatures they might meet ;
Warrachie,* Pingo,† Boorachie,‡
Or tasty lamb, if such should be
Abandoned, when in slumber deep
It lay, unnoticed by the sheep
When they for home had drawn away
A little past the turn of day ;
In fact, those dogs would tear the throat
Of valiant ram, or sharp-horn'd goat.

They ran with noses to the ground ;
And ears keen cock'd to catch each sound ;
But they heard nothing save the cry
Of ghost-like night-bird sailing by,
And the wild moaning of the breeze
Among the scrubby sandhill trees ;
And they saw nothing save the bird
That gave vent to the cry they heard,
But which, with noiseless, stealthy flight,
Was quickly lost unto their sight ;
Besides, their eyes were elsewhere bent,
Searching each nook with fell intent,
While from them glared a savage light ;—
Those thieves were ravenous that night.

But they were doom'd to hunt in vain ;
For nothing did those dingoes gain,
On scrubby plain or sandy hill,
Whereon to work their ruthless will ;
For hunters swart, (as keen as they),
Had hunted there that very day ;
So Boorachie and Mudla§ small,
Swift Warrachie and Coodla‖ tall,
Were either captured in the chase,
Or fairly scar'd from off the place.
Our dingoes, therefore, noticed naught

---

* Emu, † Large blue anteater. ‡ Kangaroo rat. § Small wallaby. ‖ Kangaroo.

In shape of game that could be caught ;
Though, when across a creek they pass'd,
They saw, as up their eyes they cast,
A ring-tailed 'possum, fine and fat,
That on a lofty gum-branch sat ;
Where, supping heartily on leaves,
He cared not for the canine thieves ;
Which on him glared with longing glance,
Altho' they knew they had no chance,
Of making off that tasty beast
A very temporary feast.
So,—like the fox, in Æsop's fable,
Who said, because he was not able
To reach the grapes, that they were green,
And pass'd on with a look of spleen—
Our brace of dingoes cantered on,
And said the brute was carrion ;
Which, looking down with cunning glance,
Hoped they would have a fruitless dance,
And that they both might 'scape nightmare,
By reason of their meagre fare.

Onward those dingoes went until
A light they saw, beneath a hill,
Which shone as steady and as clear
As planet from its azure sphere ;
While a strange sound upon the breeze
Came borne, as tho' a hive of bees
Were swarming ; but with booming roar,
As loud as breakers on a shore !
For in a yard a thousand lambs
Were bleating loudly for their dams,
Which last, with motherly concern,
Were bleating loudly in return !
In tenor, treble, and in bass ;
The whole, combined, invading space
With such a din, as nature can
Sometimes thrust on the ears of man,
To soothe or irritate his mind
Whichever way he feels inclin'd !
This sound, like music of the spheres,
May seem unto one person's ears !
Another, in a surly mood,
Would use a word extremely rude,
And ban it as a horrid noise,
As bad as that some organ-boys,
In an excruciating way,

Grind to the tune of " Old Dog Tray !"
Music may " soothe the savage breast,"
But 'gainst " sheep music " I protest.

Not so those dingoes ; it to them
Was sweet as sacrificial hymn ;
For be it known they both loved lamb,
As common people love fried ham,
(Or bacon, should their slender hoard
Not furnish ham to grace the board) ;
And that strange sound, which they knew well,
Invited, as a dinner bell,
Or gong, does human dinner waiters
Who, of delay, are such known haters,
And our two friends were ready then
To take pot luck, we'll say, like men !
But I have heard that " 'twixt the lip
" And cup, there often is a slip ;"
These wild dogs found that proverb true,
As I may soon explain to you.

I said a bright and steady light
Appeared unto those dingoes sight.
It shone from out a window small—
(If you a window it could call,
For it was but ten inches square,
And not a pane of glass was there
To shut in hot, and out cold air)—
Of a pine hut, with roof of thatch,
And paling door, with wooden latch,
Which shut within that narrow den
Four very dirty-looking men,
One woman, and three children small !
I marvel it contain'd them all !

And in the rough stone chimney, bare,
(No mantelpiece or grate was there,
Or whitewashed plaster to efface
The cracks in that rude chimney-place),
A large wood fire was brightly blazing,
(Just what a Paddy would call " plasing,")
A fine shin roaster ; and its light
Put in the shade the " slush-lamp " quite,
Whose fat-fed, flaring, smoky flame
Was quite in keeping with its name.
(A pannican, in which some clay
Is kneaded down in such a way

As to support a piece of stick,
Round which is rolled a large rag wick,
Then refuse fat is added, and
A slush-lamp's made, you understand).

The lintels and the rafters, too,
Were smoke-stained to an ebon hue ;
For when the wind was from the north,
The smoke in volumes issued forth
Toward the roof-tree, wreathing blue,
Instead of flying up the flue,
And often brought unbidden tears
Into hard eyes, that had for years
Seldom been seen as aught but dry,
Undimm'd by grief or sympathy.

Along the wall-plate, o'er the jambs,
Hung several salted mutton hams,
Which, quite divested of all bone,
Were hams by courtesy alone ;
Beside them hung some wooden crooks,
To serve the housewife as pot-hooks,
Wherewith to shift the three-legg'd pot—
A most unwieldy thing when hot—
And very apt to burn or scald one—
(For it was like a witch's cauldron,
Or the great pot the gipsies use,
Or pitch-pot known to vessels' crews).

The article in question stood,
Together with some kindling wood,
Beneath a bunk, upon the floor,
Between the chimney and the door.
This bedstead, rude, was rough and strong,
Size, two feet wide by six feet long,
And so it just filled up the space
Between the door and chimney-place ;
Some sun-dried sheepskins on it lay,
To serve as cushions thro' the day,
As bed and palliass at night—
(For bushmen need no feathers light,
Or snowy curtains round them spread,
But sleep where'er they lay their head).

And next the chimney, on the bed,
Were roll'd a pair of blankets red ;
The sleeping kit of him who lay

Upon them in a careless way ;
For he was coiled, quite at his ease,
With left hand thrust between his knees,
His dexter held a dark dudheen,—
A blue cloud issued from between
His parted lips,—while in the blaze
He peered, and mused on bygone days ;
For he, as any one might see,
Was far gone in a reverie.

A mate upon the other side
A like position occupied,
For there a similar rough settle
Was placed, and near to it a kettle.
Upon its handle sat a Scot,
Who raked among the ashes hot,—
(With a burnt-ended mallee poker,
Extemporised by that old stoker),—
And fancied as they changed in hue
That visages which once he knew,
Were pictured in those embers bright,
Only to vanish from his sight
Before he well could call to mind
Whose face he fancied was outlined !

But soon he poked right viciously,
As if a bogle he did see ;
Then quickly turning, said, " Friend Pat,.
" Just let us hae the story that
" Ye promised."   Now the man nam'd Paddy
(Of those sweet children three the daddy)
Was with his darlings taking tea,
With hunger keen, as one might see ;
Or rather supper, for 'twas late,
And the hot mutton on his plate
Seem'd to affirm the meal was what
Some folks would call a " supper hot."
But all his meals were just the same,
And varied merely in the name,—
A course of mutton, bread, and tea,
Recurring everlastingly.—
For here—which makes the growlers mutter—
In summer time there is no butter.
So Pat ate meat three times a day ;
Except on Friday, by the way,
When he ate eggs, if to be got,
Or bread alone, if they were not.
As for his wife she did the same,—

For both of them in deed and name
Were Catholics, sincere and staid
As ever *Pater noster* said.
Both had the bump of credence, too,
For both believed the story true,
Which, Pat—his hunger being sated—
Somewhat as follows then narrated :—

PAT MURPHY'S STORY.

A LEGEND OF THE COUNTY CLARE.

1

Well, thin, d'ye see, 'twas in the County Clare
 I lived afore I lift ould Ireland,
In a swate shpot as ye'd see anywhere,
 Where blackthorn wis familiar to the hand,
And flourished at aich faste, an' wake, an' fair,
 As it was wont to do in that green land,
Where there has lived no shnake, nor bug, nor toad,
Since Great St. Pathrick in it once abode.

2.

I held on rint a little patch of land,
 The quality of which wis pretty fair,
Jist the right shpot to grow good praties, and
 Anything else which might be planted there ;
But praties wis the things, ye understand,
 I mostly put in ; they need little care—
At laste they did not in thim good ould days
Afore the blissed fruit tuck the disase.

3.

I kipt a pig or two to pay the rint,
 A lurcher, and an ould flea-bitten mare.
The dog shtuck to me ivery where I wint,
 And wis the baste that jist could grab a hare ;
He used to git upon the crature's scint,
 While I kipt out upon the thoroughfare,
And thin he'd grab thim in their forms ere they
Had half a shlant to shtart an' git away.

4.

And, thin, beside, me and me brother Phil
 Had got a pot and worm, and used to make
Some poteen in a hole benathe a hill,
 Which came in handy at a faste or wake ;
'Twis mild as milk, and niver made ye ill,—
 Atho' it was the shtuff to make ye shpake
Of absint friends, and private matthers such
As ye'd not like repated overmuch !

5.

Me landlord wis a tall and black-haired man,
  And had a big black bushy beard to match ;
And sich a bright and piercing eye ! Bad scran
  To it ! ye'd really fancy 'twas Ould Scratch
Wis looking thro' ye, as they say he can !
  And troth, I never since seen eyes a patch
Upon the piercing pair that gentleman
Wis owner of ! his name wis Nid McGan.

6.

A married man he wis, and his poor wife—
  (A purty lady, as ye'd wish to see),—
Wis sid to lade a virry wretched life,
  By rason that they niver could agree.
But what at firsht shtirr'd up their conshtant sthrife
  I niver heerd the rights of properly ;
I think it wis becase a nashty crature
He liked too well, of gipsey air and fature.

7.

'Tis said, the wife, (a pious Catholic),
  Would be a wantin' to attind confission,
When bully Ned, the grate big herritic,
  Would git into a mosht infernal passion,
And cruelly illthrate her wid a shtick
  In a cantankerous an' brutal fashion,
For which (altho' she might have give him tongue)
There's no mishtake, he ought to have been hung.

8.

They used to kape three sarvints, that is, they
  Had work for three, and would have kipt thim on
If they could have persuaded them to shtay ;
  But that wis much more aisy thried than done,
For all of thim was sure to run away,
  And long before their hiring time was run ;
For what with divils, and McGan, indade,
They in their graves would have been betther laid.

9.

For all the pisanthry did use to say
  He'd nightly dalings wid the Evil One !
For often of a night he'd shtale away
  To an ould room, where murther had been done,—
Of which himsilf did always kape the kay
  In his own fob, and thrusted it to none ;—
An' to him there there's plinty says there came
The Prince of Darkness, Nicholas by name,

10.

And sundhry of his imps, both shmall and great ;—
    For boys wis sometimes bould enough to shtray
About the house he livcd in rather late,
    (As 'tis mesilf has often heard thim say,)
And seen things that had caus'd thim to retrate
    Much quicker thin they wint ! and long e'er they
Could make out wither it wis ghost or man
That hild ungodly rivils wid McGan !

11.

But all agreed that on that windey blind
    Queer shaddys danc'd like Jacky Lanterns there ;
And strange wild sounds past on the midnight wind ;
    Which they considhered warnings to beware
Of peeping farder, list that they might find
    Thimsilves give over to the kindly care
Of thim dark visithors, which they wis sartin
Wis cratures, that a body might be hurtin.

12.

And so they started home, wid hair on ind,
    Shtartin at iviry shaddy deep that fell
Acrass the pathway, and ye may dipind
    They did not loiter much or take a shpell !
In fact, me brother Phil—the divil mind
    Him !—coming home from there fell down a well !
But whither fear or whiskey made him fall,
I niver could find out at all ! at all !

13.

For he had been to ould Tim Casey's wake,
    And had drank lashins of fine sthrong poteen ;
So whin he thravelled home wid Paddy Blake,
    Who liv'd on the nixt sixion—patch I mane,
They both resolved that they would thin betake
    Thim to McGan's, to see what might be seen ;
And if they mit The Divil on the road,
They'd tan the hide of that ould skulkin toad.

14.

Talk of the divil, and his horns he'll show,
    Is an ould sayin, and I think a thrue ;
And thim two boys found out that night as how
    'Tis aysier to threaten than to do ;
Espicially if 'tis to have a row
    Wid the Ould Gintilman—ah ! wirrasthru !
Betune him and the grog they made a miss
That blissed night, as both had to confiss.

15.

Av coorse Phil said it wasn't thro' the grog ;
　He wis as sober as a jidge he swore ;
But said that as they throtted past a bog,
　They heerd a dhredful scraming, and they saw
A hare close followed by a big black dog,
　And at a distance by a many more :
The hare a cryin' as she bounded by—
" O, blissid virgin ! save me, or I die !"

16.

And thin the dogs sit up terrific cries,
　While from their gaping jaws there did ascind
Red jits of flame, and thin their wicked eyes
　Like livin' coals blased out !　Ye may depind
They did jist frighten Phil and Pat !　O, boys !
　Their hair as shtiff as shtubble shtood on ind,
While their two pair of eyes prothruded out
Like you've seen crabs, or maybe heerd about.

17.

A tall dark rider rode upon each horse,
　The biggest looming up to such a height
As proved him, out and out, past mortial force ;
　Besides, both Phil and Paddy caught a sight
Of something shticking from behind ! (av course
　A tail it was !) which so increased their fright
That they saw nothing more, till Pat in bed
Awoke next morn.　And Phil wis fish'd half dead

18.

Out of the shaft I tould ye of jist now,
　Where he was yilling like a lunatic ;
An' Paddy Connor, hearin' sich a row
　Come from his well, got a long laddher quick,
And shoved it down so quickly, that I vow,
　It risted on the back of poor Phil's nick.
Whin down Pat wint—a heavy man, bedad—
To find he'd nearly finish'd the poor lad.

19.

Av coorse the laddher poked poor Philip's head
　Benathe the wather, an' 'tis rally thrue,
Near killed the boy, for all thought he wis dead,
　Altho' they thried great manes to bring him to.
They rouled him on a barrel, so they did,
　Wid head hung down ; but that same would not do ;
And thin they shtood him heels up in the air ;
Thin laid him out quite dacent, I declare !

20.

They thought that he wis passed all earthly strife ;
 But Mary Connor differed, and said, " Sure
" Afore they wint away and tould his wife
 " They'd bether thry another splindid cure,"
And that wis " jist the shmallest tashte in life
 " Of poteen ; there was some benathe the floore,
" And he would take it kindly, if so be
" He wis not clane gone dead intirely !"

21.

They thried him wid a noggin !   In a crack
 It disappeared like rain-dhrops in the say !
As nate as whate into an impty sack,
 Or donkey's head into a bag of hay ;
And thin he give his lips a knowin shmack—
 And thin he muttherd to himsilf this way—
" Bedad, but Purgathry is not so bad
" If shtuff like this is always to be had !"

22.

O ! thin there wis some laughing and some noise
 Wid thim around the bed, where poor Phil sat !
Which put to flight his unixpictid joys,
 And made him lape up like a startled cat,
When off he boulted, followed by the boys
 Headed by Paddy Connor, wid no hat
Upon his head, and nothing but his shirt
And throusers on ! and thim all smear'd with dirt

23.

And wather from his ducking in the well
 Whin he wint down to take me brother out ;
And so he could not hit out up the hill,
 Becase his throusers they shtuck close about
His ligs ; the same wid master Phil, but still
 About *his* running there was little doubt !
Ould Nick and crew were afther him, he thought,
And so he did not mane to be soon caught !

24.

Away he wint, and as it happened, sthraight
 Up the bye-lane in which his sheelin stood ;
Which he jist rached as Katty from the gate
 Wis coming out ; and then, bedad, she could
Not undherstand why Phil ran at that rate,
 Followed by such a many, young and old ;
But thinking he'd been at some divilmint,
She opened wide the gate, and in he wint.

25.

Acrass the pratie-patch, jist like a hare,
  Round the backway, and out of sight he wint ;
While Katty could not shpake, but only shtare
  After him with the greatest wondhermint.
She thought the whole affair wis virry quare,
  Altho' she had a strong presintimint
That Phil had got into some party fight,
And killed a Murphy, somewhere in the night.

26.

But whin Pat Connor came and tould her how
  He'd found the crature roaring down his well,
She found the way to shpake agin.   Ow, wow !
  She vow'd she'd make me brother quickly tell
What he'd been up to—ye should hear the row
  She made by way av wilcome to poor Phil !
And said, the nasty, dhrunken, dirty baste
Disarved a good sound bating at the laste.

27.

I don't know how the pair of thim got on,
  For Paddy Connor and the boys wint back,
Laving the two to go in *pro* and *con*.—
  (That's Latin, I belave, for scratch and whack !)
I know there wis a scratch or so upon
  Me brother's face, and that his eyes wis black
Whin nixt I see him ; and she used to boast
She soon persuaded him *she* was no ghost !

28.

But here the Scot broke in with—" I say, Pat,
  " Your brither maun hae been a stupid fule
" To let the limmer crack the like, the caut !
  " I would hae comb'd her hair wie the first stule
" I could hae lain my haunds on ; wantin' that,
  " I would hae gotten something else to cool
" The wratches temper, and I would hae hung
" But I'd hae stoppit her blactherskiting tongue !"

29.

" Maybe ye would, maybe ye wouldn't, now,"
  Said Pat, giving his rib a knowing wink ;
" Ive heerd yer own ould woman for a row
  " Is always mighty ready, and I think,
" If she did be about and heerd ye crow,
  " Ye'd virry likely have a nashty kink
" About yer back afore ye wint to bed,
" If ye got off widout a brokin head."

30.

(For Mack's old woman was, or rather is,
   A regular " old nut," in the full sense
Of that slang phrase ! Now for her vixen phiz—
   Low forehead, hungry-looking mouth, from whence
Her teeth had fallen, but where still doth biz
   Her hornet tongue, which darts full oft from thence
To propagate malicious and foul lies ;
While malice gleams from out her snake-like eyes !

31.

These sunk within their sockets, are o'erhung
   By grizzled eyebrows, which completely span
Her long, coarse nose, which seems form'd to be wrung ;
   And would be often, were she but a man,
And did allow her ever active tongue
   To wag as only such a vixen's can ;
But she's a woman, tho' the great display
Of beard upon her chin says almost nay !)

32.

That villain Mack just laugh'd, and said—" O, aye !
   " Yere reight there, Paddy, but ye brawly ken
" She's far away the noo, and so ye may
   " As well gie's oor bit story quick, and then
" We'll gang to bed in gunyah ower the way,
   " For time's a reiver, and is weel on ten,
" And we maun rise the morn by caundle leight,
" For they auld yowes are drappin fast the neight."

33.

" Well, thin," quoth Pat, " I wish ye'd hould yis jaw,
   " Or kape yis tongue shtill wid a clout-head nail,
" And thin I'll tell ye how *I* afther saw
   " The hounds, an' hare, and hunther wid the tail !
" As thro' the counthry side one night they tore
   " In a big shtorm ov lightning an' ov hail,
" Ov which same, me an' Phil, we got our fill
" Whin boultin' from the thraps to hide our shtill."

34.

Well, to their shtory Phil and Paddy shtuck,
   Whin quishtiond be the boys whin all wis right,
But did not thry agin to run a muck
   Wid Ned an' Nick ! They got a mortial fright !
Indade they did not think it promis'd luck
   To be too near that silf-same house at night,
For 'twis thim worthies, they would shtoutly swear,
Wis huntin' Nid's poor wife in shape of hare.

35.

And sure now we belaved thim, for indade
  That innociut poor crature tuck to bed
That virry night, in troth ! an' there she stay'd,
  Wid bad pain in her back an' swimmin head !
While her shwate face to dead carpse-white did fade
  Whin cryin' to hersilf—her womin said—
And her two eyes would shtart, like frighten'd hare's,
At creakin noises on the ould oak shtairs !

36.

The praste she wantid thin, but Nid said, " No !
  " Come to yis juty, if ye likes, to me !
" If praste comes here, (and thin he laugh'd, Ho ! ho !)
  " 'Tis glad his riverince will likely be
" To git outside agin, for my boot's toe
  " Shall make the shtairs one shtip to him, dye see !
" For, be the ' Rock of Cashel !' he shall rue
" The day an' hour he dares to visit you !"

37.

As darkest midnight thin his eyes grew black,
  And his poor lady shrank from his fierce eyes,
While her own shwill'd till they did seem to crack,
  And, O ! she give a cry, that rach'd the skies !
A cry like hare's sharp scrame, whin in her back
  She feels the greyhound's fangs, and quickly dies !
An' thin her wits for three long weeks did lave her,
While it wis sid about she had brain faver.

38.

But afther that the ginthry, one and all,
  Cut Nid McGan, and would not shpake to him ;
And if they chanced to meet him at a ball
  Or racecoorse, sure their eyes got mighty dim :
They didn't see him ! which made him feel small,
  And want to put a ball in some of thim ;
And he'd ha' done it too, for he could shnuff
A candle wid a bullet nate enough.

39.

But faix, they did'nt give him half a chance
  To lit the daylight into thim, bedad !
They knew he'd virry likely make thim dance
  An ugly stip ; for once before, a lad
He had shot dead, in some hotel in France,
  For thramping on a dressing-gownd he had,
Wid tails that draggled half a yard or more
Behind him whin he walked acrass the floore.

40.

The chap he killed wis a young Englishman,
   Jist out upon his thravels, so they say,
A younger son of some great nobleman ;
   And at his death there wis the deuce to pay,
His people thrying hard to git McGan
   Hung or transpoorted ; but he ran away
To Spain, or Portingale, or India,
And stayed there till the row had died away.

41.

But while he wis abroad, the ould man died,
   And lift him all his property in Clare,
Wid a fine fortin in the bank beside,
   By rason that he had no other heir ;
And Nid invited all the counthry side
   To come and have a grate housewarmin' there ;
And thim most sit agin him—which was funny—
Seemed his bist friends whin he came to his money.

42.

And thin he married, but could not agree
   Wid his poor lady, as I said afore ;
And thin, 'twas worse as ye might think, whin ye
   Tuck to that girl, whom on some furrin shore
He'd seen too many times afore, maybe,
   For his own good ; 'tis sartin no one saw
Her in thim parts, till wid a caravan
She came, some tin months afther Nid McGan.

43.

And thin he lit her have a splendid cot,
   Wid a fine gardin and a pratie patch,
In a nice, quiet, purty little shpot ;
   And sure himsilf did often raise the latch,
No doubt wid that dark gipsy queen to plot ;
   And there wis thim as said that cottage thatch
Was as unburnable as stone or brick,
For they had thried it wid a lighted shtick,

44.

And 'twouldn't catch ; oh, no, it wouldn't light,
   It was bewitched, they said ; I think so, too,
For that girl wis a witch, and rode at night
   Upon a broomstick, wid the demon crew
That hauntid Nid's poor wife. I caught a sight
   Of her, as past like lightning on she flew,
Giving a scrame like Banshee's boding cry,
Jist at the moment whin she bundled by.

45.

And now I'll tell ye how I came to see
 That divil's hunt on that same shtormy night.
Ye ricolict me saying Phil and me
 Had got a shtill, and made some of the right
Sort of poteen—rare stuff it used to be ;
 We tippled lashings, and shtill sold a sight
To boys that kipt the sheebeen shops about,
Until, bad luck to it ! we got found out !

46.

Into thim parts the gaugers sildom came,
 Or if they did, they ginerally wint
Away much quicker, if not dead or lame ;
 They moshtly having a presintimint
That they wis likely to be shot like game ;
 And with the same benivolint intint—
That is to make a hash of thim, but not
By manes of aither fryingpan or pot.

47.

Until one time there came a lameter ;
 A bully boy he wis, an' no mishtake !
And his short lig did not the laste deter
 His thrampin off to ivry fair and wake,
Attindid always by a crass-brid cur—
 An ugly baste, that look'd as if he'd take
A leg of mutton from a butcher's shop, .
Or wantin that, a beefsteak or a chop.

48.

His master used a shtick uncommon nate ;
 If he got mixed up into any row
Wid friend or inimy, he'd sure to thrate
 Him to a tidy tashte of it ; somehow
He seem'd to know jist where to tap a pate
 To floore his man. I think I see him now
Giving his shprig an illigant twisht round,
Whin, sure, a boy or two would bite the ground.

49.

All thought he wis a pidlar whin he came
 Around their firsht, for thin he had a pack
Wid knives and ribbins, rhubarb and could crame,
 Scint, small tooth-combs, and any shmall nick-nack
As women buy, but which I need not name ;
 But this I'll say, him and his shiny sack
Wis always wilcome in ache wayside sheelin,
For he wis free and asy in his dalin ;

50.

And wis, beside, a jolly chap, for he
 Could dhrink poteen, and fight wid any lad
I've seen out here, or in the ould counthry ;
 And the desateful beggar always had
A friendly way wid him as if, maybe,
 He'd been your mate for years thro' good and bad ;
And had no ind of yarns, how the Excise
He'd chated, right afore their virry eyes.

51.

In fact, the villin once declared to me
 He did be lamed whin fighting wid the thraps
Upon the coast of England whin, d'ye see,
 He thried to run a lot of fine Dutch schnaps,
Besides tobaccy, and some fillagaree
 That the great ginthry put in their caps—
I mane the ladies, bliss their sowls—whin they
Attind the praste, to give thimsilves away ;

52.

And sure now, now I think of it, they call
 It Brusshell's lace—'tis mighty scarce I hear ;
And landin' it, this chap he got a ball
 Into his knee, which cost the fellow dear
Who fired the shot, for he in turn did fall,
 Niver agin a cuther taut to steer !
For sure the pidlar said, right thro' the head
He put a pistol ball, and kill'd him dead.

53.

And thin, with all his mates got clare off, for
 They fought for life, and kipt the thraps at bay
Until their lugger, running close in shore,
 Tuck thim on board, and made all sail away,
Not caring thin to sittle up the score ;
 For will they knew their nicks would have to pay
For their night's work, if they fell in the claws
Of thim hell-hounds that carry out the laws ;

54.

And as it was, the crature said that they
 Was almost run down by a revenue,
And only jist conthrived to git away
 In a tremenjus heavy squall, that blew
The cuther's topsail clane into the say,
 And sthrained her mast so badly that her crew
To fish the spar had all their hands full quite,
And lost the lugger in the dirty night.

55.

She made nixt day the friendly coast of France,
    But where about I disremembers now,
And lift the lameter to take his chance ;
    His shipmates caring very little how,
So that thimsilves got clare and did not dance
    On nothing for their share in that night's row ;
Thin takin in some brandy, made a shtart,
To thry their fortin in some other part,

56.

Laving the chap at a small wine shop, where
    A praste from the ould counthry found him out,
Thin tuck him home and docthor'd him wid care,
    Till his wound haling, he could git about,
Whin he gave him sich coin as he could spare,
    His blissin, and a Frenchified rig out ;
For which he kindly thanked him, tuck his hand,
And found his way back to ould Ireland.

57.

Bad luck to him, for a big lying villin !
    And him a blashted gauger all the while !
He wis so kindly thrated in each sheelin ;
    Sure, even now, it raises up my bile
To think how he found out each private shtill in
    The villages around for miny a mile,
And how he wint away, but soon kem back
Wid a full score of peelers in his thrack.

58.

But sorra one he cought tho', afther all,
    For Phil's wife's sister (Honor Mooney) got
Her man—one of the " thraps "—jist to lit fall
    The saycret of the dirty gauger's plot ;
Thin, unbeknownst to him, she sint a shmall
    Gossoon to tell us all to hide aich pot,
And worm, and head, and all our maut away,
For the excise would be on us nixt day.

59.

We work'd away that night, ye may depind,
    Thramping wid loads of maut upon our backs,
To hide among the shtones ; there wis no ind
    Of thim upon the hills, besides big cracks
Betune the rocks, which shtrangers could not find,
    Excipt be chance, or running up our thracks ;
No asy matther, tho' a gauger's eye
Is, like thase dirty nagures', horrid shpry !

60.

While Phil and me wis gitting all things shnug,
  A big black cloud rose in the western sky,
And brewed a shtorm, while we two brewed a jug
  Of whiskey punch, wherewid to wit our eye,
Afore we wid the pot and worm did jog ;
  We tippled that, and as we shtill felt dhry,
We thried another, jist as Paddy Flinn
Flung back the doore, and out of breath rushed in.

61.

" 'Tis asy ye are takin it," sez he,
  " And all thim thraps a coming up the road."
" The thraps ?" sez we. " I'm not desaving ye,
  " They're handy now, and that big skulkin toad,
" The gauger's at their head ; and now, maybe,
  " Ye won't be long in taking up yer load
" And thramping wid it ; but now, be me sowl,
  " Jist listen to the thunder roar and growl !"

62.

" A purty night ye'll have, so dhrink yer grog,
  " I'll help ye wid the same.—' Here's to ye now !'
" A plisint journey to yez round the bog,
  " And don't be rowling in it like a sow ;
" Ye've got the worm ? have up the pot now, jog,
  " 'Tis time ye did !   Och ! murther ! hear the row
" They are makin up the village ; be the noise,
  " The thraps are at a scrimmage with the boys !"

63.

He boulted down his grog, thin boulted out,
  The lightning flashing fiercely through the doore,
Which blinded Phil, and made him reel about
  And dhrop the pot down on the shanty floore,
Whin crack it wint, not being over stout,
  And there we lift it, for 'twis past all cure ;
Besides, in ividence it would not tell,
Widout they got the head and worm as well.

64.

Away we wint, and soon the noise behind
  Wis dhrowned in the peltin of the shtorm,
The growling tundher and the howlin wind ;
  But with the grog in us to kape us warm
We thramped along, tho' often nearly blind
  Afther a flash of lightning showed the form
Of all the counthry round, thin lift it dark
As it would be at night in Noah's ark !

65.

We got on fine for the first mile or so,
    By rason of the finces, lift and right,
And thought we'd soon be where we wished to go,
    For sure the head and worm wis only light,
And handy things to carry ; for ye know
    A wooden " head," so that it is does fit tight
And doesn't lit the stame out, is as good
As if 'twis cast ; and this same one wis wood.

66.

The worm wis of shquare pipe, and made of tin,
    Which answers jist as will as copper, and
'Tis much more asy to be got ; and thin
    We wanted chape and useful things, not grand
Expinsive ones, and did not care a pin
    For their appearance, so that they would shtand
Some wear and tear, and brew the sort of shtuff
To raise the sowl of any but a muff.

67.

But to me shtory : all at once the rain
    Lift off, and one or two bright shtars shone out
Jist as we enthered on a sort of plain
    Of heath and bog, and as we had no doubt
The shtorm would soon be coming on again,
    We lighted our dudheens, and looked about
To see if we wis follow'd, and to take
A lunar observation, so to shpake,

68.

And findin all wis clare, we thought we might
    As will turn off to old Tim Rooney's cot
Up in the hills, a short stip to the right
    From the main thrack, and see what he had got
By way of tipple, and to shtay the night
    Wid him, if anything like whiskey hot
Wis to be had, our damp insides to air,
While our ould coats wis dhrying on a chair

69.

Afore a good turf fire ; but " O, ulloo!"
    Says Phil, while thramping up a steepish hill,
" Look at thim lights out on the bog below,
    " And, holy mother ! listen to that yill !
" 'Tis Nid McGan again and Nick, I know,
    " Come wid a clutch of imps, frish out of hell,
" To hunt Nid's wife ;" but 'fore he could say more,
The shtorm bursht on agin wid horrid roar.

70.

The lightning ran along the ground like flame,
  The tundher rowled as if the clouds would fall,
While out of thim, like pibble shtones there came
  A heavy fall of hail, that did bate all
I iver see before ; beside the same
  A flight of good-sized hin's eggs would be shmall ;
And whin Phil hild the worm to save his hat,
They in a jiffy bather'd it quite flat.

71.

On came the howlin and the scrames more near,
  And Phil sit up a horrid yilling chorus ;
And thin a big brown hare, half mad with fear,
  And eyes that shone like shtars, ran close afore us,
While afther her, above the ground quite clear,
  Came on the hellish pack, which might have tore us
In half a jiffy into smitthereens,
And ate us, sowl and body, widout greens.

72.

On wint the hell-hounds wid a mighty yowlin,
  While a shtrong shmell of sulphur floated round,—
On wint Ould Nick and Nid McGan all scrowlin
  Upon us as we cowered on the ground ;—
Whiz wint that gipsey on a broomshtick, bowlin
  Like a big scrache owl, wid a rushin sound
Till jist above us, whin a scrame she gave
Would scare a dacent corpse out of its grave !

73.

The tundher rattled and the lightning flashed
  Down came the hail, I think a thrifle harder,
So did a big oak-tree, by lightning smash'd,
  Which nearly shtop'd meself from goin farder ;
While in the darkness on the demons dashed
  To grab the hare for their infernal larder.
I look'd at Phil, and Phil he look'd at me,
And both wis white as dirty min could be.

74.

On wint the hunt till out of sight and hearing,
  And wid it, too, the shtorm soon pass'd away,
And one by one, betune the dark clouds peerin,
  The shtars came out wid bright and plasing ray ;
Thin, as no imps or gaugers wis appearin,
  We to ould Rooney's cottage tuck our way ;
And as the bather'd worm could not be minded,
We threw it in a big hole, and so inded

75.

All cause for running from the gaugers ; so
  We stipt out quickly for Tim Rooney's cot,
And in five minutes more wis all the go,
  Afore a good shin-roaster, blasin hot,
A tellin him what ye already know,
  About the divil's hunt and gauger's plot ;
Thin dhrank poteen, till rowling off the form
We dream'd of divils, gauger's, and the shtorm.

END OF PAT MURPHY'S STORY.

―――――

  " But listen ! be the holy fly
  " There is the same infernal cry
  " That I heerd by that quakin bog !"
Said Mac, " It is a dang'd wild dog
  " Close to the yard ; hark ! there again,
  " And Spot and Rover's on the chain !"
Which said, he opened wide the door,
And gave vent to a lusty roar ;
Then rush'd to where the dogs on chain
Strove hard their liberty to gain,
Giving the dingoes howl for howl,
And now and then a bark or growl.

He loos'd them quickly, off they went,
Seeming on dingocide intent,
Close followed by old Mac and Pat ;
The latter minus coat or hat,
But with a stick stuck in his fist,
A thing few skulls could well resist,
When wielded by the pliant wrist
Of him who was the boy to dig
Potatoes, or to wield a sprig
Of blackthorn at a dacent wake,
To break a friend's head by mistake ;
(But that was e'er he left the land
Of peace and praties—old Ireland).

Yet still he liked to have one by,
If merely up the flue to dry ;
For a stout stick, with knotty end,
He always looked on as a friend :
But as for coaxing you to tread
Upon his coat, so that your head

Might so be duly qualified
To have its strength and thickness tried,
By introduction to that waddy,
Had not been lately tried by Paddy.

But now when starting, his hand sought
His caubeen, but the waddy caught,—
And seeming satisfied with that,
He forthwith rushed out, minus hat
Or jumper, tho' the night was keen,
But did not catch a cold, I ween,
Nor any other thing that night ;
For neither tame dog cared to fight
The wild ones, which oft made a stand,
Until the men were close at hand,
Then, with raised bristles and slow gait,
They trotted on, again to wait
For those two curs, and seemed to jeer
At them, and taunt them to come near,
And try their prowess in a fight
Beneath the stars' uncertain light ;
But Spot and Rover e'er to-night
Had learn'd that dingoes snap and bite
In such a disagreeable manner,
As to make worthless to a tanner
The skins they tore ; and furthermore,
The wounds would long continue sore :
For poison lurks their teeth around,
To canker each deep gaping wound
They tear in dog, or timid sheep ;
And so our cowards thought they'd keep
Out of harm's way, and this they did,
Altho' old Mac and Paddy bid
Them "hould him !" till they both were sick
Of bawling ;—and Pat shook his stick,
And vowed he'd " give thim dogs a batin,
" If they for him would jist be watin !"
He'd " lave thim in a purty plight ;"
And furthermore, that " not a bite
" Of supper should they get that night ;"—
But they took every kind of care
The wild dogs should not raise *their* hair.

Dingoes will kill for slaughter sake,
And often a great havoc make
Among a flock of sheep, and slay
A number in a reckless way,

To drink their blood, but not to eat
The mutton ; so a stock of meat
Is left for curs, which else would find
Themselves to hunger oft consigned,
Because a fruitful married pair
Must exercise no little care
To make a forty-pound old ewe
Feed for a week their hungry crew ;
And so two dogs, on paunch and head,
Can't be considered over-fed !
In fact, they often want a meal
Of victuals, if they do not steal
Food for themselves—or catch a rat—
And then, if caught, they're thrash'd for that !

And thus I think I've proved right well
That each cute canine sentinel
Should claim the dingo as a friend,
And soundly sleep, or else pretend
To do so, till the slinking beast
Has slain sufficient for a feast !
Then wake to sound, and scent, and sight,
And rouse the echoes of the night
With warning bark, and savage growl,
And melancholy long-drawn howl,
Which, striking on the shepherd's ear,
Apprises him of wild dogs near !

Yet though their masters use them ill,
The shepherds' dogs are faithful still ;
So, in reverse, they all begin
To make a most tremendous din
Directly they can smell or hear
A friendly dingo prowling near,
Thus fully warning ev'ry one
Before the slightest harm is done ;
And so they lose, by their hot haste,
Full many a good mutton feast !
But lest my readers' patience fail,
Causing them to consign this tale
To a warm corner in the grate,
And wish me some such pleasant fate,
I'll quickly shift back to old Mac,
Friend Paddy, and the canine pack,
Who now far from the hut had got,
Altho' the chase was much less hot ;
For both the men began to find

That they were falling far behind,
Also that both were out of wind,
And that it would be useless quite
To follow up the chase that night,
So called the dogs, for fear that they
Might get a poison'd bait, which lay
Beside a circular bush-yard
With woven fence, built high to guard
The weakly lambs, which else had been
An easy prey to dingoes keen.
For often in this dry hot clime
Feed is so scarce at lambing time,
That save dry grass or herbage sear,
The produce of a former year,
The sheep can nothing else obtain
On scrubby hill or saltbush plain,
And e'en for that they have to stray
Some three miles from the yard each day ;
So lambs, a few hours only old,
Are much to weak to reach the fold,
And what is more, they will not try,
As they, in fact, would rather die
Than freely walk the homeward road ;
For each long-legged bleating toad
In obstinacy far surpasses
The most pig-headed mules or asses :
For switch them smartly as you will,
They will run back or stand stock still,
And while you well belabour one,
The other little wretches run
In all directions, though the sun
Declares his daily duty done ;
But heedless quite they race away,
To be pick'd up some time next day,
Minus their intestines and breath,
For they run to the jaws of death—
Or dingoes—it is much the same,
Differing merely in the name.

O, Job ! if you with your own hand,
Join'd with your brown-skinn'd shepherd band,
To drive the pertinacious lambs
And their most perverse stupid dams
Home to the fold at eventide,
When from the rugged mountain side
Came down the famished lion's roar,
Which made the sweat from every pore

Stream with anxiety and fear :
While ewes and lambs ran there and here,
And tried what scattering would do
To lose of lambs a goodly few.
If then you kept your temper cool,
And called no one a—something—fool !
Nor kicked the lambs, nor swore amain,
When half the ewes broke back again,
I say, you earned your appellation—
Of Man most patient since creation.

But then the sheep of eastern breed
Were very different indeed,
And varied much in many ways
From their descendants of these days ;
In fact, I've heard that shepherds led
Their flocks, and stalking at their head
Would, gaily piping on a reed,
Conduct them to their daily feed,
And, *never* getting in a plight,
Would march them home to roost at night.
I'd like to learn their method, for,
As I write this, my feet are sore
From running after, not before,
Three mobs of ewes and lambs that would
Race everywhere but where they should ;
Trying most stubbornly all day
To get boxed up or else astray ;—
As I myself have, by the way,
Strayed from my story, for I find
I've left my subject far behind ;
And so friend Mac and Pat we'll send
Home to the hut, their yarns to end,
And tie the sheep-dogs up, if they
Can only catch them by the way.

And now, to make all matters plain,
I must retrace my steps again
To where those dingoes twain that night
First heard the sound and saw the light,
Which then occasioned them to pause,
Altho' they knew right well the cause
Of both—yet on their hams they sat
To have a little canine chat—
A consultation how to act
In case they chanc'd to be attacked—
And to decide upon the way

To reach unseen the fold's gateway,
At which a lamb or two, they thought,
Might very easily be caught,
If some (as lambs will often do)
Had left their ewes and scrambled thro'
Between the hurdle-bars to play,
Not having had enough all day ;
Then, once outside, their eyes grow dim,
Or else they think themselves less slim—
Like " Æsop's weasel," that when thin
Crept thro' a hole into a bin,
Where eating wheat till he grew fat,
(Queer for a *weasel* to do that !)
Could not repass the slender crack,
To tread again the homeward track ;—
And so these lambs (tho' nought but air
They feed upon while playing there)
Find it insuperably hard
To win back safely to their yard !
A camel thro' a needle's eye
Could enter just as easily !
They wriggle forth, and, once outside,
No friendly space, however wide,
Entices them to enter, when
They would be safer in the pen ;
And so they run about and bleat,
A very tempting dish of meat,
To lure the ever watchful eye
Of some gaunt wild dog prowling nigh.

Of this those dingoes were aware,
For both had sev'ral times been there,
And had arrested, there and then,
Some foolish lambs outside the pen ;
An *habeas corpus* writ served they,
Which proved those lambs a lawful prey
To Nature's sanguinary laws,
Administered by teeth and claws ;
Laws which doom helpless creatures all
Before those fiercer beasts to fall,
Which shun the light, and prowl by night,
With this their motto—" Might is Right !"

Our dingo friends then thought of Spot,
And tho' they did not care a jot
For him or Rover, yet they knew
There'd be a terrible to do ;

If they should smell their pleasant scent,
Spoiling their villanous intent
By bringing noisy fellows out
To run like " red shanks " and to shout,
Also to see that all the lambs
Were in the yard beside their dams,
And so frustrate with noisy clatter
Our dingoes' efforts to grow fatter ;
Therefore they soon agreed that they
Should take a circuitous way,
So as to get the hill behind,
And thus approach against the wind,
Then carefully they gain'd the yard,
Prowling around, unseen, unheard,
Only to have their patience tried,
By finding not a lamb outside ;
Which so upset the bitch's temper,
That she set up a peevish whimper ;
And as a pair of gaping jaws
In church or chapel is the cause
Of setting others gaping too,
In yawn on yawn, from pew to pew,
Until, affecting e'en the parson,
His face divides, and makes it pass on
To the grave deacon and gravedigger,
Who stretch their jaws with utmost rigour ;
So howling, with the canine race,
With that phenomenon keeps pace ;
Then ere the sound quite died away,
Her mate took up the dismal lay,
Which rising high in cadence shrill,
Rang mournfully o'er plain and hill ;
And tho' it might have pleas'd *them* both,
It wrung from Mac that sudden oath,
Followed by his and Paddy's noise,
Joined in with vigour by the boys ;
Added to which the dogs on chain
Gave each a most discordant strain,
Till with a horrid uproar wild,
The startled welkin was defiled !
And then that wild-goose chase began,
In which men, dogs, and dingoes ran,
Only to halloo, snarl, and ban ;
For nothing suffered hurt or death,
(Saving a little loss of breath),
As I before tried to explain,
So will not touch on it again,

But keep in view those dingoes twain,—
They still kept up a slinging trot,
Their tongues loll'd out (for they were hot),
With lower'd tail and heaving flank,
Until they reach'd a gum creek's bank,
On which a small erection stood,
Formed of short unhewn logs of wood,
Which, planted as a pallisade,
A sort of strong, stout kennel made ;
To form the roof more logs were placed,
Which, like the others, were not faced ;
And on these blocks of rock were stack'd,
To keep all steady and compact ;
A sliding door there once had been
To close the end, for still were seen
The grooves and lever, which of yore
Sustained and work'd the fatal door.
The whole resembled a device
Once used at home for catching mice,
Before the block, with holes indented,
And fatal springes were invented ;—
And this one (baited with a scrap
Of mutton) was a dingo trap ;
Or rather, he who built it meant
It for one, but his kind intent
Was frustrated by reason that
The wild dogs rather " smelt a rat ;"
For tho' their tracks were often found
Imprinted thickly all around,
They rarely caused the door to fall ;
The artful " varmints," one and all,
Distrusted both the trap and bait,
And trotted off, e'ere 'twas too late ;
So that like every antiquated
Useless invention, it was fated
To fall into disuse and ruin,
When it of dogs had had but few in ;
For then nux vomica came out,—
Was boil'd with meat and strew'd about,
(Killing no end of shepherd's dogs,
And gave a turn to some few hogs),
But did not poison many dingoes,
Who would much rather eat blue pingoes
Or 'possums, for to them no treat
Was visible in parboiled meat ;
(Tho' there are bushmen who still say
That in boiled liver is the way

F

To lay the poison, so that all
The dogs which come that way may fall
Victims to confidence misplaced,
In choosing provender by taste) ;
But to return to dogs betrayed—
Nux vomica was not long laid,
Till strychnine (from the self-same bean),
More deadly, portable, and clean,
Came into universal use,
And *this* with death ne'er holds a truce ;
For dingoes swallowing a grain,
Yield not again to hunger's pain !
But to return to our two dogs—
They scratched and sniffed around those logs
As tame ones in a friendly host
Hold solemn levee round a post ;
And then they squatted on their hams,
To muse upon the meat of lambs.
Then up and spake that dingo grim,
In language plain enough for him,
A vile patois, which I opine
Is 'twixt the canine and lupine,
Which nobody would understand
E'en if I had it at command ;
And so in English I will write
What that old wild dog said that night.

But e'er I do, I can't resist
Railing at authors who insist
On quite astonishing the weak
Nerves of their readers with choice Greek
Or Gallic extracts, which they might
Judiciously keep out of sight,
For these most readers do appal,
As broken bottles on a wall
Small longing urchins, who would fain
The inside of the garden gain,
To revel on the fruit they see,
But fear the sure phlebotomy
That would attend their enterprise ;
And so those words to readers' eyes,
Present an obstacle, which they
Can not surmount, and so they say,
" Confound the fellow ! what a bore !
" What did he put this French in for !
" We think with mischievous intent,—
" It really is no ornament

" Or use, except it be, indeed,
" Unlearned readers to impede,—
" And air *his* erudition deep,—
" Wish to goodness he would keep
" His hard words to himself, and give
" In English his plain narrative."
So shall the dingoes' talk·by me
In plainest English written be,
(Especially, as French or Greek,
Latin or Hebrew I can't speak,—
And, therefore, it is very clear
I cannot give you any here,
Which may, perhaps, account for the
Foregoing spiteful rhapsody.)
And now for what that dingo said :
He thus a fair beginning made—
" Look ! Lupulina, at that trap,
" For which we never cared a rap ;
" Mankind must really have thick skulls
" To think that we should be such gulls,
" As to be taken in and sold
" By such a thing ! we are too old,
" And know a thing or two too much
" To be betrayed by such a hutch,
" Which mars the scenery around,
" And should be levelled with the ground ;
" Besides, it will soon pass away,
" A prey to fire or swift decay,
(" Tho' white ants will not near it go,
" They like not salt soak'd pine you know—
" A sandalwood would please them better)—
" But what the mischief is the matter ?
" Why do you whimper in that way ?
" Do let me know at once, I pray."

" Matter, indeed," the bitch replied,
" My patience you have sorely tried
" With your extremely stupid chatter ;
" And then to ask what is the matter ?
" Well, then, beyond the slightest question,
" I suffer not from indigestion,—
" Nor am I likely to, I fear,
" If you intend to dawdle here.
" I thought you said, as we came up,
" You knew where we could go and sup
" On tenderest of dainty lamb—
" I think that story was all flam,

" Invented merely to deceive me ;
" So now just listen, and believe me.
" If I am destined thus to wait
" In vain for supper, sure as fate
" I'll leave you for another mate !
" A common practice with the whites,
" When wives are cheated of their rights,—
" And maintenance is one I'm sure ;
" You know the case, devise the cure."

" Indeed, my dear," the dog replied,
But with a look which quite belied
The quiet language he employed,—
(For he was really much annoyed
At this spiteful interruption,—
Which caused the most complete destruction
Of the complacent self-esteem
With which he had pursued his theme ;
Causing it from its niche to fall,
And him to feel extremely small
And rather vexed,—and so no doubt
Would you yourself, if dining out,
Inspired by best of wine and meat
You spouted what yourself thought neat,
But which some nasty, ill-bred fellow,—
Made cross by wine instead of mellow,—
Cuts up, till in a fit of rage
You'd kill him, only for his age !)

" Indeed, my dear ! you should not blame
" *Me* for the scarcity of game !
" I know that hunger's hard to bear,
" But then, you must be well aware
" That I have hunted since sunset
" A meal of game or lamb to get
" For you ; but through adverse events—
" And *I must* add *your* petulance,
" In whining, when we might have made
" Upon the lambs a famous raid ;
" And now to lay all blame on me
" I say, and really think to be
" Injustice, very hard to bear !
" You don't mean what you say, my dear."

Replied the bitch, " I do indeed,
" And as I stand far more in need
" Of supper than your idle talk,

("Which I hate worse than Jews hate pork !)
" I think you now had better start—
" Except you wish that we should part—
" And so exert your every sense,
" And let us have no more pretence
" About the scarcity of game,
" When 'tis yourself that is to blame."

" There, that will do," replied her mate,
" 'Twill hurt you in your present state
" To get into a passion so ;
" I think we may as well now go
" To that small yard I spoke about,
" At which I've not the slightest doubt
" A lamb or two have been left out."

He waited not for her reply,
But struck into a sheep-track nigh,
Followed by his *cara sposa*,
Both intent to see or nose a
Ewe or lamb, or aught beside
With woolly skin or hairy hide ;
For anything in shape of meat
Those hungry dogs would kill and eat ;
But they saw nothing, till the dog
Began to sniff, and said—" Some prog
" Of a high odour he could smell."
The bitch, she whimpered, and said " Well,
" Why don't you follow up the scent ?"
He said " All right," and off he went,
But all at once exclaim'd—" Look here
" At this big trail ; 'tis rather queer,
" No beast I know a track would make
" Like this, except a booming snake ;
" And tho' 'tis not a reptile smell,
" I think it would be just as well
" To keep your eyes wide open, dear ;
" That is, we ought not to go near
" Until we can quite plainly see
" What kind of creature it may be."

" There, do leave off," replied his mate,
" Don't talk such stuff ; you know I hate
" To hear you prate such nonsense vile,
" But you can't help it, 'tis your style ;
" Right well you know no snake of size
" Inhabits here ; tho' to your eyes

" They be of vast and horrid shape,
" You wretched, chicken-hearted ape.
" Proceed at once, and don't you dear me ;
" Quick march, I say, do you not hear me ?"
" Well, yes, I rather think I do ;
" Who could escape from hearing you ?
" Would that your tongue within your head
" Was close confined, or I were dead,
" Or deaf as any blue gum tree,
" That I might 'scape the misery
" Of hearing your eternal nag,
" You execrable, spiteful hag ;
" Whate'er I do, whate'er I say,
" To pleasure you in any way,
" Appears to your distemper'd sight
" In an unfavourable light ;
" 'Tis truly said, that ' evil folks
" ' See evil in all facts or jokes ;'
" And now, if from me you would part,
" I will say *yes* with all my heart."

Now, as this did not suit the book
Of his dear spouse, she put a look
Of tender trouble in her eyes,
Where water seemed about to rise,
And murmur'd—" Ah ! you cruel creature,
" I did not think 'twas in your nature
" To taunt me, when so delicate
" I am in this my present state :
" When really you ought not to heed
" My little temper, for indeed
" I'm always sorry afterward ;
" And so I trust you'll not be hard
" With me this time, and I will be
" A pattern of propriety."

Of course the dog was near gain'd o'er,
Tho' feeling still a little sore ;
And so he said—" There, that's enough,"
As if he yet were in a huff :
But at the same time going on,
Quite evidently bent upon
Finding a supper of fresh meat
For his most amiable mate,
Who thought it prudent to abstain
From saying aught against the grain—
At least, until she could obtain

The supper she was longing for—
That is, a young lamb taken raw.

And so she trotted silently
Behind her shaggy mate, while he
Employed his ears, his nose, and eyes
To find the much-desired prize ;
And soon he said—" A track I see,
" Which from its shape appears to me
" To be that of the raw-boned Scot,
" Who makes the place for us too hot,
" And to his flock sticks like a burr,
" Attended by his surly cur—
" Which stirs the lambs up when asleep,
" And keeps them moving with the sheep,
" So that when supper-time comes round
" We vainly beat o'er all the ground.

" And now 'tis very clear to me
" That this queer trail, which here we see,
" Is from a ewe, which this same Mac
" Has dragged along upon its back
" To tie up to a bush or stake,
" Because her lamb she would not take :
" I saw him serve a ewe that way
" When I chanc'd here the other day !
" Then thinking (as I should) of you,
" Resolved at once to save the two
" From future fatal butcher's knife,
" By quickly ridding them of life
" In nature's quiet kindly way,
" Directly Mac should go away.
" I got no chance—he stayed all day,
" And then to make the case more hard,
" He drove the weak lambs to the yard,
" Loosing the ewe—which joined the flock—
" The lamb he thrust into his smock ;
" Then making that tall hurdle tight,
" He drove the flock home for the night,
" Leaving me here to beat the plain
" For a long time, of course, in vain.
" But here the track turns off again—
" And see ! depending from that bush
" Is a large kidney, nice and fresh,
" And which, within most easy reach,
" Is red and juicy as a peach ;
" And as 'tis merely a small bite,
" You take it."   She replied—" All right."

She made a snap, which cut the twine,
One bite to taste, and vowed 'twas fine ;
Less hasty would she have been then,
Had she divined that crafty men
Had strychnine sprinkled in its heart—
Or rather, in its inside part—
Like to the ashes at the core
Of apples on the Dead Sea shore ;
So pleasant to the passer's eye ;
So filthy, if their taste he try ;
But this the bitch knew not, and so,
As I just said, she was not slow
In making that fine kidney skip
Into her stomach, as would slip
A medlar into that of pig,
Or oyster down the throat of prig ;
But no bad taste could she detect,
And therefore did not then suspect
Her danger ; and so urged her mate
To go in search of other meat.

So off they trotted on the track
Of sheep's fresh paunch, which canny Mac
Had dragg'd in spreading circle round
The yard, thus leaving on the ground
An odorous and potent clue,
Intended to lead dingoes to
A poison'd kidney or a tongue,
Which by a piece of twine is hung
About a foot above the ground
On any bush that may be found,
When the drag-bait is drawn around,
So that the spotted native cats,
Bush mice, or active leaping rats
Can not detach it and convey
It to some place, where it next day
Might be picked up by " Spot " or " Bob "—
To him a melancholy job.

Those dingoes swiftly ran the track,
Which led them nearly to the back
Of that brush-yard, where stiff and cold
Lay a small lamb, some two days' old.
" There is your meal," the wild dog said ;—
The bitch was silent, but she laid
. Upon its neck her grimy paw,
And tore its side with ruthless jaw ;

Then drawing out, began to eat
What dingoes all prefer to meat ;
That is—the liver with the gall ;
In fact, the whole of the offal,
Including chitterlings and caul.

And as she ate voraciously,
Her mate began to fear that he
Should very likely fare but ill
If he politely waited till
The bitch had finished her repast,
And so began to break his fast,
Contriving to secure the heart,
Which chanced to be the poison'd part ;
In fact, he found a bitter taste,
But did not heed it in the least,
So keen was he for that fell meal,
That was his deadly fate to seal.
And both so busy were that they
Permitted not the least delay
For observation, or regard
Of ewes, excited in the yard ;
Which, rushing madly to one side,
With starting eyes and nostrils wide,
Shrill whistling, showed the abject fear,
They always feel with dingoes near.

But all at once the bitch cried, " Oh !
" There's something wrong with me, I know ;
" I really am in horrid pain,
" And will not touch a lamb again ;"
Which said, with somersault and bound
She beat herself against the ground ;
Her blood-stain'd teeth were lock'd full tight,
Her grinning lips left them in sight ;
Upon her side she lay at length,
Her rigid limbs were shorn of strength,
Her eyes were set with backward stare,
Convulsions' foam-flakes stain'd her hair ;
Near to death's door she seem'd to be,
Terrific in her agony,—
And thus, with muscles fixed she lay,
Until the first fit pass'd away.

The dingo left the blood-stain'd bones,
And listened mutely to her moans,
But quickly found in his own mouth

A bitter and a burning " drouth,"
Which made him long for water more
Than he for lamb had craved before ;
While horrid pains his vitals rending,
A dark, ensanguined foam was blending
With the lamb's blood, which to his eyes
No longer was an envied prize ;
And once or twice he tried to howl,
But from his stiffen'd, upturn'd jowl
A quaver wild alone arose,
As if his life was near its close.

But the sharp fit in which both lay
Did shortly pass from them away,
But left a burning pain behind
So fierce, that neither felt inclined
To tax the other with the blame
Of having lighted up the flame,
Which like a jagged two-edged knife,
Was severing their cords of life ;
For both with fits were seized again,
And death usurped the place of pain.

At early morning came old Mac
With eager eyes upon the track
To hunt along the trail he'd dragg'd,
And see what " varmints " he had bagg'd ;
And how he chuckled when he saw
Those dogs, whose thievery was o'er.
" You wratches, you are dead," quoth he ,
" Your tails are worth five bob to me,
" And you will look much better dockit ;"
Which said, from out his trousers pocket
He drew a long, keen clasp-knife, and
Above the dingoes took his stand ;
And then, with vicious slashes cut
Off each one's tail close to the butt ;
Then spurn'd the stumps, so cold and gory,
And with that action ends this story.

THE THUNDERSTORM.

A TRUE STORY.

I lie on my stretcher with wakeful eye,
For the storm outside is no lullaby,
And I feel no approach, I must confess,
Of light-finger'd slumber's benign caress !
But bother my brains with the cares of life ;
Sufficient for me—tho' I have no wife !

But see ! by the glare of that vivid flash
How those scare-crow forms for my log-hut dash !
And list to the patter of naked feet
As they splash along in their swift retreat
From the pelting rain which the clouds throw down
On those luckless heads, as tho' they would drown
All nature—at least on the Western Plain !
So its ancient lords would a shelter gain
More potent than that which their wurlies give ;
(For *these* all leak like a coarse mesh'd seive,)
And thus they are bent on a night with me—
An honour indeed of the last degree !

Their goal soon gain'd, they grope for the latch,
While a flood pours down from the rain-soak'd thatch ;
So, rising at once, I fling wide the door,
And the lightning gleams on the flagstone floor ;
When the natives—frighten'd and wet I ween—
In the fitful glare show a pale pea-green
As they puff at the brands in the chimney-place,
And range themselves round with no studied grace.

For, jabbering glibly amongst themselves,
They look like a crew of dark demon elves,
With their deep set eyes and glittering teeth
Shining out, their shaggy black locks beneath,
As they squat on the flags like toads or frogs ;
While mix'd in between are their mangy dogs,
And pups are produced from I don't know where
By wrinkled old gins with the greatest care ;
When I savagely say—" You turn 'em out
" All about wilka*, or else, without doubt,
" Into the cowie† the lot of you go !"
(At the same thrusting a leg from below

---

* Dog.   † Rain.

The blankets, as if about to perform
My threat of driving them out in the storm,)
But my words avail, for with cropp'd-in tail
Forth go those vile curs to the storm and gale !

'Tis a motley crew that is squatting there,
With steaming rags on the flagstones bare !
In family circles not fair to see,
Though all of them smile as the talk runs free,—
Till I greatly fear that each occuput
Will backward fall e'er the mouth can shut !

Hark ! a dusky brat with the stomach-ache
Starts doing its best with its yells to wake
The echoes which sleep round the cobwebs old,
Festoon'd 'neath the roof by their spinners bold ;
And it fiercely fights with its swart mamma,
(Who wears widow's weeds for their late papa,
Whose " carkata-peepa "* was crack'd, poor man,
A short time since by his loving clan !)
So I give the lone creature an ancient rug,
And tell her the little one's mouth to plug
With nature's own bottle (I might say jug !)
Which she quickly does, and, to my delight,
To the land of dreams the young imp takes flight !

Now a nice old man, with fine open face,
Steps gingerly up to the chimney-place,
(With nature's sole garb on his soul's black case !)
And easily chats to the young gins there,
While two or three brands he selects with care,
And carries them off as a reek ascends,
And in graceful curls with the light steam blends !
Oh ! happy is he when a blaze springs up,
(Which brings to light a small smuggled pup ;)
But dashed from his lip is the cup of bliss—
For his fire, to me, comes rather amiss ;
For though I put up with my friends so dirty,
My eyes won't stand the sharp " erdla merty,"†
So I tell that " poolka,"‡ as sure as fate,
I'll turn him out at a double quick rate
If he keeps the hut in this smoky state.

He tries to raise a facetious whinney,
Observing " Him only a pe-ckanninny,"

* Scull.   † Wood smoke.   ‡ Old man.

And " him big one warm," but I won't relent,
So he tells his gin, with much discontent,
To put back the sticks to the hearth again ;
For he plainly thinks on that flooded plain
No black or white, in his sense quite right,
Would wish to pass such a terrible night !

And now my sweet guests, all whispering low,
Declare 'tis Jemmy, they very well know,
Who, out in his camp on the sand-hill near,
Is up to his tricks for his lost wife dear !
The " wirra-wirra's "* fierce scathing flash,
And the awful " arndoos "† volleying crash
From the storm-vex'd clouds, are his work, 'tis plain,
And the constant dash of the hissing rain !
And they say that " a big one poota "‡ next
He'll raise to her manes when next he's vex'd !

But I try to explain, (though of course in vain),
How the thunder, lightning, and heavy rain
Can be caused by none save the Mighty One
Who made the mountains, the clouds, and the sun—
Who breathed into man the first breath of life,
Before to the world came sorrow and strife,
When unknown was death, and the bright young earth
Was filled with peace, plenty, and harmless mirth.

But they hear with scorn all my reasons warm,
And say it *was* Jemmy who raised the storm,
And " tintoo "§ jump up, weather fair or foul,
With that old man they will certainly growl.
But as they begin to get warm and dry,
Their longing for vengeance they soon lay by,
For huddled together upon the floor
They yield to sleep, and I hear no more,
Save an occasional deep-toned snore,
And, from the outside, the elements roar.

But they are not pleasant lodgers, I trow,
For a steam is arising from them now
Of an odour certainly not the thing
That floats about when the laughing spring
Calls forth from their tangled wild hiding place
The modestly beautiful floral race,
Bespangled with gems by the morning dew,
So gaily sipped by the butterfly crew,—

---

* Lightning.   † Thunder.   ‡ Dust storm.   § The sun.

But a horrible scent, which, to my nose, is
The very reverse of a bright fragrant posy's.

And I'm very glad when old Sol again
Rolls darkness away from the Western Plain,
For the storm clouds hang o'er the eastern range
With various forms and colouring strange,
While the happy birds, in blithesome play,
From rain-laden boughs shake showers of spray,
And the kangaroos, in ungainly crews,
Find the mud their efforts to hop confuse.

So now my delightful lodgers I warn
To quickly decamp from my bushland barn,
When they and old Jemmy, without a grunt,
Go off in a mob to a " coodla "* hunt,
And the old woman comes with a sour face,
And inwardly growls as she cleans the place.

A DINGO HUNT.

A TRUE STORY.

1.

Upon a station, years ago,
    I lived as overseer :
A situation, you must know,
    At which no one need sneer ;
For hunting, tho' a pastime thought
    At home by sporting men,
Was business to me, for I sought
    Each idle vagrant then.

* Kangaroo. These are easily caught when the ground is boggy, as their toes sink
in and throw them forward—almost on their nose.

THE DINGO HUNT.

2.

Which far from where it should have been,
    In safe and lawful thrall ;
Search'd eagerly for herbage green
    Beyond stern duty's call.
I hunted up, which was no joke,
    The bullocks one and all,
With likely steers to put in yoke,
    And cows with young calves small ;

3.

The cows to grace a rustic bail,
    The calves in pen to fast,
To bring their mothers to the pail,
    Themselves to take the last
(And often very scanty) drop
    Of milk, the maids or men
Leave, when drain'd udders bid them stop
    Till morning comes again.

4.

I hunted up stray station steeds
    Which, poor and weak when lost,
Would soon career o'er verdant meads
    With manes and tails high toss'd ;
I hunted wethers and old ewes,
    I hunted weaners small ;
I hunted too—and did abuse—
    The shepherds one and all

5.

When they would leave the sheep and go
    Off home to nurse " the kids "—
(A name colonial, you know,
    For human chickabids !
Of whom their mothers are so proud :
    Small angels, minus wings,
Who cry for ever, shrill and loud,—
    The interesting things !)

6.

Then on one sultry Sabbath morn,
    I am ashamed to say,
I hunted—tho' I lacked a horn,
    Foxhounds, and red coat gay—
A wild dog that I chanced to see,
    While running in two steers ;
I vowed his tail my prize should be,
    I valued not his ears.

7.

I never should have made that vow,
 But hied home with my steers ;
I was in fault, I see it now,
 In these my sober years ;
But *then*, it was another case,
 I was but young ; and so
Resolved at once to go the pace,
 And slay that shepherds' foe.

8.

The facts, just as they did occur,
 To you I will relate ;
Altho' no doubt you will concur
 In saying that the fate
Which waited on my enterprise
 Was well deserved by me ;
And that for aye by dust and flies
 I should tormented be

9.

For breaking so the Sabbath-day
 With such ungodly sport ;
And to be candid, I must say,
 I really think I ought ;
But then, again, 'tis hard to shun
 Temptation in the guise
Of a fine wild dog, that *will* run
 Right in before your eyes

10.

When you are mounted on a prad,
 That can and will hit out :
Tho' it be wrong, tho' it be bad,
 And wicked without doubt,
You quite forget what day it is ;
 And as Sam Slick would say—
" Your dander being fairly riz,
 " You yell and put away."

11.

You yell not at, nor put away
 Your evil impulse—no !
You tickle up your bay, or grey,
 Give him his head and go
After the dog like winking, or
 A shot, or what you will ;
Of your great sin not thinking, for
 Your conscience then is still.

12.

You only think how you shall knock
    The dingo on the head,
And steer your horse clear of each rock,
    Each tree and sandy bed,
And " crab-hole "—which is worse than all
    The other things beside,
And oft will cause a nasty fall
    To those who rashly ride ;

13.

(For if a horse shall fairly set
    His fore feet into one,
He turns a flying summerset,
    And comes down with a run :
Most likely on his rider's back
    With horrid crushing force ;—
To test the strength of rib and back,
    There's nothing like a horse !

14.

This I with certainty can say,
    For I have tried it twice—
Or rather, I've been tried that way ;
    And did not find it nice ;
For some six hundred-weight or more
    Upon one's carcass thrown,
By old Sir Isaac Newton's law,
    Would make a giant groan.)

15.

Upon one sultry Sabbath morn
    I went into the yard,
Where horses stood, *sans* hay and corn—
    A case you may think hard ;
But they, like worms upon a hook,
    Get used to it no doubt,
And so for feed they do not look
    Till to the bush let out.

16.

But you will say I'm wasting time ;
    And so I to my story
Will turn, and state ('twill help the rhyme)
    The sun, in all his glory,
Was sailing in a sea of blue,
    Where not a cloud was seen,—
Just as the herbage, then in view,
    Show'd not one tint of green,—

17.

When I old Teaser bridled, and
  The saddle on him toss'd
To get, as I o'er night had plann'd,
  Two steers Flash Dick had lost,
And which I'd heard a shepherd say
  He'd seen a short time back
Upon a plain nine miles away ;
  And so I took the track

18.

That led thereto ; and rode along,
  Tormented by the flies,
Which sang to me their buzzing song,
  While sporting round my eyes ;
Or sunn'd themselves upon my back,
  Or on my old felt hat ;
While scores of others on my hack
  With great decorum sat.

19.

I wish'd them all to Jericho,
  But they were quite at home,
And would not take a hint to go—
  They did not care to roam ;
For when with motion, swift and sly,
  I dash'd my hand with force
Upon my fly-besprinkled thigh
  I did but scare my horse,

20.

For much too knowing were those flies
  To be so simply caught ;
Wide open were their keen, bright eyes,—
  They dodg'd, as quick as thought,
To light again, quite merrily,
  Upon my punish'd leg ;
Making me wish that every fly
  Had perish'd in the egg.

21.

But wish or slap would not avail
  To keep at bay those flies,
And as I could not sport a veil,
  They frolick'd round my eyes,
Or got entangled in my hair—
  Bizzing, I guess, with fear ;
While others did for fun repair
  Into my shady ear.

22.

But tho' they would not go, they went—
  That is, they would not go
Away *from* me—they were intent
  On teasing me, and so
They stopp'd, and went *with* me until ·
  I saw beneath some trees,
Upon a low and grassy hill,
  Some cattle at their ease,

23.

And with them lay the pair of steers
  I sought, but which soon caught
The scent of me, when with cock'd ears,
  Cock'd tail, and frightened snort,
They ran like redshanks with the rest
  Along a cattle track ;
But gallant Teaser did his best,
  And quickly turned them back ;

24.

Then dashing in among the mob
  The steers he dodg'd about,
And, understanding well the job,
  Soon cut them neatly out,
And put them on the homeward track,
  When I soon check'd their pace,
To breathe my sweating, panting hack,
  Much winded by the chase.

25.

Slowly I traced the sylvan way
  To where three gum creeks met,
I knew that there some water lay,
  So thought a drink I'd get ;
But just before I reach'd the spring,
  I by some chance look'd back,
And saw a wild dog following
  Quite close upon my track ;

26.

His eyes were red, he was athirst,
  His tongue loll'd from his jaws ;
Oh ! Teaser, we will have a burst—
  Your hoofs against his paws ;
I gave a yell and touch'd his side,
  He answered to the call,
And quickly getting to his stride
  The dog did overhaul.

27.

Away for life that dingo hied,
　We followed close behind ;
He ran into the gum creek wide,
　Some cover there to find :
But as no burrow met his sight,
　He dash'd out on the plain,
And trusted to his speed in flight,
　Some shelter safe to gain.

28.

But Teaser closed up with him fast,
　I swung my stockwhip round,
The dog turn'd short, the horse dashed past,
　And lost some lengths of ground.
Now both are at their utmost speed—
　'Tis to the creek we rush !
Lay out, old Teaser, gallant steed,
　We'll have that fellow's brush !

29.

The dingo was the first to gain
　The gum creek's stony bed :
But then he seemed to run in pain,
　With drooping tail and head ;
We quickly ranged up on his flank.
　To strike him I was bent ;
There was a hole beneath the bank
　He saw, and in he went.

30.

Then down I sprang with active heat,
　The brute I saw quite plain ;
He seem'd to me to be dead beat ;
　So I dropp'd Teaser's rein.
To poke him out was my intent
　By aid of stick or stone ;
He bolted out, and off he went,
　And I was left alone :

31.

For I had no idea, of course,
　On foot to catch that dingo ;
And so I turned to mount my horse—
　He too had gone, by jingo !
I saw him up upon the plain,
　He'd hunt no more that dog !
For with raised head to clear the rein,
　He went off at a jog.

32.

Of course to catch my truant steed
　　Became my chief intent :
He sometimes stopp'd as if to feed,
　　Then onward slyly went ;
And so he led me up and down
　　O'er stony hill and plain,
Till I, just e'er the sun went down,
　　To give him up was fain.

33.

And by that time the heat and flies
　　Had played the deuce with me ;
The perspiration filled my eyes
　　Till I could scarcely see ;
My feet were sore, my throat was dry,
　　My clothes were all wet through ;
Nine miles from home ;—and by-the-by,
　　My boots were small and new.

34.

There was an empty sheep-hut by,—
　　To it I bent my way ;
The water-tank was nearly dry,
　　Tho' some still in it lay ;
But how was I to get some out
　　Tho' ever so inclined ?
There was no tin or string about—
　　No dipper could I find.

35.

That iron tank was four feet wide ;
　　It was the same in height ;
No tap appeared on any side
　　Unto my prying sight ;
But, then, the round hole in the top
　　Was fourteen inches wide ;
I found my head it would not stop,
　　And so my arms I tried.

36.

I first put in one arm and wrist,
　　Then thrust my head in too,
And by a most determined twist,
　　My shoulders I got thro' ;
With scooping hands the water then
　　I lifted to my mouth,
And tho' much trickled back again,
　　I soon dispelled my drouth.

37.

Out from that hole I tried to win ;
  My shoulders would not pass ;
My trousers would not let me in,
  So stuck was I alas !
But feeling round with fingers fleet,
  I tugg'd my trousers wide,
Pulling them downward pleat by pleat,
  Until I fell inside.

38.

Forth from that dungeon dark and dank
  I got, and homeward sped,
Resolved again into a tank
  I ne'er would thrust my head ;
Ah ! when I next ran down a dog
  I would not leave my steed,
But with my whip the " varmint " flog,
  Till nothing more he'd need.

39.

'Twas late when I got home that night,
  Minus my horse and steers,
And in a rather wretched plight—
  With dust in eyes and ears.
I had a pair of blistered feet,
  Which fill'd me with dejection !
Like Æsop's dog, I'd dropp'd the meat
  To grasp a vain reflection.

BLOWING BUBBLES.

TO A CHILD.

RATTLE the pipe in the water and soap ;
  Through the stem steadily blow ;
And forth from the bowl, an emblem of hope
  With radiance all aglow
Shall issue in pride, like a fairy thing.
  There ! give it a wave and send
It forth in the ambient air, to wing
  Its course to its journey's end.

A beautiful sphere, of colouring rare !
  Look, look at each tint so fine !
O, its rainbow hues, are wondrous fair
  As the sunbeams on them shine.
So airy and light, it glides in its flight,
  On a zephyr's viewless wings,
And is welcomed along, by the magpie's song,
  Which forth from the gum creek rings.

'Tis hollow, 'tis frail, and it will not last ;
  Ah, there ! it has burst, my dear ;
And its form collapsed to the earth is cast
  Like a beggar's falling tear.
No more shall that bubble your eyes delight,
  'Tis lost like all bygone things ;
But many another as passing bright
  Will soar if you give them wings.

'Tis so with our hopes, when in youth's springtime
  We start on our path so gay,
And to castles in air attempt to climb,
  Nor reck of the toilsome way !
And though like delusive bubbles of soap
  They suddenly disappear,
We'll gain a bright home, if we cling to hope,
  And valiantly persevere.

THE FLOOD.

A TRUE STORY.

1.

An old Scotch woman and a lass,
Called by the matron " oor wee Jass,"
Lived for some time with great content
In an extemporary tent,
Erected on the shelving bank
Of winding creek, 'midst herbage rank,
Which promised creeping things galore,
To crawl upon the earthen floor.

2.

The gude man he had sallied forth
Unto the regions farther north ;
Upon an old bay mare he went,
To find a shepherd's place intent ;
And weeks flew by, but still he staid
Away from anxious wife and maid,
Whose great concern did not prevent
Their taking proper nutriment.

3.

And thus they lived, until till one night
They got a most terrific fright ;
For after two days' heavy rain
The drainage from each hill and plain
Brought down a flood, which swiftly swept
Around their gunyah while they slept—
Dreaming, perchance, of the gude man,
When they from danger should have ran.

4.

But all at once a horrid din
Was made by articles of tin,
Which, as they hung on bent nail hook,
The water violently shook ;
Then woke those women in a fright,
And hurried forth in dismal plight
Thro' rising waters now knee high,
Toward the high land looming nigh.

5.

They waded on in great distress,
Each having but a thin nightdress
Upon their bodies, tho' each head
Had on the " night-mutch " worn in bed ;

No other covering had they,
For all the rest was wash'd away,
With rations, tenement, and all
Their household goods both great and small.

6.

For when the sun rose on the scene
Next morn, no vestige could be seen
Of goods or gunyah ; all were gone
Upon the angry torrent borne,
To be left here and there piecemeal,
For wretched blacks to pick and steal ;
Or planted snugly in the mud
Till the subsidence of the flood.

7.

So on they strode thro' waters dark,
Wishing themselves in Noah's ark—
Or clumsy mud barge, or a skiff,
With cheering drop of something stiff ;
For all around them, flashing white,
The foam swept past in bubbles light,
While in their ears the creek's fierce roar
Made them stride madly for the shore,

8.

Which they soon gained half dead with fright,
But with no lucifers to light
A fire to warm each shrinking form,
Drenched by the creek and pelting storm ;
For rain in torrents fell again,
While lightning flashed across the plain,
(One moment an unearthly gleam,
The next thick darkness reigned supreme),

9.

But showing with its transient blaze,
The public-house and laden drays,
Which stood upon the other side
Of that dark, rolling, roaring tide
That dashed against the gum trunks grey,
Which stubbornly withstood its sway,
Bearing the current on each side
In seething foam upon its tide ;

10.

And growling thunder ;—low at first,
But growing louder till it burst
In awful tumult overhead,
With mighty crash would wake the dead,—

(Could those be roused by any sound,
Who deeply slumber 'neath the ground,
Before the final trump and word
To summon quick and dead be heard !)

11.

Went rolling onward on its course,
But seemingly with lessen'd force,
Till o'er the mountains in the east
It in dull distant echoes ceased,—
To be close followed by the flash,
And most stupendous roar and crash
Of the next lightning and thunder,
Cleaving the black storm clouds asunder.

12.

And those poor creatures' faces fair
Showed ghastly in the lightning's glare,
As 'neath a bush out on the plain
They tried to shelter from the rain ;
Vain hope !—it seemed with forceful sway
Into their forms to find its way ;
Causing their good warm Scottish blood
To stagnate in their veins like mud.

13.

And so like souls by dreary Styx,
Those two were rather in a fix ;
For no old Charon was there there
To punt them over for a fare.
So tempest-beaten and forlorn
They felt like lambs just newly shorn ;
And, longing for the morning light,
They murmured at Old Time's slow flight.

14.

But Phœbus showed his face at last,
And half their troubles then seem'd past :
For soon he caus'd to flow again
The life-blood freely through each vein,
While in the bright blue morning sky
No cloud appeared unto the eye,
Save those, which lay in masses strange
Above the lofty eastern range,

15.

Whose rounded forms in heaps were roll'd,
With edgings of pale pink and gold,
Thrown by the glowing god of day
Upon them in a careless way ;

And fitfully the lightning's flash
Suffused them with a roseate blush ;
While distant thunder's low report
Could by the ear be faintly caught.

16.
Those women noticed neither cloud
Nor rosy tint, but long and loud
They cooey'd, till, above the din,
'Twas heard by those within the inn ;
Who quickly sallied forth in force,
And hastened to the creek of course,
To see what troubled Mrs. Dill ;
They hoped she was not taken ill.

17.
And O, how grieved they must have been—
(Or rather ought to have, I mean)—
At seeing those poor women's plight ;
In draggled nightgowns, long and white,
With hair dishevelled, hanging down
Upon the back of each white gown,
In long elf-locks, which, by the way,
With one was brown ; with t'other grey.

18.
But I have heard there was a laugh,
And that some man began to chaff
The women on their doleful plight,
Instead of sobbing at the sight ;
But Bully Bill was standing by,
And swore that he would black the eye
Of any cove who said too much ;—
" He'd very likely want a crutch."

19.
So then their tale the women told,
And begg'd that someone would be bold
Enough to cross that deep dark tide,
And bear a bottle to their side.
But Bob and Bill, and Jim and Tim,
Were not inclined for such a swim :
To risk their lives for ladies, for
The days of chivalry are o'er.

20.
But Edwin, minus coat and vest,
The other fellows thus address'd—
" I'm blowed if I don't try my luck,
" For I can swim like any duck ;

" So give the bottle here to me,
" And then aquatics you shall see.
" I've often swum across the port,
" And after that this ere is nought."

21.

He took the bottle, in he went,
To do the business quite intent ;
But ere he'd flounder'd scarce a yard
An eddy took him off his guard,
And whirl'd him up and down and round,
And all declared he would be drown'd ;
But when it seem'd that all was o'er,
He floated in toward the shore :

22.

When William—strong as any bear—
Contrived to clutch his coal-black hair,
And lugg'd him lifeless to the bank,
With eyelids closed and garments dank ;
But quickly much revived was he
When they gave him some *eau de vie ;*
Tho' as for swimming in again
He did not mean to, that was plain.

23.

The other fellows all had seen
Too much to venture in, I ween ;
And so they stood and gave advice,
Till William hit on a device :
He said—" A bottle in a shirt
" Will roll up tight, and 'twon't be hurt,
" So Jimmy Kenny, go and bring it,
" And then Big Billy there can fling it."

24.

The bottle in the shirt was tied,
And round the whole, a piece of hide,
To give it greater slinging force,
And urge it onward in its course ;
Then Billy whirled it o'er his head,—
The missile on its mission sped :
All watch'd it, breathless, as it flew,
It fell far short—and Bill looked blue.

25.

The publican then made a cast,
And this fresh parcel safely past
To those with roses red at tip ;
Who were so anxious for a nip.

'Twas quickly seized, each took a draught,
Which made them neither drunk nor daft,
But tended much to cheer their hearts,
And soothe their craving inward parts ;

26.

Then other wants they quickly found—
Their feet were naked on the ground,
Some socks would give them great delight ;
Two pairs of boots would charm their sight ;
Some lucifers to light a fire,
To make their draggled nightgowns drier ;
And sundry other things beside
They wish'd thrown o'er that raging tide.

27.

Some bread, the boots and socks were thrown,
Likewise a meaty mutton bone ;
Of lucifers, a little store ;
All that they ask'd—in fact, far more.
Then they were left to meditate
Upon the harsh decrees of fate,
And as to where the turbid flood
Would plant its plunder in the mud.

28.

But ere the close of that spring day,
The flood had nearly pass'd away,
Leaving a dingy, dark-brown rill
To bubble o'er the boulders still ;
Those women's troubles then were o'er,
For wading to the other shore
They soon, like daws in peacock's feathers,
Appeared in borrow'd prints and leathers.

NO FRIENDSHIP IN BUSINESS.

1.

If you have business with a friend,
You'll find it better in the end
To treat with him as you would treat
With perfect stranger in the street.
That is, with *care* your bargains make,
No matter what may be at stake ;
Then shall he say—" My friend is wise,
" *His* friendship it were well to prize ;
" Right honestly I'll deal, and still
" My vows of amity fulfil."

2.

But should you lean to friendship's side,
And lead his profits *far* too wide,
His latent greediness awakes,
And *Honour* in her castle quakes.
For generosity appears
To indicate an ass's ears ;
And, as an ass is not a beast
Well-fitted for true friendship's feast,
You quickly feel the rod of scorn,
And, what is worse, you lose your corn !
Your *friend*, ere this, you've lost, and *he*
Has lost far more—his probity !
Then recollect, lest friendship cool,
" Good-nature's garb proclaims the fool !"

AN ECHO.

An old man to the altar led
A gay and frisky lass ;
Then afterwards, like Echo, said
A-las ! A-las ! A-las !

THE FOURTH OF JANUARY, 1864.

1.

THE sultry night has pass'd away,
  And Phœbus once again
Mounts in the east, and opes the day
  O'er valley, hill, and plain ;

2.

But not upon the human race
  Looks he all smiling, down ;
For with a wrathful, lurid face,
  He seems on men to frown.

3.

The magpie sitteth silently
  Upon the gumtree's limb ;
He sendeth not toward the sky
  His mellow matin hymn.

4.

The diamond sparrows round the spring
  Crowd thick with panting breast,
With gaping beak and drooping wing,
  By sultry heat oppress'd.

5.

The gasping emus now betake
  Themselves into the creek,
At reedy pool their thirst to slake,
  And gumtrees' shade to seek ;

6.

There eagerly the sheep all speed,
  Nor linger by the way
Upon the saltbush sere to feed,—
  They feel but thirst to-day.

NOTE.—The day described in the following poem was the hottest I ever experienced. I was driving a team on the road from Port Augusta, and had started from Yadlamalka with nothing save a bottle of very brackish water to last me the stage (twelve miles on a treeless track), and this only augmented my thirst, for before I had got six miles from my starting point my tongue began to feel too large for my mouth, while my lips cracked, and I experienced the greatest difficulty in respiration, the air being too rarified to properly distend my lungs, and I believe I should have fainted had I not remembered that in the waggon there was a bottle of sarsaparilla, of which I drank nearly half. This cleared my senses as if by magic, and I got within a mile of Warrakimbo, when the dust-storm burst on me. I subsequently learned that the thermometer stood at 122 degrees between two open doors in Malcolm Gillies's hut. Birds of many kinds, including magpies and crows, died by hundreds ; and even bullocks, dogs, and sheep succumbed to the terrible heat. I continued to drink water, at short intervals, for nearly 24 hours before I could quench my inordinate thirst. I wrote the poem while making my next day's stage, and it appeared shortly after in the *Observer*.

7.

Now rugged range and arid plain
  Seem waving in the light ;
Their barren glare inflicting pain
  Upon the weary sight.

8.

And from the portals of the north
  The simoon's sultry breath,
Like furnace blasts comes sweeping forth,
  A burning wind of death.

9.

For upborne on its pennons strong,
  Vast clouds of dust arise ;
Whirling like smoke, they rush along,
  And darken all the skies.

10.

The native sparrows leave the springs,
  The magpies quit the creek,
And, faintingly, on flagging wings,
  In huts a shelter seek ;

11.

With them come dotterel, and whole flocks
  Of feather'd creatures small ;
The simoon all their efforts mocks,
  And numbers lifeless fall ;

12.

For, even as they fly, the band
  Is wither'd by its breath,
And strew the burning wind-waved sand,
  Their wings collapsed in death.

13.

The shepherd on the glaring plain
  Shrinks down a bush behind,
With cracking lip and eye of pain,
  Beneath the scorching wind ;

14.

He sees the dust-storm coming high,
  With side-wings spreading wide ;
There is no friendly shelter nigh,
  No place in which to hide !

15.

He crouches low, he bows his head,
  O'er him it howling flies,
As if the storm-king in it sped
  Beneath the frowning skies.

16.

Dust, filth, and broken herbage fly
In one black stifling cloud ;
The sun is hidden from the eye,
While thunder, pealing loud,

17.

Rolls through the sky with awful crash ;
And through the murky air
Fork'd lightnings in sharp zigzags flash
With sickly baleful glare.

18.

Now from the icy southern sea
A wind comes strong and chill,
Before which scatter'd raindrops flee,
And sprinkle plain and hill.

19.

The shepherd feels the welcome blast ;
He raises up his head ;
The dust has from the landscape pass'd,
Upon the south wind fled.

20.

From off his brow he wipes the grime
And sweat with heavy hand ;
And lays a curse upon the time
He came into this land ;

21.

And well he may, for day by day
'Tis naught but dust and wind ;
His sheep are starving and astray,
Himself is almost blind.

22.

The very air he breathes is foul
From sheep and cattle dead ;
While dingoes thrive and nightly howl,
And kites sail over head.

23.

Then ye who would a picture view
Of desolation drear,
Come, Anti-squatters, all of you,
Come North and see it here !

A DREAM OF THE DROUGHT, 1865.

With harrass'd mind I lay and thought
Upon the drought, that ruin brought,
    And desolation spread
O'er all the cheerless dusty plain,
Whose leafless shrubs for want of rain
    Had for long months been dead.

I thought on all my fruitless toil
On this most unproductive soil ;
    I thought on prospects fair,
Which for a time well pleased my sight,
Like buoyant bubbles passing bright,
    To burst like them in air.

And so I call'd in vain on Hope,
For far too faint was she to cope
    With Ruin grim and vast ;
But fled at once when on her ear
Rang out his bitter mocking jeer
    From dreary howling blast,

Which, sweeping round the chinky walls
In quick succeeding heavy squalls,
    Did clouds of dust detach
From where it had, from day to day,
Been gathering, in masses grey,
    Up in the dry rush thatch.

I gave my mind to form some plan
To save the stock ; but what is man
    When under God's dread frown ?
And so I thought and thought in vain,
Till weary grew my aching brain,
    When gentle sleep flew down,

And on mine eyelids set her seal,
Though still my brain no rest could feel,
    For then, as if the steam
From some unholy magic pot
Bewitched it with its vapours hot,
    I dream'd a fearful dream.

For swift unfolding to my view
A panoramic picture grew,
    Till spread before me lay
The plain, with dust-clouds driving fast
Before the ever-hissing blast,
    Against the face of day.

And silent horror shook my frame,
For from the earth hoarse murmurs came ;
   While sandhill, tree, and rock,
All reel'd and tottered to their base ;
Convulsed was nature's sterile face ;
   It was an earthquake's shock !

Shock followed shock, and dust-clouds grew,
And changed from grey to pitchy hue,
   Through which fork'd lightnings burst,
To meet the flames which from the ground
Flash'd fiercely forth through rifts profound,
   Like Tophet's fires accurs'd.

And from each blazing red abyss
Arose a mingled roar and hiss,
   As if the fiends were risen
In arms once more to try the might
Of Him who drove them from His sight
   Down to their awful prison.

I heard unnumbered thunders roll
With ceaseless crash from pole to pole,
   Above the ebon mass
Of smoke which on the plain now fell,
Like to the pictured roof of hell—
   No sunbeam could it pass.

But soon again all things did rock—
Three times I felt the earthquake's shock,
   And then a spire of flame
Shot from the lofty eastern Pound,
And shed its baleful glare around,
   While molten lava came

In one red, rushing, roaring tide
Of blazing billows down its side,
   And quickly fell'd each tree,
Which flash'd with flame, and then was lost
Beneath the flood, like snow-flakes toss'd
   Into a stormy sea.

Onward that raging torrent swept,
In awful cataracts, which leap'd
   Downward from dizzy height,
Till soon 'twould reach the spot of ground
Where, horror-struck, I glared around
   Upon the dreadful sight !

But now from that volcano vast
A roar came down like cyclone blast !
    I gazed in fresh amaze ;
For just above the crater's rim
Three fearful Phantoms, huge and grim,
    Were thron'd amid the blaze

High on a vast putrescent heap
Of ghastly oxen, steeds, and sheep,
    Which well became the three !
They seem'd to grin with horrid mirth
Upon the God-forsaken earth,
    And on unhappy me !

Despairing wrath within me grew,
And I address'd that ghostly crew ;
    I asked what they might find
To raise their mirth ?   When one and all
Affirmed they had been, since the fall,
    The scourges of mankind.

That human dread was their delight,
A trophy of their ruthless might ;
    Murder, and deadly strife,
Earthquakes and plagues, were pastimes rare,
With famine gaunt, and wild despair,
    And all the ills of life.

I then perceived, that as they spoke,
A name, in flaming letters broke
    Out on each livid brow ;
At which the grimmest cried—" Behold !
" For to *us*, all the North is sold—
    " Our wretched slave art thou !

" To me thou dost unwilling pay
" A teeming sacrifice each day
    " Of oxen, steeds, and sheep,
" Which these my servants, good and true,
" Wring from vile earthworms such as you,
    " And on mine altars heap.

" And now the solemn rites to crown,
" Thyself shall soon be stricken down—
    " To me resign thy breath ;
" For tortured in that burning sea
" A prey thou shalt become to me,
    " Thine enemy—King Death !"

At once those characters of flame,
To my enlightened eyes, became
    An alphabet of ease,
Which told me that the comrades dread
Of Death, were those who long had spread
    Starvation, and Disease.

But now the burning lava near
Its awful volumes did uprear
    In one vast roaring wave,
Which, rushing with resistless might,
Presented to my awe-struck sight
    A greedy, yawning grave,

Which in an instant more would hide
My calcined corse within its tide.
    I felt its burning heat,
Like to some deadly dragon's breath,
Boil my hot blood with blast of death,
    Yet there was no retreat.

It seem'd to burst ; when loud and clear
Came down a fell demoniac cheer,
    And startled slumber fled ;
For with a stifled cry I woke
To find thick dust, in place of smoke,
    In clouds above me spread.

The sweat had stream'd from ev'ry pore,
And mud was darkly coated o'er
    My visage as I lay,
With thicker masses round my mouth
And eyes, while bitter-burning drouth
    Had made my throat a prey.

I rose, and from a jug did drain
The water of the western Plain,
    Defiled with grimy sand,
And wished that either rain would fall,
Or sweeping ruin swallow all,
    That I might leave the land

Where I for six long years had toiled,
To be in every object foiled
    By drought's effects most dread ;
Till, harass'd out in frame and mind,
I curse the destiny unkind
    That here my footsteps led.

THE LIFE OF A WORKING BULLOCK.

1.

A PRETTY bull-calf, red-spotted and sleek,
　　Is sporting with other calves small ;
They frisk about on the bank of a creek,
　　Unheeding each cow's loving call ;
They flourish their tails about in the air,
　　And battle each other in sport,
For they know nothing of trouble or care,
　　Or anything else of the sort.

2.

But a stop is quickly put to their play,
　　For a horseman, stockwhip in hand,
Comes galloping up and drives them away,
　　To suffer by knife and by brand ;
For 'tis to the stockyard now they all go ;
　　They are joined by more on the way,
And the air resounds with whip-crack and low—
　　'Tis a general mustering day.

3.

Now learns our young calf a lesson in life,
　　And also the nature of pain,
For the stockwhip cuts his skin like a knife
　　When weary he lags on the plain,
And he joins the herd with a bleat of pain ;
　　He finds that he should not delay,
And fagg'd tho' he be will not linger again,
　　But keep up the rest of the way.

4.

The calves are shut up apart from the cows,
　　Which to them incessantly low,
While a fire is blazing, of dry gum boughs,
　　To keep all the brands at red glow.
Through a hole in a post is a hide rope small,
　　With a noose on the inner end,
While two men are outside, pulling left and right,
　　And the brands and the fire to tend.

5.

A stockman spreads the loop on a stick,
　　And nooses the neck of our calf :
At which he begins to plunge and to kick,
　　And his enemies rough to laugh.

He bellows with impotent rage and fright
    As his tail receives a sharp twist,
While the men outside, pulling left and right,
    Care little how he may resist.

6.

Then a noose on his near hind foot they cast,
    This then is triced high to a rail,
His near fore foot they too make fast,
    And drag him to ground by the tail.
Now his head is fast 'neath a stockman's knee,
    Another, not at all tender,
Kneels on his flank, and our calf soon will be
    A case of the neuter gender.

7.

With a glowing brand on his hide they scar
    His owner's known cypher or name ;
Then the station mark they cut in the ear,
    To know him by, far on the plain.
His eyes and his nose with foul dust get fill'd,
    His hide it hath many a smear ;
The cords are removed by which he was held,
    And he starts on the life of a steer.

8.

Two or three years have since glided away ;
    He has roam'd at his own free will,
Has lain in the shade thro' each summer's day,
    In the shady creek or on hill.
His horns are wide spread with an upward curve,
    His limbs have grown brawny and strong,
And the overseer is heard to observe—
    " I will rope that steer before long."

9.

He is penn'd again in a stockyard high,
    Like a restless bear in a cage,
And shakes his head at the stockkeepers nigh,
    While pawing up dust in his rage.
But soon a few rugged old slaves of the yoke
    Are turned in to act as a blind,
For an active man with stick and rope
    To lassoo his head from behind.

10.

By his brawny neck he is dragg'd again,
    And he roars and plunges around,
But that only adds discomfort and pain,
    For the rope is of texture sound.

He stubbornly stands till his eyeballs crack,
   And his tongue lolls swollen and white,
When the men are obliged that rope to slack,
   Or he would soon strangle outright.

11.

But they quickly drag on the rope once more,
   With a stick they thrash him, and then
For the fence he bounds, with a smother'd roar—
   Fine sport for those reckless men,
Who, hauling the rope in, hand over hand,
   As quick as he rushes almost,
Soon force the half madden'd creature to stand
   With his head drawn tight to a post.

12.

Now a big old worker, crabbed and strong,
   Is made to stand up to his side,
While a coupling chain by a green hide thong,
   To the base of his horns is tied ;
Then the other end to a worker's neck
   Is made quite secure with a rope ;
His liberty now is a shatter'd wreck,
   And he a dumb slave without hope.

13.

His surly old bondsmate he circles round,
   Which by Ranger will not be borne,
For the veteran meets his next wild bound
   On the point of his nearest horn ;
And he leads that steer a captive away,
   And will beat him into submission ;
For many another, before to-day,
   Has he brought to the same condition.

14.

Our bullock now drags the lumbering dray
   Thro' the midsummer's terrible heat,
And wearily toils on his dusty way,
   Tormented by flies and sore feet ;
And should the dray be fast in the sand,
   He suffers a world of abuse,
For the whip is plied by a heavy hand,
   Which is perfect quite in its use.

15.

And so he toils on, and is bought and sold,
   But never by change does he gain,
For still he must work, tho' starving and old,
   A slave of the yoke and the chain.

At last when from weakness he cannot obey,
    He is scourged with the whip in vain,
For, staggering down in front of the dray,
    The slave leaves his life's load of pain.
16.
In the stony pass, where our bullock died,
    Still lies a foul festering heap,
Whence dry bones gleam from the once glossy hide,
    Where sarcophagus beetles creep.
And the lizard lurks 'neath his cavern'd flank,
    In wait for its sun-loving prey,
While clustering masses of herbage rank
    Flourish greenly on his decay.

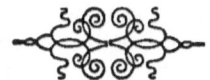

THE DEATH-BLOW.

A TALE OF DARKNESS.

Oh! ye who dwell in busy towns, where Law, with iron hand,
Guards well your lives and properties,—ye cannot understand
The hardship which a bushman bears, or perils round him spread,
When, in the howling wilderness, he lays his weary head.
So, readers pay attention now, while to you I relate
How one misguided wanderer went blindly to his fate.

The night is dark and overcast, and chilly is the air,
When, by a giant gumtree's foot, is seen a flame's bright glare;
And there, beside it, in his rug, a weary bushman sleeps,
While, with an uprais'd heavy club, a naked savage creeps
Toward the solitary man, with stealthy step and slow,
As with keen, gleaming, vicious eyes he meditates his blow.
But still his victim lies supine, all helpless on the ground,
When crash! the swift descending club a mortal part has found;
And, as the body writhes about, more sounding blows descend;
When, suddenly, the man awakes! and starts right straight on
    end!
Then nimbly leaping to one side, he cries out, "Well done, Jake!
"Him big one lucky you jump up, and kill 'em that one snake:
"I'm plenty glad I fetch 'em you to track 'em sheep 'long me;
"Here bacca. Now, you ketch 'em smoke, and boil 'em pot of tea."

A FISHY LEGEND OF DORSETSHIRE.

In Dorsetshire, one autumn day, beside a shady pool,
A well appointed fisherman sat on a rustic stool.
His polish'd rod, with rings and reel, stood planted on the ground,
While he, as if he loved it well, a luckless croaker bound
Unto a hook,—two cruel hooks,—which back to back were bent,
And seem'd to threaten everything with mischievous intent.
O ! once loquacious, happy frog ! bad company you've found !
'Tis lucky your amphibious, or you'd be surely drown'd,
For sunk within that silent pool you presently will be,
When lots of old acquaintances you may, if watchful, see ;
But no, a deadly foe lurks there, with appetite more keen
For delicate frog provender, than Frenchman's e'er has been ;
But, bah ! 'tis only loss of breath to tell you all I know,
So go yourself, my spotted friend, and beard him down below.

The fisherman, self-satisfied, surveys his bait so neat,
And as it dangles helplessly he rises to his feet,
Then carefully resumes his rod, and with a cunning eye
He notes the best locality for lurking " Jack " to try ;
When seeing that his line is clear, he makes a handsome cast,
And froggy to the shades below right suddenly has pass'd ;
But o'er him still the painted float is dancing on the tide,
While circles, which at first were small, now ripple far and wide.

Then smiled that gentle fisherman, and from a pocket flask
He takes some soothing "medicine,"—to him no painful task,—
And lights a mild Havanna ; but, ah ! he drops it quick,
And gives a sharp, decided jerk unto his jointed stick ;
Then presently low rounded waves are plying to and fro,
And though his line is paying out, his rod bends like a bow,
Right skilfully he plays his fish, until a gleaming side,
Like flash of light an instant shows above the troubled tide,
Then disappears ; but slowly now the ripples mark his way ;
For master Jack, with gasping jaws, has drunk too much to-day,
And soon the handy landing net has got him in its bounds,
A mighty fish of three feet long, and fully fourteen pounds !

Now gasping on the sedgy brink the robber lies supine,
When by that dandy fisherman a dog is heard to whine.
With sudden start he glances round, and there a "lurcher" lank
Is standing by a little boy amongst the herbage rank.
No child of gentle parentage can be that urchin brown,
Whose pleasing, open countenance smacks nothing of the town,

But wears that sweet simplicity which marks the rustic race,
And goes so far to compensate for their known lack of grace.
His boots are heavy hobnail'd ones, of polish guiltless quite ;
Brown leathern gaiters occupy near half of his small height ;
O'er these a pleated garment hangs in graceful folds around,
While with a round top'd " billycock " his shaggy locks are
    crown'd.

The dog *might* once have had a tail, it now has but a stump—
A melancholy sort of thing ! an elongated lump !
From which some straggling hairs depend, which plainly do
    denote
A shaggy tail he *ought* to have, as well as shaggy coat.
And as he meditates the pike, he hath a knowing glance,
As if he'd take it home with him—if had but the chance.
And so perhaps he may, but not as he no doubt would wish,
(There's " other way save in the mouth " of carrying a fish !
And now his biped friend observes unto that fisher wight—
" Be golly, Meastre, that ur fesh looks jeast as ef ud bite."
The gay and festive fisherman replied—" Ah, yas, perhaps,
" Just try him with your finger now—you're used to rabbit
    traps."
But Johnny Bumpkin shook his head—Ah ! what a happy
    thought !
Instead of finger, Pincher's tail !   O, wouldn't that be sport !
" Meastre ? " (he bashfully remarked), " I'll tell 'e what ull do,
" We'll let un pin oud Pincher's theare, if be the same to you."

The unsuspecting gentleman rejoined—" Just try him, then."—
He called himself soon afterwards the stupidest of men ;
And *well* he might ! for when the pike to Pincher's knob froze
    tight,
That much astonished quadruped betook himself to flight!
Like pigeon, that some fancier, on racecourse or at fair,
With note to it securely tied, throws upward in the air,
To take to his far distant home, the news unto it bound.
So circles round, a time or two, that active tailless hound !
And if he made a yelping noise, 'twas no doubt just to tell
His playful patrons that he thought his " rudder" answered
    well ;
But then, as if he felt asham'd when he their laughter heard,
He made a bee-line for some place, just like that home-sick bird.

And now a chevy chase began, which ended soon indeed,
For nought save electricity could touch that dog in speed.
And clench'd upon his " narrative," just like avenging fate,
The fish, fresh from his element, pursued him o'er a gate.

But after that (tho' I can't tell where those queer comrades
    hied)
The gentleman jump'd on his hat ! while Bumpkin, by his side,
Like flea-vex'd poodle, roll'd about, and laugh'd until he cried!
Till with a rousing kick reprov'd, he started to his feet,
And from that frantic fisherman effected his retreat.

And Mr. Pincher from his home for days a truant stayed,
(Though he, perhaps, not all that time pursued a porter's trade.)
But if he did, most probably he shifted his queer load
To somewhere, else where it might be more comfortably stow'd.
And as he look'd quite satisfied when he returned again,
It is surmised he much enjoy'd what gave at first such pain !

Of Walton's gentle follower I will not say much more.
His language was peculiar,—though I will not say he swore !
At any rate, 'twould only grate upon your polish'd ear ;
And, therefore, you'd have long to wait before you find it here.
So let him fix his sever'd line, and catch another frog ;
Or bundle up his fishing kit, and inn-ward grimly jog.
One thing I may as well just state—that is, to Pincher's tail
He will not hang his fish again, but send it home by rail !

MORAL.

And now, my gentle readers all, no chance should e'er be missed
Of taking morals from true tales ; and so I'll try to twist
A very short, but warning one, from this my story plain—
Thus, " Do not trust to reckless dogs, what *you* may need again !"

LYRES AND LIARS.

Old Homer swept his sounding lyre
    With grand fierce fire supernal !
While " Nick " sweeps each astounding liar
    Into fierce fire infernal !

GOOD ADVICE.

O 'TIS a most delightful thing to tender " good advice "
Unto our frail acquaintances, it is *so* cheap and nice.—
I know I've very frequently advised my friends for good ;
Yet somehow, shortly afterwards, in like position stood.
But you, no doubt, have often heard the adage old—O dear,
From being in *their* company, I must have err'd, I fear.

O, is it not a friendly act, to tell your old friend, Max,
(Who matrimony meditates) that his fair sweetheart lacks
Each admirable quality that sweetens married life ?
And he just goes (the stupid ass) and makes her his *dear* wife !
Then tells her in the honeymoon, for lack of else to do,
Your blindness in mistaking her ; O, how she then loves you !

You say to Mr. Moneybags (whose father made his pile
From some dark, dirty copper mine, or well of stinking " ile ")
You wish you had *his* capital, *you'd* double it right soon
In such a stunning little speck !—A railway to the moon—
(We'll call it that !) For when he goes, and lays his money out,
He does not get it back again ! *and quits* when you're about !

A wicked little boy you hear to *shocking* words give vent ;
Severely you then lecture him with virtuous intent,
And tell him to what dreadful place such language leads in time !
But, ah ! what *something* vagabond is that you see to climb
Into your loaded bergamot, and shatter down a branch ?—
O ! what *expressive epithets* you at the culprit launch !

Tom Trotter (who has money made) would start a "trap and
    horse,"
You know about " the very thing," a bargain quite, of course,
And *such* " a first-class quadruped "—he has not got one fault !
Poor Trotter buys the whole concern ; but here I fain would
    halt,
For when you go to borrow it, *a hearse* just leaves his door,
And his *afflicted relatives* will speak to you no more !

O ! what a mournful man are you, as homeward then you speed,
Or go to freely *give your mind* to him who sold the steed.
No more, you *firmly* do resolve, will you your friends advise—
When, you encounter neighbour Jones, a green shade o'er his
    eyes :
And as consolatory talk you pour into his ear,
You recollect a " splendid cure " you heard about last year.

Minutely you explain to him how he should lotion make—
(Some awful liquid flame of fire), and what he ought to take.
But poor old Jones is rather deaf, and stupid too—O dear,
How sorry you are afterwards, when from his wife you hear
" That Joseph to the hospital has gone in sorry plight,
"And 'tis thro' using *your vile stuff* that he has *lost his sight !*"

Well, these events, so tragical, should certainly suffice
To be a stoppage magical to your insane advice.
But *will* they ? Here I answer, No—if you are mortal ! Still
You'll trot about and doctor folks when they are taken ill,
And tell them what they *ought* to do when trouble hems them
    round,
And then, *be sorry afterwards !* for that I will be bound !

And still my friends I do not say, look to yourselves alone,—
(Forgetting thus the Golden Rule),—but pity Trouble's moan ;
And any little thing you know that can do good to others,
Explain it well, and help them on ; for are we not all brothers ?
And now to close this prolix lay, with which you have been
    task'd,
I say, *be ready with advice*, and give it WHEN YOU'RE ASKED !

SLOTH.

SLOTH is a Vampire, which by day and night
    With maw unsated, battens on men's lives ;
As doth insidious and fatal blight
    On some fair tree ; and when it settles, thrives
On wasted time, till it all prospects bright,
    Fair fame, and fortune, from its victim rives !
Yet leaves him not when they are lost, but still
    Clings to his wreck, a genius of ill !

TO A BLOW-FLY.

Oh, filthy vulture of the insect world !
  The loathing you inspire no tongue can tell,
When, with loud buzzing busy wings unfurl'd,
  You sally forth upon your mission fell,
  Guided afar by keenest sense of smell,
That laughs to scorn the bloodhounds !   Thing of ill !
  Fiend-like, your business you perform too well !
The poor maim'd lambs with living tortures thrill,
When from fierce wild-dog's fangs they 'scape for *you* to kill !

Your horrid zeal to propagate your kind
  Outrivals e'en the mad dog's rage to bite,
Or tigers, to destroy !   Oh, wretch ! designed
  For foulest work !   You, with obscene delight,
  Gloat o'er destruction ; and, with headlong flight,
Speed to the carnival that death may spread,
  Or strife strew broadcast.   To all creatures' sight
You are a pest to shudder at and dread ;
And, could deep curses kill, then were your kind all dead !

"GO TO THE ANT, THOU SLUGGARD."

" Go to the ant, thou sluggard," do !
  And sleep upon his nest ;
Then, if you rise not early, you
  A " sluggard " lie confess'd.

THE NATURALIST AND ICHNEUMON FLY.

1.

A very benevolent, bald-headed mortal
  Loved butterflies, moths, and the whole of their race ;
In fact, with his yellow gauze net he had caught all
  The insects, and ranged them in glass-cover'd case—
With one grand exception—a moth of great beauty ;
And so a strict watch for it formed his chief duty.

2.

He offered rewards, and the bumpkins then brought him
  Privet-hawks, peacock-moths, and old ladies a stock ;
While one saucy fellow a *bat* saw, and caught him,
  But got nothing for it to line his smock-frock ;
And as for himself, why, he roam'd in the gloaming,
While great was the mess that he often came home in.

3.

But all was in vain ; till, one day in a thicket,
  His eyes from their sockets near leap'd with delight,
For, ah ! its great chrysalis !—yes, 'twas the ticket !
  'Neath sheet of loose bark just appeared to his sight.
And oh ! as he carried it home to his study,
A smile quite usurp'd all his countenance ruddy.

4.

In a box with dry moss he bestowed his rich treasure,
  And covered it safely with gauze like his net ;
While first thing each morning, with keen, anxious pleasure,
  He'd lovingly gaze on his curious pet.
Till oh ! his vexation, and dire aggravation,
Were plainly betray'd by a sharp exclamation !

5.

For there, I declare, from the chrysalis broken,
  A villanous ichneumon fly had come out ;
And, if that old gentleman's thoughts had been spoken,
  His tongue some strange words, had then utter'd, no doubt.
As it was, thro' that slender, black, wasp-looking pirate
He stuck a sharp pin, and felt soothed, tho' still irate.

6.

But then, like the ass of bad Balaam, the prophet,
  The ichneumon spoke, and these words did he say :—
" You think I've been cruel, so send me to Tophet,
  " Though *you* are much more so to moths every day ;
" For while *we* are sent, by the All-wise, to eat them,
" *You,* just for sheer mischief, impale and maltreat them."

THE VILLAIN AND THE HERO.

1.

A GALLANT old colonel, a country J.P.,
  Was pompous and stern in his manner,
And thought a rope-noose was a rare recipe,
  And its burden the law's chiefest banner.

2.

Well, one day, a fellow, who'd murder'd his man,
  Was dragg'd up in handcuffs before him,
And, the charge being proved, his stern worship began
  With vicious tongue, scourging, to score him.

3.

" You rascal ! you're sure to be hang'd till you're dead,
  " And ought to be whipp'd well directly,
" And put in the pillory, thence to be led
  " To the gallows, if treated correctly."

4.

The culprit here gazed at that irate J.P.,
  And said, " Sir, I thank you sincerely ;
" But if a hemp-collar is fitting for me,
  " Why you, yourself, ought to feel queerly.

5.

" But there, my friend Blair has so aptly declared,
  " ' One murder will make a great villain,'
" While, as a ' grand hero,' a soldier is chair'd
  " Who has spent all his life in man-killing !"

STUPID PETER.

DEDICATED TO WHOM IT MAY CONCERN.

AIR—" *Juanita.*"

1.

LEANING o'er his liquor
  Lingering lolls the fledgling fop ;
Grins a senseless snicker,
  Strokes his chin's " down crop."
On the barmaid slender
  His sheep's eyes they love to dwell ;
Fuddled looks, yet tender,
  Throws this would-be swell.

Peter, stupid creature !
   She don't care a pin for you ;
Peter, stupid creature,
   What I say is true !

2.

He'll take to pawning,
   Nought cares he, but drinks again,
And, prudence scorning,
   Looks his love in vain.
Grog his breath all scenting ;
   Like an oyster is his eye ;
Oh, he'll be repenting
   Ere the night's gone by.
      Peter, stupid creature,
         You that yet may be a man ;
      Peter, stupid creature,
         By " Darwin's plan."

SONG OF THE FAR NORTH MAIL.

[AFTER HOOD.]

WITH action weary and spent,
   With eyeballs sunken and dull,
Four over-worked, half-fed horses strive
   A lumbering coach to pull.
      Drag ! drag ! drag !
In the midst of a scorching clime,
   Oh ! fain would stop each poor struggling nag
For a moment's breathing time.

      Drag ! drag ! drag !
With the fierce sun glaring above,
      And drag ! drag ! drag !
While the *fares* get down and shove.
'Twere better in a cart
   As stock of the cat's-meat man,
Where horses have ever to take a part
   When past cab, coach, or van.

Drag ! drag ! drag !
Though their strength begins to fail :
Drag ! drag ! drag !
While the whip makes many a wale !
Plain and sideling and creek,
Creek and sideling and plain,
And over the gutters they stagger weak,
The end of the stage to gain.

Oh ! mail with letters fraught,
Oh ! mail that hurries and drives,
It is not leather you're wearing out,
But starving horses' lives.
Drag ! drag ! drag !
In suffering, hunger, and grime ;
Away up here in the dreary North
Horse-killing is no crime !

But why should those steeds fear death ?
Those spectres of skin and bone,
Which crawling on in skeleton shape
Would melt a heart of stone—
Would melt a heart of stone
To think of the fasts they keep ;
Oh, shame ! that horses thus should starve
Though hay now be not cheap.

Drag ! drag ! drag !
The whipcord never flags
While a man for wages still will ply
The scourge on those wretched nags:
A hayless rack, and a barren plain ;
Starvation is everywhere.
From the well alone can they get their fill
And sometimes not e'en there.

Drag ! drag ! drag !
A weary stage and long,
Drag ! drag ! drag !
Urged on by ruthless thong,
Creek and sideling and plain—
Plain and sideling and creek,
Till the lifeless action and drooping head
Of a broken spirit speak.

Drag ! drag ! drag !
With the noonday sun too bright,
And drag ! drag ! drag !
Through the sultry summer night—

Till the driver falls asleep—
To wake with a sudden start,
   As *they* soon know by the whip's sharp crack,
   And *" long-oats " burning smart.

Oh ! for a hearty feed
   Of lucerne or hay so sweet—
Or e'en the town nag's bed
   Trod down beneath his feet,
   For only one short week
In the farmer's rude brush shed,
   Before them stretched the well-filled racks
Where perchance they once were fed.

Oh ! for a respite brief
   From galling collar and whip,
From sweat-soaked trace and bit and rein,
   And dusty toilsome trip,
A little feeding would give them heart ;
   But pity nought avails.
† *There is no feed* for those starving steeds,
   Gaunt slaves of Her Majesty's mails !

With action weary and spent,
   With eyeballs sunken and dull,
Four overworked half-fed horses strive
   A lumbering coach to pull.
      Drag ! drag ! drag !
In the midst of a scorching clime,
Oh ! fain would stop each poor struggling nag
For a hasty bite from a feeding-bag,
   And a moment's breathing time.

---

*Whipcord.

†This poem was written in 1876, when the horses on the Blinman line had to subsist on what they could pick up on a country where *sheep* were starving !! They were like the " Frenchman's horse," they died before they got used to it.

BURNING OF THE COSPATRICK.

BURNING OF THE COSPATRICK.

THE glowing sun is sinking out of sight
Behind a spreading circle's western verge ;
The winds of southern summer, soft and light,
Breathe o'er the billows, which have ceased to surge
Since the last tempest hath withdrawn its scourge ;
Yet still their huge unquiet forms arise
(Like half-quelled rioters a word would urge
Again to fury), but the tranquil skies
Proclaim a peaceful night, and daylight slowly dies:—

Leaving a lofty ship, with spreading sails,
To roll and toss upon her lonely way,
Urged by the lazy breeze, which nearly fails
To fill the canvas, looming ghostly grey,
Beneath the young slim moon's faint silver ray.
Slowly she sails, while floating o'er the deep
Are wafted melodies, now sad, now gay—
Songs of bright hope, to make men's hearts to leap
And plaintive ballads old, would force the blithe to weep

For her wide decks are crowded with a throng
Of emigrants from Britain's islands twain,
Who seek the lagging time to speed with song,
While idly rocking on the restless main,
Far from the homes they ne'er may see again.
Gaily the laugh and sportive jest goes round,
As to bright fancy they allow the rein ;
For are they not to certain fortune bound,
In those fair Southern isles where plenty reigns around ?

But hark ! sharp measur'd chimes from stricken bell
Rise o'er the other sounds with cadence clear,
And to the hardy sunburnt seamen tell
That the short watch at eve, so justly dear,
Is past and gone.   And soon a man to steer
Steps quickly aft the helmsman to relieve.
He takes the wheel, while plainly in his ear
His shipmate gives the course, then turns to leave
With quick-glanced comments queer, as plain as words could
    weave.

Upon the forecastle the look-out man
Patrols the narrow space with careful tread ;
Stopping at times the vessel's path to scan,
To see that dangers do not lurk ahead,
Watching for ships, or floating wrecks more dread.

While his rough comrades of the watch bestow
Themselves around, where'er by fancy led,
In friendly knots to talk in voices low,
So to avoid complaints from wakeful tars below.

And presently the landsmen slowly go
Down to the 'tween decks to their berths to sleep,
Though some remain to watch the starlight's glow
In quivers play upon the restless deep,
While little sparks, like shining soft eyes, peep
From out the patchwork of white-sheeted spray
Formed when the waves against the vessel leap,
And fall with sullen splash, then pass away
To the wide wake astern in masses dull and grey.

Now the last lingerer unwilling goes,
Leaving the officer the poop to pace ;
To con the sails, and ascertain whence blows
The languid breeze which scarcely fans his face ;
While now and then he calls his men to brace
The yards around, to meet the shifty wind,
Which they, not differing from all the race,
Do with strong arms, while with low words unkind
They growl beneath their beards, and wish him dead or blind.

Thus they on deck, and nearly all below,
In their rude berths, are now beneath the spell
Of gentle sleep—the sweetest mortals know,
When undisturbed by fevered visions fell,
As every honest weary soul can tell—
And these, quite confident in ship and crew,
Without one thought of fear, sleep sound and well ;
For all their hopes rose-tinted are in hue,
And their lives' pictured paths are pleasant to their view.

They do not heed the wash against the bends,
The sounding bell, or heavy rollers' shock,
Or on the deck the clatter of ropes' ends,
Or noisy banging of a tackle-block,
The creaky fittings, or the vessel's rock,—
Nor are they wakened by the seaman's tread,
Which, echoing hollow, slumber seems to mock,
But as a lullaby it serves instead,
Becoming food for dreams in many a pillow'd head.

And restless brains, ignoring sleep's control,
Indulge in visions strange and manifold,
Which wizard Fancy—artist of the soul—
Paints with a majic pencil free and bold,
To suit the young, the middle-aged, and old !

The past, the present, and the future bring
A strange mixed medley of designs untold
To fill his canvas. Mirth, on glancing wing,
And Guilt and Trouble, too, to him their subjects fling.

The young strong man, with health and courage blest,
Unknowing yet the force of Time's fell hand,—
Who feels for dangers rude a burning zest,
Treads with firm stride the yet far-distant strand;
Or breasts the flood, or views his well-tilled land ;
On gallant steed outstrips the bushland flame,
Or singly combats with some savage band ;
Sees beauty his, grasps opulence and fame,—
And is the winner, sure, in Life's swift changing game !

The buxom lass, her red cheek on her arm,
Meets once again the lover left behind—
Or, what for her hath still a greater charm,
One still more handsome whom she yet may find
Should blind Dame Fortune be to her but kind !
Gay scenes of pleasure, dresses rich and bright,—
All these combine to fill with joy her mind ;
Let anxious care assail with morning's light—
She hath fair visions now to charm her dreaming sight !

The tender infant by its mother's side,—
E'en it hath dreams to stir its slumbers deep ;
Its soft lips work as if they draw the tide
Which doth its baby life in pleasure steep,
And sends it satisfied each night to sleep.
Faint wreathing smiles play o'er its dimpled face,
Its rosy limbs from 'neath the blankets peep ;
And surely o'er it from the Throne of Grace
A guardian angel stands and keeps its resting-place !

'Tis now of night the silent solemn noon ;
And once again the clangour of the bell
Proclaims the changing of the watch, and soon
The weary seamen—thinking all is well—
Turn in to sleep their brief allotted spell ;
While their bronzed brothers, yawning as they go,
Creep into cosy nooks old yarns to tell,
To pass the time which drags for them full slow,
While still the sleepers sleep, and dream their dreams below.

One man, now past his prime, from Erin's Isle,
Moans in his dream, and even seems to weep;—
For ah ! he stands amidst a concourse vile
Of black-mask'd monsters, who a circle keep
Around a house whence half-clad creatures leap

To 'scape those flames, which, redly rushing high,
The night's black clouds in lurid crimson steep !
Oh God ! the fiends ! they hurl them back to die !—
The horror is too great—he wakes with stifled cry !

What pungent odour steals up from below ?
What stealthy hiss, as from some hidden snake ?
Oh ! 'tis to him a far more deadly foe,
For at its name the boldest-hearted quake !
" Fire ! fire !" he cries.   The dreamers all awake
In wild confusion and in dread affright.
Their very lives with death are now at stake
Out on the ocean in the darksome night,
For fire and flood are leagued to crush themwith their might!

The boldest don what garments they may find ;
The women rush upon the deck to shriek ;
While crew and captain, as one man combined,
Unite the fire within its lair to seek,
With steadfast purpose, but with blanching cheek.
Too late ! too late !   On sails and cordage fed
It gathers force, and rushes forth to wreak
A swift destruction on each helpless head,
So lately laid secure in slumber void of dread.

In vain a deluge from the sea they send ;
In hissing steam the fire but flings it back
Up through the hatchway with the mists to blend,
And pass to leeward with the heavy track
Of pitchy smoke which rolls in volumes black !
While the dread foe, fierce, hydra-headed, flies
At those who on it bravely make attack,
Like famished lion that with blazing eyes
Beats back the hunter band, and bears off one a prize!—

Or like the fires which in these southern lands
Rage through the cornfields when great heats prevail,
Mocking the efforts of the sweat-drenched bands,
Who fight against them, but with small avail,
As borne upon the pinions of the gale
They dart with sullen roar upon their prey,
Filling with ruin all the peaceful vale
Late rich in vineyards and in gardens gay—
And so the flames spread now, and all is wild dismay !

The frightened women to the workers cling,
Or screaming children to their bosoms fold ;
While men with pumps and buckets madly fling
Tons of salt water in the burning hold.
E'en fearless hearts with sudden dread run cold ;

For all in vain their failing force they try—
The whirling flames beat back those seamen bold
Breathless and scorched—and then exultant fly
To claim the foremost boats, and climb the rigging high !

The fated ship, now head to wind, sweeps round,
And the tall foremast falls with horrid crash,—
(Like some vast forest tree unto the ground
Beneath fierce lightning's devastating flash),—
While to the boats the fear-struck people dash,
And overcrowd one—by their terror driven—
Till with the weight the iron davits smash,
And the dark sea by struggling forms is riven,
Whose awful cries for help rise madly up to heaven !

They cry in vain to God and fellowman !
Their time is come to cross the gulf so drear !
Their earthly course is shortened to a span
Of awful anguish and ungoverned fear,
Which like a red-hot iron seems to sear
Those bursting hearts, which now must quickly stay
The varied pulse of joys and sorrows here !
For Death in all his terrors stalks this way—
The wild waves work his will, which fainting souls obey.

The mate, brave Lewis, and McDonald try
With the third mate the pinnace large to turn ;
But no one answers to their earnest cry
For needful help, and so 'tis left to burn ;
And leaping flames soon rage from stem to stern.
But still another boat is hanging near.
To lower it becomes their chief concern,
While others, not yet overcome by fear,
Secure the fallen boat, and quickly bail her clear.

Meanwhile some throw the gig into the waves
With clumsy haste, to drift half-swamped away
Upon the spar-encumbered sea, which raves
And surges round in eagerness to slay !
Now many who a greater fear obey,
Flee from the fire but to be quickly drowned,
And sink in ocean's depths cold lifeless clay ;
Save those who, clinging to the wreck around ;
A cruel respite gain, in such frail succour found.

Densely the boats are peopled with a crowd
Of reckless men who down the tackles slide,
Or wildly leap ; while splashing all around
Strong swimmers battle bravely with the tide,
And scramble fiercely to surmount the side !

Both crafts at once are crowded to excess—
The crews push off, and from the wreck they glide.
They cannot aid amid this wild distress !
Their feeble chance of life, each moment renders less.

Upon the ship rolls aft the fiery pest,
And from the great main hatchway roars on high ;
While soon, by e'en the bravest, 'tis confessed
No hope is left for any but to die,
And prayers and shrieks go up in one wild cry ;
While to the crashing mainmast's thunder dread
The awful groans of victims make reply,
Mixed with the wailing whirr of flames o'erhead,
Which light with lurid glare the living and the dead

The two frail boats are heaving on the deep,
Throng'd with pale inmates, who with horror view
Despairing wretches from the vessel leap,
And yet to succour them can nothing do.
Gazing with faces of an ashen hue,
They see the captain throw into the waves
His much-loved wife—then swiftly follow too !
The doctor, with their child, the same fate braves—
Then, with a shrieking crowd, they sink into their graves.

(How strong the love of life in men must be
When they can tamely sit, while all around
Their fellow-creatures in their misery,
Crying for help, are yet, all helpless, drowned !
If now no ark of safety can be found,
Do not they think that they may well die too,
And pass away, with deathless honour crowned,
Rather than live for evermore to view
By day and night, in thought, that lost beseeching crew ?)

The mizenmast falls headlong in the sea ;
The waters surge, while with explosion dread,
As of a score of cannons, forcefully
The stern blows out.   And soon the flames are spread
O'er all the vessel, for by spirits fed
They mount on high with rushing whirlwind roar,
And in the midst the last sad souls are sped—
Divorced from earthly clay—above to soar
To work their Maker's will elsewhere for evermore !

The hull floats on, infested by fierce fire,
Which eats her massive frame, while jets of steam
With angry hiss above the flames aspire,
When through her shattered stern the waters stream,
Or dash into her through the ports abeam.

And one by one the swimmers strong go down ;
And men drop off from coop or floating beam
With choking cry, beneath the waves to drown,
Each fear-wrung visage pale fast settling in a frown.

And near the wreck, with their large living freight
Of human salvage, those two frail craft lie,
When bright Aurora opens wide the gate
For blushing Morning in the eastern sky,
And all around the seamen's glances fly
In eager hope that some tall saving ship,
Approaching slowly, may now greet the eye.
They gaze in vain, with indrawn breath and lip ;
Sea birds alone they see, which in the waters dip !

Now as the cutter has no chief to guide
Her future movements and control her crew,
McDonald goes on board, while by his side
Bentley and Cotter and brave Lewis too
Attend their officer his will to do
With prompt submission ; and though lacking sail,
Compass or chart, with land far from their view,
Undaunted hearts may help to turn the scale
Against gaunt Famine's tooth, and Ocean's ruthless gale.

The day wends on, the sun resigns his reign,
And night's long weary vigils too are past,
While once again above the watery plain
The morning breaks, as hopeless as the last ;
For, though all night the wreck's red beacon cast
Its warning light far o'er the lonely sea,
No swelling sail—no lofty taper mast,
Within the circle of their sight they see,
And from their saddened hearts faint hope begins to flee.

The second day is nearly past, when lo !
The calcined hull sends up vast clouds of steam
As with a plunge she hissing dives below ;
And as she dives her red-hot ruins gleam,
And a wild requiem startled seabirds scream ;
While rushing waters in the vortex meet,
And in fierce contest for the plunder seem !
Then rolling onward in their endless beat,
They count one vessel more to Ocean's sunken fleet !

Now on the hamper which around them floats
The shipwrecked look—then shape their hopeless course
Sans food or water, in those sailless boats,
With three oars only their slow way to force.
But now adroit McDonald hath recourse

To a torn garment which a poor girl lends
To form a sail—which might have been the source
In times more prosperous, of jests. This tends
To raise their hopes of life, as their frail mast it bends.

Onward they drift the livelong silent night,
The starry hosts reflected in the deep.
And while for succour some few strain their sight,
The others, wearied out, all huddled sleep,
And the poor women in the mate's boat weep.
The morning breaks, and Ocean's breast again
Hath not a sail to cause their hearts to leap ;
But thirst and hunger add unto their pain ;—
O ! for the crust despised !—the gently falling rain !

Another day is numbered with the past ;
Another night and still another day ;
Then o'er the ocean wakes again the blast
Which bids the waves arise—and they obey,
Rolling before it in the moonlight grey ;
And on they speed, those gaunt and wasted forms,
Who little heed the crested billows' play ;
For with the wind the hope each bosom warms
That they may meet a ship, or reach the Cape of Storms.

Now brave McDonald scans the sea in vain ;
The other boat has vanished from his sight,
And to his loudest call no voice again
Comes back in answer through the thickening night
Over the surges, gleaming crisp and white,
Onward they scud, while in each breast of care
The feeling gathers, that the weary fight
With wolfish hunger, thirst, and deep despair
Must now be, all uncheered, for them alone to bear.

The Sabbath dawns—no peaceful time of rest !
What day it is they scarcely know nor care ;
For as they gaze beyond each billow's crest
Their sinking hearts give way to dull despair ;
Their burning thirst becomes too great to bear,
And—all regardless of wise counsels given—
They drink the brine, altho' it seems to tear
Their very vitals, till by madness driven
They glare like savage beasts, and rave of Hell and Heaven.

And one by one their anguished souls depart,
Leaving their bodies to the sea a prey.
Poor Bentley, steering, wakes with sudden start
From a deep doze, and, falling, drifts away.
They see, they hear, but have no power to stay !

On, on, they drive !   While, like a rushing pack
Of famished lions, all intent to slay,
The angry billows follow in their track,
And o'er the gunwales leap, to be bailed hardly back.

Still howls the gale ! And now, by hunger driven,
The ghoul-like living feed upon the dead !
For from their breasts all human qualms are riven,
For they must die if not on something fed,
And naught is there save those whose souls have fled.
And they are many—for each awful day
Sees raving wretches die, whose veins are bled
To keep those living who have strength to slay,—
The life-sustaining law, so ruthless to obey !

Now just before the breaking of the dawn
Of the eighth morning, through the shades of night
There bursts upon those voyagers forlorn
What is to them most welcome, dearest sight !
A barque ! full sail before the breeze, now light !
They try to shout, and raise a feeble noise,—
But disappointment like a deadly blight
Falls on their hearts—none hear their weak " ahoys !"
And the swift craft speeds on, and all their hope destroys !

O ! who can tell the anguish that they feel
As the good ship upon her voyage steers ?
Their strength is gone, their shattered senses reel,
And their hot eyes distil yet hotter tears
As Death in ghastly form so close appears,
He seems to grasp them.   Yet brave Lewis now
Pours words of hope and comfort in their ears
(Though agony's cold dew is on his brow)—
" We're on the track," he cries, " which homeward vessels
    plough."

Nine dreary nights, nine weary days are flown,
And still floats on that ark of horrors, where
The mangled dead are midst the living strewn ;
For near them crouch like wild beasts in their lair,
The gaunt survivors, who no longer care
For life or death, but 'neath the cold grey skies
Sleep in dull sleep, or round them madly glare
Upon their comrades with red frenzied eyes,
Till, like a hungry wolf, one on McDonald flies,

And bites his flesh, who, starting from his trance,
Then rises feebly to repel his foe.
But what is that which meets his waking glance,
And makes with hope his bosom once more glow ?

A noble ship ! He tries to shout " Sail ho !"
But has no voice—then to the gunwale clings,
And gazes mutely on the gallant show
The coming vessel makes with snowy wings,
While o'er the crested waves her captain's hoarse hail rings.

Now are his comrades one and all awake !
Watching the vessel, as with bird-like sweep
She meets the wind until her white wings shake
With nervous twichings o'er the dark blue deep.
While, fawning on her, swelling billows leap !
Her fore and mizen sails again soon fill,
Her mains are thrown aback, and serve to keep
Her near the spot, while with a hearty will
Her crew stand by to save with promptitude and skill.

Oh ! who shall know the feelings of those men
Who gasp for breath as they that ship draw nigh !
Lost from their thoughts their loathsome blood-stained den,
And fixed upon their saviours every eye,
While to their homes their minds exultant fly !
Brave friends are near, whose honest faces glow
With eager kindness, but whose warning cry
Is changed to horror when the truth they know,
As 'neath their vessel's lee glides up that charnel low.

The active seamen hoist the saved on deck,
And wash away each filthy gory stain,
While the poor dead—sad relics of the wreck—
With decent rites are given to the main
To sleep the sleep devoid of dreams or pain,
Until, aroused by that dread trumpet's call,
They shall awake with perfect forms again
To be arraigned before the Judge of all.
Here let the drama end—here let the curtain fall.

MOODS OF THE OCEAN.

1.

I RIPPLE on my sandy shore,
When the winds repose in their airy hall ;
In murmurs soft my wavelets fall,
 As if at peace for evermore.
And the sea-birds dive for their finny prey,
While the ship scarce moves on her trackless way.

2.

A restless wind awakens now,
And wings its way o'er my peaceful breast,
Whence wavelets leap to be caress'd
 And don foam-crests of sparkling snow.
While the watchful sea-birds wing their way
With the ship, which speeds on her path of spray.

3.

Now howling blasts, like furies fly !
And my bosom vex to a foaming waste,
Whence all, save wrath, is soon effaced,
 As Titan waves insult the sky !
While the sea-birds speed to the distant shore,—
And the ship goes down, and is seen no more !

IN MEMORIAM.

OLIVER WATSON HARRIS—DIED, JUNE 1, 1875.

Farewell, dear friend ! a long, a last farewell—
 For I have heard that thou hast pass'd away
From this fair world, where thou wert loved so well,
 And where the best so often shortest stay.

Oh ! can it be, that I no more shall hold
 That strong right hand, so cordial in its grip ?
Shall ne'er again that comely face behold—
 The broad fair brow and smiling eye and lip ?

Those honest eyes ! whose open, steady light
   Beam'd forth so kindly from their depths of blue ;
'Tis hard to think they are no longer bright,
   Hid in the grave for ever from our view.

That manly form—fit home for the brave heart
   Which knew not guile, and never bowed to fear—
Is stricken down by Death's unerring dart—
   That dart which ends at last each bright career !

Tho' not to me allied by blood or birth,
   Yet, like a brother, I have loved thee well,
And many friends who knew thy sterling worth
   Mingle their tears with mine in this farewell.

LOST.

FOUNDED ON FACT.

1.

ONE summer's morn, in Adelaide's far north,
Phœbus glared down with lurid glance of wrath,
While, from his flaming face, a flood was cast
Of scorching heat, as if the world to blast ;
Steeping the mountains, till their faded hue
Deepen'd from grey to one intensely blue ;
While their rude outlines show'd unto the eye
In bold relief against the paler sky.

2.

At foot of one, behold there did appear
A lovely scene, drawn in the atmosphere ;
A shining lake, with fringe of sombre pines,
The water sleeping in bright silver lines ;
While at each side, and backing it, were high,
Bold, time-worn crags which seem'd to kiss the sky ;
Forming a picture, beautiful and grand,
Like some great artist's dream of Fairy-land !

3.

And, as a dream, 'twas merely a delusion,
Which, like the fairies, would not brook intrusion ;
For, on approach, that vision passing fair,
Dissolv'd itself, and vanished in thin air ;
While to the eye there then appear'd instead
Huge sandstone rocks, all time-worn, bare, and red,
And black-oak scrubs which clothe the southern face
Of the tall range which bears the name of Chase,

4.

Which there encroach'd upon a saltbush plain,
Whose sun-crack'd surface told that needful rain
For months long pass'd had never fallen there ;
While o'er it play'd, suspended in the air,
A lesser mirage, like to water waving,—
Which mocks the sight of thirsty bushman craving
For the pure element, as onward toiling,
With dry canteen, he feels his blood near boiling.

5.

Deep silence reign'd, like that of lonely grave,
And no stray zephyr caused the leaves to wave ;
Though, spectre-like, some whirlwinds to the sky
Raised their vast heads of thin grey dust on high.
No bird or beast appear'd unto the sight,
Saving an eagle, which, with lazy flight,
Wheel'd on broad pinions, buoyant, in mid air,—
A dusky speck amid the sultry glare.

6.

For, urged by thirst, all else had gone to seek
For shade and water in some cool gum-creek ;
There to remain till Phœbus should resign
His mid-day reign, and to the west decline.
But soon a man appear'd upon the scene,
With hurried step, and agitated mien ;
Who, as he sped, with keen suspicion peer'd
Around his path, as if he danger fear'd.

7.

A timid man !—far better had he stay'd
To gain his bread by some dull, useful trade,
In town or village of his native land ;
His life the care of Law's far-reaching hand:—
For curlew's scream, borne on the midnight breeze,
Or sighing wind, among the rustling trees,
Caus'd him to start with keen enquiring ear,
As if he thought some deadly foe lurk'd near.

J

8.

Then his faint heart with frenzied fear was fill'd
When rumour told how savage blacks had kill'd
A luckless shepherd, on adjacent run !
Its promptings urged him, ere the rising sun
Glanc'd o'er the range, to leave his sheep to fate,
Death threat'ning him if he relief should wait.
And so we see him, like a hunted deer,
Fleeing for safety to a station near.

9.

But soon in doubt he paused, and gazed around,—
Then bent his eager glances to the ground ;
For now two paths his puzzled sight confused,
Both faintly mark'd, and neither lately used ;
One trended south,—the other crossed the bed
Of stony creek, and to the station led,
Which, though from this, but two short miles away,
Was screen'd by hills, 'midst which it nestling lay.

10.

But he, as others would no doubt have done,
Soon chose the plainer and the broader one ;
And it,—like that to everlasting ruin,—
Became the cause of that poor man's undoing !
For it led out upon the saltbush plain
Where nothing lived, except when winter's rain
Caused pools of water in the holes to lie,
Which summer's drought leaves deeply crack'd and dry.

11.

With nervous haste he strode upon his way,
With growing dread lest it should be astray ;
While agitation, and the sun's fierce beams,
Wrung the salt sweat from him in trickling streams ;
He heeded not the pertinacious flies
Which swarm'd around and in his mouth and eyes ;
Too much by fear his mind was occupied
To notice, now, how else he might be tried !

12.

The marks grew fainter, as he onward went,
Till with the plain they finally were blent ;
He had pursued a once-used cattle track—
He turn'd in haste, and hurried swiftly back,
But, by sad chance, found not the path he left,
As if of sight he had become bereft,
Or careless grown, from stupid haste and fright,—
He gave no thought to what was wrong or right.

13.

For then,—instead of gazing calmly round
At ranges near, and guided thus, have found
His morning's track,—he wandered on the plain,
As if intending to go home again.
But no such thought was present to his mind !
'Twas fate relentless that his steps inclined !
For so bewilder'd was he by his fright,
That well-known hills now mock'd his puzzled sight !

14.

When leaving home, so hurried had he been,
That quite forgotten was his large canteen ;
And thirst was added to his mental pain !
Oh ! that in England he were once again !
Her meanest puddle would to him have been
A priceless boon ! tho' garb'd in stagnant green !
A willing gift had been his hoarded gold,
For one large cup of water, clear and cold !

15.

Oh, ye ! who live in England's favour'd land,
With purest water always at command ;
A draught of it gives you but little pleasure ;
You do not know the value of the treasure !
So with all blessings, if too cheaply bought—
Upon their worth we seldom give a thought ;
But let us lose one, be it ne'er so small,
'Tis straightway sought, pursued, and prized by all !

16.

And so with him who pines for water now.
Oh ! how he long'd, while wiping his hot brow
At some clear stream, to take a breathless drink !
Compared with which the choicest wine would sink
In estimation,—left untasted till
His thirst was banish'd at the sparkling rill !
For tho' in praise of wine so many sing,
All those who thirst would quickly choose the spring.

17.

On, on he ran ! still harass'd by the flies,
With cracking lips, and painful sweat-dimm'd eyes ;
A bitter slime pervaded his hot mouth,
His swollen tongue and throat were rack'd with drouth ;
While on his head, convuls'd with throbbing pain,
The sunbeams struck, and seem'd to scorch his brain.
His feet were blister'd, and his state of mind
Can neither be imagined nor defined !

18.

But soon he struck the beaten road again,
Where Chase's range abuts upon the plain,
To trace once more that fatal erring track,
And on the plain to wander, hopeless back.
In senseless haste he paced the fatal round,
E'en when the sun, with golden glories crown'd,
Swept with his train of wide, diverging light
Down in the west, and left his realms to night.

19.

He sank, at last, exhausted on the ground,
And scarcely breathing, mark'd each sylvan sound ;
The gauze-wing'd locusts, shrieking from the trees,
And dingoes' howl borne faintly on the breeze,
While *" oolka boorachie" hopp'd close around,
Adding their short and most peculiar sound,—
As hungry night-hawks stay'd awhile their flight,
Then flitted on like spectres of the night.

20.

He might recline,—he vainly tried to rest ;
For, with wild fear and bitterness oppress'd,
His heart beat audibly, as if 'twould burst !
He tried to pray—but, raving madly, cursed !
He started up, sat down, then rose again,
As fearful fancies crowded thro' his brain ;
While thronging fast before his mental sight
A medley strange of past scenes sped that night !

21.

No charms for him had constellations bright,
That richly gemm'd the majesty of night,
But through the gloom he peer'd with eager eyes
For fair Aurora's advent in the skies.
Tears down his cheeks pursued their silent course,
Wrung by despair from their long pent-up source ;
Till tired nature could no longer keep
That fearsome vigil,—and he fell asleep.

22.

Sleep ? yes, 'twas sleep ! but of the fever'd kind
That seals the eyelids, but permits the mind
To live tormented by a phantom host—
The evil genii of bright dreamland's coast !
Of varied shapes, and various terrors, they
'Midst night's dark shadows hold their horrid sway !
Gaunt, grinning spectres o'er the starving flit—
Vile shapes enormous on gorged gourmands sit !

*Kangaroo-rat ; Native name.

23.

But to the man who slept unhappy there,
A savage seeming did the phantoms wear.
Huge naked blacks to him appeared to rage
Around a hut where helpless he was caged ;
Eager for blood, they shook their horrid spears,
While fiend-like yells assail'd his startled ears ;
And then, one demon, darting from the band,
Soon gain'd the hut with uprais'd, flaming brand !

24.

The thatch ignites ! at once, with whirlwind roar,
Devouring flames towards the heavens soar !
Oh ! he must die an agonizing death !
He writhes beneath the conflagration's breath !—
It was too much—the awful spell it broke,
He started wildly, and at last awoke
To find himself beneath the midnight sky,
Consumed by thirst—no friend or water nigh.

25.

He slept no more, but watch'd with aching sight,
For those faint rays which herald morning's light.
Oh ! would that day, so longed for, *ever* dawn
To cheer his heart, by gnawing anguish torn ?
Those weary hours seem'd lengthen'd into years,
Each one full crowded with a lifetime's fears !
He thought Old Time, with folded pinions, stay'd
His wonted course, and daylight long delay'd.

26.

But those dread hours of darkness fled at last,
And night's black mantle from the plain was cast,
Which soon again in glowing light was dress'd,
Yet comfort came not to that wanderer's breast.
For on his march he sped with early dawn,
And with quick steps pursued his way forlorn.
But whither bent ?—'tis to no haunt of man,
But to that fate which yesterday began.

27.

For now, again, as on the bygone day,
Out on the plain he wends his weary way.
The hills, confused, seem whirling in his sight,
His eyeballs burn with wild and frenzied light !
Deeply his nails he digs into his palms,
And, all unknowing, waves aloft his arms ;
His mental tortures, acting on his brain,
Fast sap his reason !—he is near insane !

28.

He hurries on, with scarcely any change,
O'er arid plain, and by the frowning range !
As barque round Mäelstrom, in Norwegian sea,
To sure destruction, ceaseless circles he !
But, worse than on sharp jagged rocks to burst,—
He soon must die of all-consuming thirst.
Of hunger's pangs he scarcely is aware,—
They are as naught to thirst and deep despair !

29.

Again fierce Phœbus, from his mid-day path,
Regards the earth with unabated wrath ;
Till the scorch'd plain flings back its sullen glare,
And mocking mirage vapours in the air.
Yet onward still, with redly gleaming eyes,
The luckless one from foes imagined flies ;
With steps uneven, in erratic lines,
For to no track his course he now confines.

30.

Anon by suffering and madness driven,
His scanty clothing from his form is riven
By trembling hands, which heed not what they do,
As on the saltbush they the garments strew,
Till naught remains ! yet still he feebly strays,
Nudely to bear the dreadful solar rays ;
While like a furnace, all its flames close pent,
With horrid heat are his vex'd vitals rent !

31.

Far o'er Lake Torrens' wild and dreary shore
The sun sinks redly in the west once more.
Then staggers down that worn-out man to die,
Unseen by any, save his Maker's eye !
Madness and fear have fled his stricken brain,
And, from his frame, its all-pervading pain !
He starts not now at any fearsome sound,
But in a swoon lies senseless on the ground !

32.

The evening hours glide silently away,
And noiseless night-hawks hover o'er their prey ;
When Death's dread call unto his spirit rings,
Which must essay its now unfetter'd wings
In flight momentous to a hidden fate
Of pain eternal, or seraphic state !
For who shall judge an erring mortal, save
HIM who, with life, his fallen nature gave ?

Now day's bright god his realm pervades again,
And, with a glance, drives darkness from the plain,
Steeping in light that body void of breath,
Which silent lies in dreamless sleep of death !
No more its eyes shall nature's beauties scan,
Or its still'd brain poor human business plan ;
Dust it shall be, and mix with kindred clay,
Till once more quicken'd on the Judgment Day !

TIME.

1.

Old Time strides on with steady pace,
  His speed he quickens never ;
Yet still he runs a winning race,
  And keeps the course for ever !
By night and day, while worlds decay,
  He strides along for ever.
      For ever, yes, for ever !

2.

He just looks down, with scornful face,
  On mortals swift and clever,
And, as each drops from out the race,
  He leaves them there for ever.
Both great and small, he leaves them all,
  And strides along for ever.
      For ever, yes, for ever !

3.

But still yourselves, ye mortals, brace,
  For *Fame*—it dieth never !
And though ye drop from out the race,
  Your name may live for ever.
Then gain a name, and let your fame
  Stride on, with Time, for ever !
      For ever, yes, for ever !

THE GUM-TREE.

Of Austral trees I am king, I ween,—
  None can with me compare !
My vast old crown is of evergreen,
  Begemm'd with plumage rare !
My limbs I wave like sceptres grand
  To the wattle-scented wind,
And I am loved in this southern land
  As a friend by all mankind !

> Chorus—
>   Then sing ye jolly corn-stalk band !
>   Loud let your praises be
>   Of the monarch grand in this smiling land,
>   The glorious old gum-tree !

My pendent sprays in sweet whispers sing
  When zephyrs round me play ;
But loudly roar, and defiance fling
  At the rage of a stormy day !
My mighty roots like anchors hold
  In earth's dark breast right fast,
And my tall trunk stands like a Titan bold,
  And laughs at the vanquish'd blast !

> Chorus—Then sing, &c., &c.

I lend my shade, in the fierce noon-day,
  To dark skin and to fair,
And the fever-fiend I drive away
  If lurking in the air.
And when bright Phœbe, queen of night,
  Reigns o'er the peaceful scene,
My magpie choir oft hail her light
  From my lofty leafy screen.

> Chorus—Then sing, &c., &c.

110° IN THE SHADE.

1.

Alack ! what are we coming to ? oh, dear !
  But two degrees 'neath burning fever's point !
Our livers will not stand it long, I fear,
    And all our functions will be out of joint !
    Save the unpleasant one that doth anoint
Our parboil'd cuticles with perspiration,
  Which might indeed be measured by the pint !
And which insists upon a perportation,
A sort of liquid loan for instant liquidation.

2.

Too hot for work !—we therefore loll about
  In just the coolest quarter to be found ;
And here, I own, I feel a lurking doubt
    That, in that bourne to which bad souls are bound,
    (To suffer anything but to be drown'd)
It can be any hotter than this place
  Near to Lake Torrens' border ; where the ground
Gasps, with a thousand fissures in its face,
For a cool breath of air, just like the human race !

3.

The covers of the books are curling up,
  As if they fain a student would invite
To pore o'er their crisp pages for a sup
    From learning's fount ; but who, with fly-vex'd sight
    Would quickly leave them in a sorry plight,
By pouring on them perspiration's rain
  In mighty spots ! just like the splashing flight
Of scattered drops, which patter on the plain
Just ere the weather-clerk turns on his thunder-main !

4.

Poor Towzer, there, is lying in a hole,—
  A scratch'd-out cavern 'neath a leaking tank,—
Nor thinks of mutton he so lately stole,
    And, from the crows, secreted in a bank ;
    But sprawls, at length, with slowly heaving flank,
Too much oppress'd to wag his bushy tail,
  He'd scarce " skedaddle " for a kick or spank ;
E'en at that caller, with his dusty swag,
He will not rise to bark, though plainly an " old lag !"

5.

The panting fowls are gasping in the shade,
  Their dingy plumage hanging loosely round,—
While chanticleers, with warfare for their trade,
    Mope side by side, and nothing now would hound
    Them on to combat ; or, indeed, to sound
The martial challenge with their clarion shrill ;
  Are *these* the birds which strut upon the mound,
And for a pullet's sake, are kill'd or kill ?
Too hot it is for love ! e'en jealousy is still !

6.

That grim grimalkin stretch'd upon the floor
  Is surely dead, so motionless he lies ;
Upon the mucine race he'll prey no more,—
    But if he's dead, e'en Death can't stand these flies !
For see, he clutches at his half-closed eyes,
With sudden claw, to scare those insects vile,
  Which shirk the blow, and all inertly rise
On lazy wing, to poise a little while,
Then settle down once more, the luckless cat to rile !

7.

Upon the ear sounds forth no songster's note,
  To break the stillness of the sultry air,
And all is silent, save where sheep or goat
    Speeds to the water with unhappy blare,
    'Neath bushes dodging to avoid the glare
Of Sol's fierce glances, who hath fever got,
  And is as pleasant as a scalded bear !
Now I must pause to take a cheering tot,—
A nasty one I mean, the water's nearly hot !

8.

Oh ! for a snow-crown'd iceberg's leeward side !
  But not too near it,—for extremes are bad.
Here I much wonder that the dogs ne'er tried
    To wile away the time, by going mad
    But no ! 'twould be a deal too hot to pad
'The hoof, in quest of legs at which to snap.
  " Johnny ! you Johnny ! just come here, my lad,
And take that water-bag round to the tap,
And fill it speedily, or you may get the strap."

9.

I'm done up, quite ! and so will guzzle tea ;
  That is, of course, when no " three-star " remains ;
But, by-the-by, it really puzzles me
    How soon that brandy from the bottle wanes !
    The footless glass must suffer little drains,

Like perspiration, through its pores to ooze.
Oh, dear, the question bothers my stew'd brains,
And so I'll try to soothe them with a snooze ;
A trial at the best, when heat and flies oppose.

THE MYSTERY OF LIFE.

" Good night ! good night " the mother said
While leaning o'er her infant's bed,
    She kiss'd his mouth so rosy :
" Good night ! good night !" she said again—
Another loving kiss, and then
    She left him warm and cozy.

And going out with footfall light
She left the candle burning bright—
    Till sleep, on angels' pinions,
Should with soft hands his eyelids close,—
While fervently her prayer arose
    To Heaven's supreme dominions—

That he, her son, should grow in grace,
And run with credit in the race
    Prescribed on earth to mortals—
And when, with years and honours crowned,
He should by kindly Death be found,
    His soul should win the portals

Of that Bright Land where sin is not—
Where pain and sorrow are forgot—
    Where tears can trickle never !
And, doubting not that she should fly
For shelter there when she should die,
    Trusts they shall joy for ever.

And soon she seeks the little bed
Where,—sleep's bright visions round his head,—
    Her darling now lies dreaming ;
While sunny smiles upon his face
Appear to her, from Throne of Grace,
    Replies of hopeful seeming.

So, taking up her light, she goes
With noiseless tread, to seek repose,
  And leaves him to his slumber—
But never dreams that her fair child
Shall grow up like a nettle wild,
  Earth's smiling face to cumber !

 * * * * * * *

Upon the past's dim silent shore,
Long years are cast for evermore,
  Since in his cot, that child
Slept, 'neath his guardian angel's care,
A happy mortal, passing fair,
  With soul yet undefil'd.

Can *this* be he, who on the sand
Lies dying in this desert land
  From thirst and hunger pangs ?
A ghastly creature, ragged, worn !
Too mean for word, or glance of scorn,
  A prey to conscience-fangs !

But see, upon his face a light
Gleams, as his spirit takes its flight !
  Yes, 'tis indeed no other !
And ah ! a soft word leaves that tongue,
Whence oft the ribald curse hath rung,—
  That cherish'd name of " Mother !"

Ah ! heart-wrung parents ! who repine
When Death, sent by the All-wise Mind
  Comes gathering your flowers ;—
Rebel not at the order given—
Ye know those " blossoms," borne to heaven
  Will deck Eternal bowers !

THE FLYING DUTCHMAN.

A LEGEND OF THE CAPE OF GOOD HOPE.

Two hundred years ago, or so, I will not be precise,
A fine old-fashion'd galliot, which look'd just like a slice
From Daddy Noah's clipper craft ! (a bottom slice of course !)
With lots of beam to carry sail, was thrashing at the force
Of snooring gale, from Sou-Sou-East, and nasty chopping sea,
As lively as she bobb'd about as such a craft could be !
And on the weather-quarter loom'd old Afric's stormy cape,
Round which the Dutch adventurer his daring course would
    shape ;
For " Vanderdecken," of that craft, was skipper bold I ween ;
(A burly, round-stern'd mariner as ever yet was seen),
Who paced upon her lofty poop, with trumpet in his hand,
As if he'd hail the natives swart, upon that savage land.

An oil'd sou-wester cased his head, above his shaggy brows,—
Who *could* believe that bear-like man once fancied by the Vrows?
His keen small eyes were like a rat's ! and then, his nose ! oh
    dear !
'Twas like a pimpled pineapple ! (he loved his schnapps, I fear !)
A long moustache, like cross-jack yard, was slung beneath that
    knob,
And fitted was his cruel mouth to take a man-trap's job !
His grizzled, bushy beard hung down upon his brawny breast ;
His antiquated doublet, brown with grease, was greatly mess'd,
And in the girdle that he wore, was thrust a dagger long,
To prove its owner in the right,—however in the wrong.
Trunk hose of leather met his boots, (of close-grain'd hard
    horse-hide),
Which on the luckless cabin-boy full often had been tried !
Who, though he doubtless fancied them *too large* a size or so,
Discover'd that, like " three-leagued boots," they made him
    swiftly go ;
And once when with great energy, and suddenness applied,
They furnish'd wings which carried him into the sea's salt tide,
Where,—as he was an orphan boy, of melancholy mood,—
They left him, just to fraternise with " Mother Carey's " brood.
But oh ! as if into the breast of Stormy Petrel small
His puny soul had entered in, so surely in each squall
One of those evil-omen'd birds, on restless wings pursued,
With other notions, said the men, than just to seek for food.
For gramercy ! right well he knows, quoth they, how we shall
    fare,

And so, to keep us company, already doth prepare ;
For since the little Johann died, hath trouble hemm'd us round,
And will, till in the fatal sea, like him shall we be drown'd:
So biscuit crumbs some to him threw, while others wished that he
To " certain burning latitudes " might on swift pinions flee !
But, howsoever they might wish, there still that sea-bird flew,
Which troubled Vanderdecken more than e'er it did his crew ;
And often, with his arquebuse, had he, with cruel mind,
Aim'd at the little wanderer, a messenger unkind !
But still a charmed life it bore, and still it sail'd along,
As if it loved the billow's crest, and tempest's weird song.

Now swallow-like it skimm'd along, on pinions strong and
    light,
A hated and reproachful thing, in Vanderdecken's sight ;
Who, as he roll'd along his deck, no words of pleasure spoke,
But mutter'd curses from his throat, in sullen thunder broke !
And, scowling on his sun-burnt crew, from foremast-man to
    mate—
He call'd down " blessings," in Low Dutch, upon each luckless
    pate ;
As if those scurvy-stricken tars could help the gale so foul,
Which in derision, through the gear, like demons seemed to
    howl !

" Now, rouse that fore-tack down," he cried, " be smart, ye
    lubbers all !"
And half a dozen tarry ones responded to his call,
While, just as sportive rabbits drive into rude dingle dens,
So dived into the seething trough the " Renaud Englekens ;"
For thus was Vanderdecken's craft from Burgomaster named,
Who little thought, when she was launch'd, that she would be
    so famed.

Now, Peter Vanderbelt, the mate, a fair-hair'd, blue-eyed tar,
Is gazing with his mental eye upon some scene afar ;
For, as against a shroud he leans, his heart is far away
To where his loving Gretchen sits, while round his children play ;
And in his ears their joyous tones, like music seem to ring ;
But him, from his bright reverie, his skipper's accents bring.
" Wake up ! you dreaming home-sick calf," he hears that
    worthy hiss,
" E'er Amsterdam ye see again, it will be long, I wis ;
" For may Old Scratch seize on my soul, if I for Holland turn,
" Before we weather yon black cape, and leave it far astern ;
" For spice ! and precious stones ! I sail'd, and mean to have
    them too !
" And so I'll stay and carry on till everything is blue.

" Besides, I never yet was beat wherever I did roam ;
" Get ye below, you foolish loon, and dream no more of home."

But ah ! what fearsome sound was that, which both those
    seamen heard ?
It could not come from albatross, or any other bird.
Tho' round them rustled viewless wings, and wierd shadows
    fell ;—
Oh, no ! 'twas like exulting laugh from mocking fiend of hell !
And with a sudden change of wind, the sails were thrown
    aback,
And stopp'd the " Renaud Englekens " abruptly in her track.
But e'er the startled seamen sprang to haul the yards around,
She fill'd again, and gather'd way, as if for Cape Horn bound.
But where is gallant Vanderbelt ? not in his berth below,
No pillow, save a " water one " will Peter ever know !
For, by the jibing main-boom flung into the raging sea,
No more will he his pleasant home, or gentle Gretchen see—
With one wild cry to Heaven sent for mercy on his soul,
He disappears beneath the waves, which o'er him surging roll !
E'en Vanderdecken's rugged heart, by what he saw, was wrung ;
For oh ! he loved his sister's son ! tho, he no hen-coop flung,
Or wore his clumsy galliot, or tried to heave her to,
Or, in a cranky cockle-shell, sent forth a saving crew.
For well he knew that fruitless all would such endeavours be,
No dingey that was ever launch'd, could live in such a sea !
Besides, he saw him fathoms down, sink like a deep sea-lead,
So turn'd upon the steersman bold, and swore at him instead.
" Just mind your helm, you lubber, you ! why, what are you
    about ?
" I do not want, you sea-cook's son, to put the craft about ;
" And 'twas *your* carelessness just now, that got her in the
    wind,
" And sent poor Peter overboard ! by ——— ! I'm inclined
" To string you up without a shrift, unto that yard-arm there ;"
The man replied, " Thou skipper mine, from further threats
    forbear ;
" No fault was that of mortal man, but of the Evil One,
" Who works for us a cruel fate, which he hath well begun !
" For oh ! that horrid gibing laugh rings yet within mine ears,
" And ever will, though I attain to all one hundred years !
" A doomed ship is this, I trow, and all that in her sail ;
" That fatal cape we'll never round, or weather out this gale !
" But I, for one, like Christian man, will bravely meet my fate ;
" I wou'd I were as well prepared as our departed mate !
" For gentle was his soul, I wis, tho' as a lion's bold !
(And as thus spake that mariner, tears down his visage roll'd)

" 'Tis thirty days since first in sight of that swart cape we came,
" And high upon the inland hills beheld the mighty flame,
" Which you said native blackamoors were making as a sign !
" An ugly blackamoor, indeed ! thought I, and comrades mine.
" And still a foul wind baffles us, while scurvy thins the crew ;
" Then hearken, Sir, to the advice I fain would offer you."

Stern Vanderdecken answered not, but turned him on his heel,
Tho' into his hard wicked heart, a doubt began to steal,
And as he wander'd up and down on those unsteady planks,
Old recollections fill'd his mind of what were worse than pranks ;
And then he mused on Vanderbelt, when (who would think it
    true ?)
Unconsciously, from his fierce eyes, stole down a tear or two !
For his good angel tried once more to turn his stubborn heart,
(That indurated pebble-stone, which stood for vital part !)
And prompted him to seek again his helmsman good and true,
And growl, " Now, Diedrick, say thy say, but let thy words be
    few."

Then spake that skilful mariner, and this is what he said ;
" Turn back, if there should yet be time, and be by prudence led ;
" And let us to Our Lady pray to help us in our strait,
" For, with her aid, perchance we may. e'en yet, evade our fate."
Here Vanderdecken stopp'd him short, with mutter'd curse and
    scowl ;
Quoth he, " Befits it seamen bold unto the saints to howl
" Whene'er a puff of wind comes down, and makes the water
    rough ?
" Pshaw ! if you call *that* good advice, you've given quite enough."

E'en as bold Vanderdecken spoke, that stormy wind veer'd
    round,
And seemingly the Englekens was fairly outward bound.
Then mutter'd that grim skipper old, as they the yards did trim,
" Not yet hath Satan clutch'd my soul ! I still will weather him.
" Ho ! steward, bring the cheering schnaps, let all the main-
    brace splice !"
That steward said not anything, but vanish'd in a trice ;
And soon each drouthy mariner toss'd high the polish'd horn,
Then pour'd into their season'd throats the blood of barley-corn.
E'en Diedrick took his liquor off, as should a seaman brave,
But still it lighten'd not his heart, or clear'd his visage grave ;
And when a comrade to the helm came aft his trick to take,
He gave the tiller up to him, then gazed back in the wake,
As if the mate once more he'd see,—then cross'd himself and
    sigh'd,

And offer'd up a prayer for him who slept beneath the tide ;
Then forward to the forecastle he silently did hie,
For something whisper'd in his ear, 'twould soon be his to die !
Now merrily the galliot runs right before the wind,
And wildly yaws, as is the wont of vessels of her kind ;
While albatross, and moleymauks, and flocks of smaller fry,
On buoyant wings wheel round and round, and keep an eager eye
Upon the boiling wake astern, for what the cook might cast,
While through the rigging, whistles shrill the mighty western
    blast !
And from the huge green-headed waves, with crests of snowy
    white,
A school of uncouth blackfish plunge, and disappear from sight.
Then Vanderdecken goes below to take another nip,
And quite forgets the adage old anent impending slip
'Twixt cup and lip, although before, unto his cost, hath he
Oft verified the truth of it upon that very sea.
And hark ! that heavy tramp of feet denotes a stir on deck,
So quickly up the booby-hatch he cranes his bull-like neck,
And sees the yards braced round again, to meet the gale un-
    kind,
For, haul'd upon a bowline taut she's close upon a wind.
Ah ! now she will not lie her course, unless they wish to land
At Table Bay ; and soon e'en that is on their weather hand ;
And,—blowing as 'twould blow its last,—the fast increasing
    gale
Soon forces Vanderdecken bold to take in sail by sail ;
And tho' she " lies-too like a duck " in ordinary gales,
There's nothing now would stand to it unless sheet-iron sails !
She therefore needs must scud away, beneath her long bare poles,
While with her yard-arms to the brine, 'midst horrid waves
    she rolls ;
And as the night comes rushing down upon the stormy sea,
E'en Vanderdecken would he were beneath some island's lee !

Oh ! how that fierce south-easter blows, so piercing, dry, and
    chill,
And stars with cruel steel-like gleam the cloudless heavens fill,
'Neath which the sailless vessel speeds, one instant toss'd on
    high
On mountain waves, whose wind-shorn crests in stinging
    showers fly ;
Then hurl'd to seething, gloomy depths, by rushing waves
    assailed,
No wonder that upon their knees the fear-cow'd seamen quailed,
And prayed unto their patron saints for help in this their strait ;—
They might have heard, but if they did, they left them to their fate !

K

For hark ! as yaws the Englekens, an awful billow breaks
With force terrific on the craft, which to her kelson shakes
Beneath the shock, which smashes in her hatches, as a bomb
Descending through some dwelling's roof, would carry wreck
    and doom !
And down into her gloomy hold invading waters pour
In torrents like Niagara, and with a sullen roar.
Bold Diedrick, and the watch below, dart out upon the deck,
While scurvy-stricken wretches pray, and moan a certain wreck ;
And well they may, for overboard the helmsmen twain are cast,
Their dying cries to leeward borne upon the raging blast.
And Vanderdecken ! where is he ? why, on the cabin floor
As full of schnapps as he can be, and has been oft before !
The tiller smashed ! the binnacle gone with the helmsmen brave!
No wonder that the boldest now expect an ocean grave !
And e'er brave Diedrick can invent, and, with the hardy crew
Rig up some patent steering gear, the vessel broaches-to,
And by the wind's terrific force is thrown upon her beam,
While through the hatchway's gaping jaws the fatal waters
    stream !
In vain those active mariners, with ready jack-knives bound
To hack the weather lanyards tough thro' rigging's dead-eyes
    wound,
For with a suffocating sob, she rights a moment—then
Dives down into the depths below, with all her dooméd men !
Whose death-shriek ringing wild and shrill, one moment peals
    on high,
Then nought is left, save raging waves, beneath the cruel sky.

Long, weary years have slowly crept into the changeless past,
And still for Peter, Gretchen waits, all faithful to the last ;
And for his safety nightly prays, and watches thro' the day,
While fainter, in her heart of hearts, becomes hope's cheering
    ray.
But hark ! the sound of culverins, upon the Zuyder Zee,
Proclaim that hardy mariners have come from ruder sea ;
And audibly her poor heart beats, as she her mantle ties,
And swiftly to the water side with her dear children hies.
But oh ! tis not the Englekens which to the harbour glides,
Although a gallant galliot with weather-beaten sides;
Which plainly tell of voyage long, as do her much patched sails,
While tawny are the visages which peer above her rails.
All, all bespeak her from the clime where Phœbus fiercely glows,
And where, in lieu of merchandise, men often meet with blows.
But ah ! what sturdy mariner makes signals from the ship,
And waves his hat, and puts his hand unto his bearded lip?

Oh, can it be her husband brave? come back to her once more,
By time and hardship changed so much upon some foreign shore
That he one moment could appear a stranger to her eyes?
No, no! it is impossible! her faithful heart replies;
But yet the form is not unknown; 'tis strange if it should be—
For oh! her brother, kind and true, and skipper brave is he.
Now, surely tidings she shall hear, her heart to break or glad,
How faint she feels, as fear declares those tidings will be bad!

Now active seamen shorten sail, till, with a splash and roar,
Her anchor, with its rusty chain, seeks holding ground once
    more.
And as they trimly furl the sails, and coil up sheet and brace,
Her brother rows unto the land, fair Gretchen to embrace.
But oh! his face is very sad, tho' fain would he be blithe,
And tears *will* start as he regards those children gay and lithe.
Poor Gretchen feels the truth at once, and with a stifled cry,
She fainting falls unto the earth as if about to die.
But soon the ruddy vital flood pursues its course again,
While silently, from her soft eyes, the soothing tears drop rain.
And when she slowly gazes round, and sees her children there,
She dedicates her life to them, and offers up a prayer
For help and guidance from above, and for her husband's rest,
Though doubt as to his future state ne'er enters in her breast;
To which she folds her children now within a sad embrace,
Who gaze with silent wonderment into her tearful face;
And then upon the mariner, whom well the eldest know
As uncle Will, who sail'd away full three long years ago;
Who used to bring them curios from many a foreign land;
And as they press around him now, and grasp his kindly hand,
They ask him why their mother weeps, and wherefore comes not
    dad,
And why so grave is his brown face, that once was never sad?
And where the shells and parrots are, and where the monkey
    small?
To their last questions he replies, " Well, I have got them all,
" But they, with lots of other things, we'll get to-morrow, dears,
" Now I must see your mother home—come, Gretchen, dry your
    tears!
" For he, that seaman brave and true as e'er the sea did sail,
" Is in a haven bright, I wis, and safe from ev'ry gale!
" Now, if you lean upon my arm, we to your cot will go,
" And there, to satisfy your mind, I'll tell you all I know."

The cottage, with its gables queer, and garden trim, they gain,
And William tells of his long cruise upon the boundless main.
And how, when off the cape of storms one wild and squally night,

Unto their startled eyes appear'd a strange unearthly sight !
For, as they ran before the wind, a phantom ship appear'd,
Which right into the very eye of strong sou-wester steer'd !
Beneath bare poles she glided past, a cable's length a-lee,
While, on her deck, one weird form was all that we might see !
But no one, who had ever known Hans Vanderdecken bold,
Could e'er mistake that misty shape, with eyes which redly roll'd.
Besides, the craft, *which left no wake* upon the troubled sea,
Was just as like the Englekens as pea unto a pea !
Though, even as the ghost on deck, a ghostly ship was she !
And then we knew that in the slime, a thousand fathoms deep,
Her luckless crew, around her wreck, were wrapp'd in death's
  dull sleep.
So, for their soul's repose we pray'd, though we misdoubted
  then,
How it might with the skipper fare, howe'er might fare the men.
But none that knew brave Vanderbelt could his bright future
  doubt,
For if St. Peter bars *his* way, why, all shall be left out !
" Then Gretchen, for your children live, and comfort take from me,
" For poverty shall shun your door, while I can sail the sea !
" And, as the little Peter grows unto a man's estate,
" Teach him his father's life to live, and fear no earthly fate."

And now, this tough sea-yarn to end, I'll tell you as a friend,
That on the perfect truth of it you really may depend,
For many honest mariners have seen the phantom sail
Upon its ancient cruising ground, and always in a gale,
When dark as e'er was Erebus the gloomy night-shades fell !
And so they could not be deceiv'd, and it could be no sell.

MORAL.

A modicum of good advice from this my tale I'll draw,—
Thus ; shape a fair straight course thro' life, and from it never
  yaw !
And do not bluster, or declare that you *will* have your way,
Or, like poor Vanderdecken's ghost, you'll find it does not pay.

THE HUNT OF GOLD.

THE world is one vast hunting field ;
 Its people, hunters all
For varied game its coverts yield,
 In cunning toils to fall.
   But gold, which lines the pockets best,
   Is by most hunters hardest press'd !

Some hunt for husbands, some for wives,
 And some, for lovers' gay ;
Truth, some pursue thro' all their lives,—
 A shy, scarce game, they say ;
   But gold, &c.

Some hunt for pleasure, some for health,
 And some, excitement's flame ;
Tuft-hunting,—open, or by stealth,—
 A toady band can claim ;
   But gold, &c.

Some hunt, their fellows to enslave ;—
 Some, liberty pursue ;
And some, unto the very grave
 Hunt mortals good and true !
   But gold, &c.

But listen, hunters, great and small !
 List ! all ye eager crew !
Death—keenest hunter of ye all—
 Is grimly stalking you !
   Then, if with him ye would be bold,
   Let honour guide your hunt for gold.

LEAP-YEAR.

IN VERY SHORT METRE.

1.

One day,
  A pair—
He gay,
  She fair—
The breeze
  Beside
The sea's
  Salt tide
Enjoy'd,
And toy'd.

2.

Said Jane,—
  "Dear Ned,
I fain
  Would wed,
(Leap-year
  'Tis now)
So here
  I vow,
I'll wed
  Thee Ned."

3.

Said he,—
  "My dear,
For me,
  I fear,
Too gay
  You'd prove.
Good day,
  My love !
You'll wed
  Not Ned !"

4.

MORAL.

From this
  True tale,
Each Miss
  Don't fail
To be
  Well warn'd ;—

For she
  Is scorn'd
Who tries,—
  Like Jane,—
A prize
  To gain.
Beware !
  Take care !

TOT AND BESSIE.

Two little bright-eyed maids love me,
  And, oh, I love them in return ;
Fresh charms in them each day I see,
  Though crabbèd I am grown, and stern.

They laugh with joy when I come home,
  While round my neck their arms they fling;
And if afar I chance to roam,
  Still, in my heart, their voices ring.

My daughters are those children fair,
  Their mother's gentleness have they ;
Earth cannot show a blither pair,
  Not e'en of birds in blooming May.

Oh ! what is fame, and what is gold,
  To that pure blessing from above,
Exceeding them a thousand-fold,—
  That priceless gem—our children's love ?

While little Tot and Bessie live,
  And love me as they love me now,
My sorrows to the winds I'll give,
  Though care sits heavy on my brow.

LINES

ON THE DEATH OF A VENERABLE AND MUCH RESPECTED LADY.

To THAT fair home, with ling'ring flight,
　Came silently the angel Death ;
And, fearless of his awful might,
　She calmly yielded up her breath.

Her friends' and children's falling tears
　Have not the sting of bitter pain,
For, full of virtues and of years,
　She's gone, a heavenly crown to gain.

Still in their faithful hearts enshrin'd,
　Her memory shall ever live,
With wreaths of love and honour twined,
　And all that reverence can give.

And as thro' life they journey on,
　The hope shall cheer their future way,
With her, of blest reunion
　In realms of bright eternal day.

DEPARTED FRIENDS.

WHEN fortune smiles, when hopes run high,
　And youth with pleasure glides along,
E'en if the best and dearest die,
　Our mourning for them lasts not long.
Yet, latent in our hearts, the pain
Sleeps but to wake in time again.

For trouble comes in sombre guise,
　And age his heavy hand extends ;
Then with sad souls and tearful eyes
　We muse on our departed friends—
The mists of years before us fall,
And we their priceless worth recall.

Oh ! hearts, by weary yearning wrung !
   How all your pains and sorrows swell,
If conscience, with upbraiding tongue,
   Of cold neglect to them can tell !
Ye writhe in torture, self-accused,
'Neath what once sophistry excused.

Then all to whom kind fortune gives
   (To glad you in your onward way),
Dear friends and loving relatives,
   Devotion show them while you may,
And when they are no longer here,
Mem'ry your lonely hours shall cheer.

SONG OF THE NEWSPAPER.

1.

Hurrah ! for the " Banner of Liberty " !
   The broad black letter'd sheet
That, round by post, a mighty host
   Each morning flies to greet
With news of the world, by light'ning hurl'd
   To Editor's retreat.

2.

Hurrah ! for the " Banner of Liberty " !
   That speaks to heart and eye ;
For its pages teem with the thrilling theme,
   Of times fast fleeting by:
Of might and right, of peace and fight,
   Of those who " do or die." !

3.

Hurrah ! for the " Banner of Liberty " !
   Its power let none gainsay ;
The soldier now to the press must bow—
   The sword to pen give way ;
For truth's bright gleam is its grand theme,
   Despite the despots' nay !

4.

Hurrah! for the "Banner of Liberty"!
   May its prestige ne'er be less!
Hurrah! for the men of type and pen
   Who deeds in language dress!
And hurrah for all, both great and small,
     Who work the "Printing Press"!

THE POST OFFICE.

1.

A GIANT dwells in St. Martin's le Grand,
   Who is mightier far than Briareus,—
For his arms stretch forth into every land,
   By "Sirius" sway'd or "Aquarius,"—
And ruled by the will of his mighty mind,
Work cheerfully on to oblige mankind.

2.

This giant will take, for the meanest man,
   A message to China or Timbuctoo,—
To famed New York, or to Astrachan,—
   To Bangalore, or to Woolloomooloo!
And all that he asks, for his service vast,
Is a paltry stamp to a note stuck fast.

3.

A priceless friend is this giant so kind,
   To comfort the heart of the wandering wight;
Of each anxious friend he relieves the mind,
   And sorrow dispels with a message bright!
What pleasure can equal, in man's large stock,
The rat-tat-tat of the postman's knock?

4.

Then here's to our friend of St. Martin's le Grand,
   For his arms and his hands Briarean,
With a special cheer for the postman band,
   From the cleanly-shaved, to the hairy-man.
And long may the picture of our good Queen
In years to come on our stamps be seen!

SUSPENSE.

1.

What equals thee for evil, pale Suspense ?
For keen malignity, and torture fell ?
Oh ! 'twould, to virtue, be a hoist immense
    Could we be sure that, in the place call'd Hell,
    Thou canst contrive thy baleful powers shall swell
The endless torment to the souls of men
    Doom'd, for their sins, within its flames to dwell !
    Oh ! if thou can'st, all I can say is, then
I'll not go willingly to that well-lighted den,

2.

But rather roam, a melancholy ghost,
    By Nova Zembla's icebound, dreary shore,
With nought save Northern Lights at which to toast
    My frozen shade ; alone for evermore
    With howl of wolf, and savage white bear's roar
By way of music ; but that desolation
    Would not protect me ; *you'ld* be to the fore,
    To tantalize me with the expectation
That other ghosts *might* come on polar exploration !

3.

When some dear friend lies at the door of death,
    What silent tortures tear the aching heart !
As by the bed, we listen for the breath
    At times near still,—till, with a sudden start,
    It strives again to baffle death's fell dart !
Then, *thou* art near, the troubled mind to rack
    With dread uncertainty's protracted smart,
    Till we are *almost glad* when, on that track,
The spirit takes its flight from whence it ne'er comes back.

4.

Oh ! what is hunger to the empty pain,
    Thy tugging at the heart-strings,—when we watch,
Month after month, for all-refreshing rain,
    And start at midnight with strain'd ear to catch
    Its welcome patter on the dusty thatch ?
A few drops fall ! when, ah ! that gusty wind,
    Veering to south, will surely overmatch
    The " weather-clerk's " intentions to be kind,—
The brooding soft clouds flee, but *thou* art left behind

5.

To jostle Hope ! till, like hermaphrodite,
  It is a mixture hard to be defin'd !
But thou, Suspense, art more than half of it,
  Therefore it needs must be a thing unkind !
  A vulture fell, to prey upon the mind.
As " hope deferr'd " beneath a friendly mask,
  You sickly tortures for your victim find,
  Till, with crush'd heart, he, with despair, doth ask
For Fortune's fellest stroke, and seeks the soothing flask.

6.

I'll write no more ! for *thou*, to all mankind
Art known too well, and hated as a pest,
Almost the greatest that a fate unkind
  Can plant, for torture, in the human breast,
  To kill its peace, and murder sleep and rest.
Not one good word can mortals say for thee,
  Though all do curse thee with a hearty zest !
  And so, farewell ! I would the same to me
Thou could'st for ever say, and absent ever be !

FAME.

1.

FAME hath a trumpet, which, with lungs of brass
  She needs must sound, with future-waking blast,
When strange things happen ; instance, Balaam's ass
  Discoursing Hebrew ! Spartans standing fast
  In old Thermopylæ !—Good Daniel cast
Into the lion's den !—Fair Juno's geese
  As Rome's best sentinels !—and, as time pass'd,
  The gentle Nero fiddling on in peace,
While conflagration vast bade Roman life to cease !

She hath her trumpet, and vast strength of lung,
   But uses both with small discrimination ;
And sounds, when horrid murderer is hung,
   As readily as at the coronation
   Of king or queen of some great thriving nation.
In fact she cannot help herself, but blows
   Her instrument with trifling variation,
   For honour's truest friends, or blackest foes,
Just as a cold-vex'd man, in church, must blow his nose.

3.

But yet we dog her steps, and fain would buy,
   Or beg, or steal a little blast or two ;
Just as tuft-hunting dowager would try
   With royalty to have an interview ;
   Or bankrupt to obtain from cautious Jew,
Or Chr'stian Shylock managing a bank—
   Another trifle on an I.O.U;
   Yet few, indeed, unless of wealth or rank,
Or villainy unique, the jade have cause to thank !

4.

At least in life ;—and after death, why, then
   'Tis very difficult indeed to say,
And therefore more so to describe with pen
   What flattering effects her trumpet's bray
   May have upon the spirit, sad or gay,
That may, perchance, an echo faintly hear
   Belauding it, and its poor house of clay
   In ruins left behind: I rather fear
It would be much preferr'd if not in such arrear.

5.

Yet two complexions hath our loud voiced friend,
   Or rather, patroness ; one dark, one fair,
And as, in chase, your eager way you wend,
   Do you on truth and honour's side declare.
   Then, arm'd with perseverance, bravely dare
Fame's frowning cousin, the dread pale chimera
   Of evil fortune ;—and a kindly blare
. Not loud, perhaps, as evil Fames, but clearer,
Fair Fame may sound for you, while you on earth can hear
   her!

THE SOD OF TURF.

A TRUE STORY.

1.

Green land of Old Erin ! thy sons and thy daughters,
    Where'er they may wander, think ever of thee !
No matter how distant, on earth's spreading quarters,
    Their hearts are still with thee, thou gem of the sea !

2.

And here, to Australia, across the wide ocean,
    Came one, whose affections were tender and true,
Her heart warm and steadfast, her life a devotion
    To stern self-denial, for friends old and new !

3.

And though of a station in life poor and lowly,
    With small earthly treasure, she did what she could
To succour her neighbours ;—and what is more holy
    Than, like our Great Master, to try to do good ?

4.

Long years had departed of mixed joy and sadness,
    When, from the Old Country, news came that a friend
Intended to join them ;—she heard it with gladness,
    And wrote to her kindred a " turf-sod " to send.

5.

For oh ! 'twould remind her, that strange, simple treasure,
    Of scenes of her childhood, in Erin's fair isle !
No jewellery costly, could give such a pleasure
    As that magic mirror, her cares to beguile !

6.

But, as o'er the billows the gallant ship bounded,
    That brought to Australia the turf and the friend,
They laid her to slumber, 'neath mound low and rounded,
    In silent West Terrace, her ashes to blend

7.

With those of the pilgrims departed before her,
    Who came from the country they loved till they died !
A love, that her children have fervently bore her,
    Unmatch'd by e'en that of a man for his bride !

THE MORTAL TO HIS SOUL.

1.

" Oh ! source mysterious of joy and grief,
  Of apprehension, and of hope serene,
That, of thyself, contains the grand belief
  Of deathless being. when the mortal screen
  That now enshrouds thee, shall, beneath the green
And fruitful surface of the earth resume
  Its state of dust, and be a lair unclean
  For crawling worms ;—whilst thou, who know'st no tomb,
Eternal glory find'st, or everlasting gloom.

2.

What art thou ?—Satisfy thyself ! oh ! say,
  (For 'tis thyself that now the question asks,)
Canst thou not give unto the light of day
  That mystery which human wisdom tasks,
  And hath, in times which hoary age now masks
In dim obscurity ? Oh ! find a voice !
  Thou that in sadness sits—in gladness basks,
  And hath a tenement of God's own choice ;
Speak of thyself, I pray, that we may both rejoice."

SOUL.

" Go, study Holy Writ, and read therein
  Of Him who came on Calvary to die ;
With His dear blood, to cleanse me from my sin,
  And make me fit for palaces on high
  To which the saved on angels' pinions fly,
There, in His presence, by His Throne to stay
  For ever, and for ever !—' *What* am I ' ?
  Will *then* be answered. *Here*, have faith and pray
That I may happy be when time shall pass away."

THE GARDEN OF THE MIND.

1.

The infant mind is a garden fair,
  And angels watch as its buds unfold,
For though God planteth his choice seeds there,
  Yet Satan soweth a hundred-fold ;
And his wild rank weeds spring up and blight
The plants so dear to the angels' sight.

2.

With firm strong hand, and with watchful eye,
  Ye parents tend to your gardens' bright,
And the weeds pluck forth, ere the flow'rets die
  And their guardian angels wing their flight
Away, in grief, with averted face,
To the garden's Lord in His heavenly place.

3.

Then strive, oh ! strive your fair plants to tend,
  Till their roots strike deep in the yielding soil,
And then, though tempests of sin may rend,
  And weeds of folly o'erwhelm and spoil,
Like a Phœnix bright, from its ashes they
Shall bloom again on a future day.

THE STORM-WAVE.

1.

Upon Gangetic Delta low
  Night's gloomy mantle falls,
While sleeping Hindoos fear no foe
  Within their bamboo walls ;
Though jackalls' cry, from jungle nigh,
  Like evil spirit calls.

2.

The cocoa-palms, like genii strange,
    Seem watching o'er mankind ;
And through the gloom bright insects range,
    With moths of every kind.
While sugar-canes Æolian strains
    Play to the midnight wind.

3.

Grotesque the horrid idols stand,
    To guard their sleeping slaves ;
But stern Fate laughs, while in his hand,
    His deadly brand he waves.
" Ah ! ah ! ye blocks ! your temple rocks !
    Death now for victims craves ! "

4.

What mighty roar, with thunder voice,
    Is rolling o'er the ground ?
The Storm-wave comes ! and gives no choice
    To flee, or to be drown'd—
Its work is done !—It rushes on !—
    Death reigns supreme around !

LOVE IN A CHURCH.

ONE summer's morning, piously intent,
To Ruthlin Church the pompous Judges went ;
A good example to afford, and hear
A sermon preached in accents mild and clear
By the High Sheriff's learned Chaplain, (who
Glanc'd oft towards that dignitary's pew !)
There sat in state, but with a chasten'd mien,
The legal magnate in his might serene.
On what his thoughts ran I care little—no !
Law and its minions to Hong Kong may go !—
So let him listen, or in slumber lurch,—
My theme is Love conceived and made in church !

A youthful gentleman upon a tour,
That morning sat to hear the sacred lore
In mild persuasion from the lips proceed
Of that disciple of the " High Church " creed
Whose pleasant task was sacred seed to sow
On Judges' souls—where it perchance might grow
Like to the " grain of mustard seed," and form
A goodly tree to brave temptation's storm,
And yield a shade 'neath which each Judge might live
In the calm peace religious faith can give.

It went no further than our hero's ears ;—
For in the pew next to his own appears
A blooming maiden, lacking merely wings
To be an angel ! (If indeed such things
The forms seraphic of the angels' grace)
Our mundane one possess'd a lovely face,
And crinoline a vast expanse,—which well
Became the figure of that peerless belle;
A piquant bonnet added to her charms ;
Her dainty hands, and softly rounded arms
Would fire a sculptor !   Then, her raven hair !
Its shining masses were beyond compare !
The nymph was faultless,—and the hard hit swain
Felt in his soul the pleasurable pain
Infix'd by Cupid's deeply wounding dart
Which now, fresh feather'd, quivered in his heart ;
And working inwards, still the smart enhanc'd
As each fresh glance, the victim more entranc'd !
Loudly his pulse beat,—dizzy grew his brain,—
While his young blood cours'd madly thro' each vein,
Fled from his thoughts were parson, judges,—all
Save she who held his ev'ry sense in thrall !
Swift to her pew he longs at once to fly—
Fall at her feet, and plead with tongue and eye !

He checks the impulse, for on shining wings
A happy thought much comfort to him brings.
A happy thought !—By Jingo ! that will do !
His gilt-edged Bible opens to his view,—
Its rustling pages turn beneath his hand,—
(The reason why, you soon shall understand)
Ah ! there it is ! His eyes now light upon
The second letter of Apostle John,
Verse 5—" And now I do beseech thee Miss,
" (Not that I say a new commandment this,
" For from the first it was, it is,) that we
" Should love each other—that is, you and me "!

With marking pin the passage he impales,
Then leaning o'er the pew's dark polish'd rails,
He gives the book to that enchanting maid
Who takes it from him with expression staid,
While much she wonders,—but her woman's wit
Finds for the riddle a solution fit.
Then in her mind resolving that the youth
Is quite " the *ton*,"—she seeks the Book of Ruth,
Second and tenth, which seems to fit the case—
' Tis this—" Then fell she down upon her face
" And said to him, while bow'd unto the ground,
" Why in thine eyes have I such favour found,
" And I a stranger "?   Here she gave the book
Unto the youth, with hand that slightly shook,
While a bright glance stole from her modest eyes
Like gleam of sunshine thro' soft April skies !
Which made him feel !—ah ! I can scarcely tell,
Though fresh young lovers know the feeling well ;—
Still, though he felt his vital fluid fly
Through every vein like lightning through the sky,
He murmurs—" Yes ! She will be mine indeed !"
Then seeks the third, and last of John with speed,
Which, when he finds he gives unto her view,
And its translation, I present to you—
" To thee I have so many things to write
" That 'twould be better far to meet to-night
" Or after service, so that face to face,
" I then can state, and you can hear my case."
She reads the verse, and gives back just a look,
Keeping in pawn that vastly useful book.
A happy omen in her lover's eyes,—
Heaven opes for him its bright unclouded skies !
That angel fair, intends to be most kind,—
Fear flies the field, and rapture fills his mind.

The Sheriff nods,—the Judges rappee take,
And cough and sneeze to keep themselves awake ;
While wakeful ladies nudge their sleepy spouses
When, dozing off, they warble through their noses.
On a gay butterfly the children's eyes
Are keenly fix'd, as to and fro it flies,—
Lighting at times on artificial flowers,
To flit at last to Nature's scented bowers ;
And all the while, the parson preaches on,—
His text, some verse most likely in St. John.

With learned piety doth he descant,
Exhorts with fervour, tho' he does not rant ;

Brings stores of reference to bear upon
His sermon's subject as he passes on
To all the points from which it can be view'd,
And fill'd with fervour, and with zeal imbued,
His eloquence glides on with steady flow,
Till hungry deacons quite impatient grow,
And muse on *cold* roast fowl and apple pie,
Though on the parson still is fixed each eye.
" Lastly, my brethren "—ah ! the end is near !
The thing most wish'd by almost all I fear
Of his rapt hearers, who at once uprear
Their languid heads, and now all life appear.

Upon the maid our hero steals a glance,
And meets her beaming eye—of course, by chance !
'Tis quick averted, while her brow of snow,
And swan-like neck with brilliant blushes glow.
These, like the lovely tints on landscape bright,
Augment her charms, and crown her swain's delight.

With gentle bang the parson shuts the book,—
Winds up his sermon, and with fervent look,
Implores a blessing on his flock, who now
Their lower'd heads in seeming worship bow:—
That is, they're putting on their gloves, and tying
Their children's hats, who, near with hunger dying,
Are most impatient to vacate their pew,—
So, too, the lady, and her handsome beau ;
At least the last is, tho' I fear I err
About the belle—too well bred she, by far,
To feel impatient in the least degree
To walk and talk with that young handsome he.

The benediction said, with solemn swell
The organ's tones the sacred building fill,—
While the large audience with decent pace
Pass down the aisles, and slowly leave the place.
The poor folks foremost from the portals go,—
To quit their seats their betters are more slow ;
To plume themselves, at first they have deferred:
They scorn e'en here to join the common herd,—
But wait till aisles and porch become more free,
Then leave their seats and sail majestically
Out thro' the porch, to where some dapper page
Attends the side of each gay equipage,—
Then take their seats, the door is bang'd behind,
And 'midst soft cushions at their ease reclined,—
Are straight borne home as if on winged wind !

And now no doubt you think that I shall tell
About the meeting of the beau and belle ;
But there you err.   Some other bard may sing
About the wedding, and that sort of thing.
Tho' I may say, to satisfy your mind,
That blind Dame Fortune for the once was kind,
For the next week the blushing maid was led
Unto the altar, where the vows were said
Which bound them fast (like cats' tails tied together)
With that queer string well known as Hymen's tether,—
When off to Coventry, by way of Chester,
They swiftly drove, with no rude boys to pester
The happy pair for largesse—which no doubt
They would have thrown had urchins been about.
But Welsh policemen kept the rascals back
From playing antics in the chaise's track ;
And chaise and ribands disappear'd behind
A cloud of dust which rose upon the wind.

GOLD.

1.

Of MIGHT untold am I " King Gold " !
    To sway the minds of men ;
For, in my cause, they laugh at laws,
    And stab with sword and pen,
And e'en would charge, for " nugget " large,
    Into Apollyon's den.

2.

From light of day I hide away
    Far down in earth's dark breast ;
But man will dig, and dig, and dig,
    Scarce taking food or rest,
Till on his sight I glimmer bright,
    And yield to be caress'd.

3.

And 'tis right odd, that though a god
    I am to mortal's view,
I buy and sell, and send to —— , well,
    Their fate, a goodly few !
Yet, e'er they burn, I serve their turn
    As servant good and true.

4.

My yellow face is full of grace
    And beauty, loved of all,—
For women smile while I beguile,
    And often work their fall.
Great king and slave,—true men and knave,—
    None can resist my call !

5.

Death stalks abroad ! for gun and sword
    Bear carnage on amain !
To strengthen laws, and freedom's cause,
    The statesman will explain.
For *me*, King Gold, those slain lie cold !
    For *me*, that crimson stain !

6.

Though I am strong to further wrong,
    I make men's hearts to sing ;
For, lacking me, mild charity
    Would be a chilly thing.
But more than all ! for great or small
    I find the " wedding ring."

MEDITATIONS IN A DUST-STORM.

1.

Oh ! —— this filthy dust and scorching wind !
  What aim hath it in blowing day by day ?
Seeks it to drive me with its breath unkind
  (Like some fell demon, with uncanny sway)
  To leave this Satan's hole, and speed away
To smiling fields within the rain-fall line
  Of our great Goyder, who, with just survey,
Could mark the limits of, and well define
  Bold Wapstraw's paradise—the land of wheat and wine ?

2.

Oh ! would there flow'd a fount of " Lager " beer,
  All icy-cold, from sandhill low and wide !
I'd make a shift through whirling dust to steer
  A hasty bee-line to its cheering tide,
  And crouch me down all panting by its side ;
Then strive to turn the streamlet in its course,
  To irrigate with it my parch'd inside ;
And, draining it unto its gushing source,
  Would visibly increase like e'erwhile drouthy horse,

3.

When in the pool his muzzle makes one dive ;
  And, like a thirsty water-spout at sea,
The fluid rises, and he seems to thrive
  Upon his liquid meal amazingly.
And so 'twould fare, I'm very sure, with me ;
But ah ! the rill would quickly choke with sand,
  Which last would blind me till I could not see
To work with judgment, and with steady hand
  To make that amber stream run purling thro' the land.

4.

And so I'll leave off longing, and will try
  To ease my feelings by a word or two,
Mild interjections such as ah ! oh my !
  And stronger ones defined by some as *blue !*
  Of which you may imagine just a few ;
Then, if you blame me for a hearty curse,
  Why, come yourself and in this dust-hole stew
For a few days, and you will utter worse,
  E'en should you tell it not, like me, in sounding verse.

PLANTING THE VINE.

A LEGEND FROM FRANCE.

1.

THE mighty ark on Ararat
For years has rotting lain ;
Its animals released from thrall
Now people hill and plain.

2.

Right merrily the happy birds
Their joyous music sing ;
And flit amid the leafy shade
On variegated wing.

3.

The gaily-painted butterflies
Among the flow'rets roam ;
And bees their pleasant business ply
To stock their woodland home.

4.

While on the stillness of the air
The brooklet's murmurs rise ;
And all is bright and beautiful
Beneath those eastern skies.

5.

E'en where a ghastly frame of bones
Crops from the teeming ground,
The mould'ring monument of wrath
Is with bright verdure bound.

6.

There lithesome lizards sun themselves,
And dart upon their prey ;
While rustling snakes amid the grass
Pursue their stealthy way.

7.

But hark ! glad children's silver tones
Ring upward from that glade,
Where an old man with shrivell'd hands
Is digging with a spade.

8.

His eyes are bright, and shine beneath
　　His shaggy brows of snow ;
His locks are long, his beard hangs down
　　His girdle far below.

9.

A sheepskin hangs about his waist,
　　And suits him to a T ;
It is a modest garment which
　　Just reaches to his knee.

10.

With chaplets green his hoary locks
　　By loving hands are bound ;
Coarse sandals keep his aged feet
　　From off the thorny ground.

11.

His spade by Tubal Cain was made,
　　And is a tool, I ween,
The like of which our gardeners
　　Have very seldom seen.

12.

But still in Cornwall, " under ground,"
　　And in each miner's hovel,
Its very model may be seen—
　　I mean the Cornish shovel.

13.

He wedg'd it now and then with bark
　　He gather'd from the ground,
And hammer'd in with handy stones,
　　But still the blade turn'd round.

14.

The patriarch disgusted grew
　　And cried out " *drat* the thing ;"
When past a bat-like creature flew
　　On noiseless leathern wing.

15.

He did not see the creature pass ;
　　But from a coppice nigh
A band of dusky children ran
　　With wild excited cry !

16.

" O, grandad, there's a " flying fox,
  Just come to eat the fruit !"
But Noah was too busy then
  To care about the brute.

17.

He merely said—" Just get some salt
  To put upon his tail ;
But first time, as I'm thirsty, dears,
  Get me some Adam's ale."

18.

They quickly brought a pumpkin full
  Of clear pellucid water ;
He took it off and wish'd it was
  A pot of Whitbread's porter.

19.

But as there was no inn about,
  Of course he wish'd in vain ;
So delved away and mused upon
  The perish'd race of Cain.

20.

Meanwhile the children with the salt
  Were searching for the bat:
'Twas vanish'd from that blooming glade,
  It must have " smelt a rat."

21.

They hunted in each hollow tree,
  And gazed high in the air,
But could not see where it might be,
  Altho' it was still there.

22.

For it had changed into a cloud
  Of black and threat'ning hue,
From which the thunder bellow'd loud,
  And vivid lightnings flew.

23.

Old Noah cried—" My dears, 'tis time
  We bolted to the sheeling ;
Oh, mercy ! how the lightnings flash,
  And how the thunder's pealing !

24.

But never mind my chickabids,
　　The rain was wanted badly ;
Those cabbage plants I set last night
　　Began to wither sadly.　·

25.

'Twill make the crooked stick take root
　　I've planted in the ground ;
I hope that healthy bud and shoot
　　May soon on it be found."

26.

And now to take old grandad's hand
　　Each dusky urchin tries:
The youngest two the favour gain,
　　And amble by their prize ;

27.

While a young chubby chap of ten
　　In triumph bears the spade,
And like scared hen and chickens then
　　The party leave the glade.

28.

No sooner are they out of sight,
　　Than with electric speed,
Down from the cloud descends to earth
　　An ugly beast indeed.

29.

His hind legs shod with hoofs of brass
　　Sustain a grizzly bear ;
His paws are arm'd with fearful claws,
　　His eyes malignant glare

30.

From out a lion's tangled mane
　　That o'er his visage hangs ;
His tongue lolls redly from his mouth,
　　And his terrific fangs

31.

Would quickly crush a crocodile
　　Into a shapeless pulp ;
And then his throat is wide enough
　　To bolt it at a gulp.

32.

It is a fearsome thing to see,
    Where'er his footsteps light,
The herbage wither instantly
    As from some deadly blight.

33.

But hark! he has a human voice,
    And says with cunning leer,
While looking at the crooked stick,
    "Why, what has he got here?

34.

I ought to know that cutting—yes!
    No! yes! it is," says he,
" A cutting of the jolly vine
    So well-beloved by me

35.

When, up in shining Hesperus,
    I held my lofty state,
Till, by ambition hounded on,
    I rushed unto my fate.

36.

But as those times have gone for aye,
    I'll drive them from my mind,
And think how this delightful tree
    Has got among mankind.

37.

It was not here before the flood;
    I've roam'd the world around,
In torrid and in temperate zone,
    But ne'er the grape vine found,

38.

Not e'en in ' Eden's blooming bowers,'
    Where, as the ' subtile snake,'
I coax'd the comely creature Eve
    That grand mistake to make.

39.

Which since has been the fruitful cause
    Of harvests ripe for me ;
And now, I think, I can contrive
    To make like use of thee !

40.

Come, let me see. Ah ! that will do,
    A splendid thought of mine ;
A faithful ally shalt thou be
    To me, my jolly vine."

41.

But all at once he hears a sound,
    It is a gentle bleat ;
And suddenly he makes a bound,
    The innocent to meet.

42.

Says he " You are the beast I need
    To expedite my plan ;
And so become, my foolish friend,
    An irrigating can ;"

43.

Which said, the frisky innocent
    He seizes in his paws,
And tears its swelling jugular
    With deeply rending claws.

44.

Then pours the ruddy life's blood round
    The vine upon the earth:
So that its juice henceforth might be
    Productive first of mirth

45.

And harmless folly to the man
    Who should one goblet take off,
And make him round a danger play
    When he should quickly make off.

46.

In fact to be a two-legg'd lamb
    In all things save the wool,
And to be anxious with a friend
    To take another pull.

47.

The last drop trickled from the veins,
    Nick throws the lamb away ;
And looks to where among the trees
    A monkey was at play.

48.

Ah! there he is, a monkey small,
  Of very long-tail'd race,
Head down he hangs beneath a limb,
  With wonder in his face ;

49.

He swings a moment and then drops
  Down to a lower bough ;
He views the lamb turn'd into chops,
  And yet he can't tell how.

50.

For tho' we see the enemy
  Of mankind well enough,
Nor lamb nor monkey could perceive
  His outline grim and rough ;

51.

Nor even smell him, tho' 'tis said
  He has a brimstone scent ;
They must have been beneath a spell—
  That's my presentiment.

52.

For down poor puggy comes until
  He gets a dreadful squeeze,
Which causes him to give a yell
  That would your life's blood freeze

53.

If you were wandering at night
  Upon some common drear,
And all at once, from out the gloom,
  It struck your startled ear;

54.

Murder, and every other crime
  You'd swear was being done,
And then with all the speed you had
  You'd very likely run

55.

To help the victim to escape,
  Or else away like winking;
The latter, were you not most brave,
  Would be your course, I'm thinking.

56.

And good cause puggy has to yell ;
　For heedless of his screams,
The evil one his neck twists round,
　And out his life-blood streams,

57.

And saturates once more the earth
　About the fatal vine ;
While Clootie grins from ear to ear,
　And says—" 'Twill answer fine.

58.

For now when man his second bowl
　Of sparkling liquor drains,
He'll feel the lively monkey's blood
　Course quickly through his veins ;

59.

He'll smile and smirk at womankind ;
　He'll practise stupid tricks ;
Wrench knockers off, sing wicked songs ;
　And oft get well-earned kicks

60.

For his tomfoolery ; but now
　More elements I need ;
To make my plan a perfect one
　Some other brutes must bleed."

61.

And as he speaks, a dreadful roar
　Rings through that fertile glade ;
The king of beasts is prowling nigh,
　Intent to make a raid

62.

On Noah's fold at eventide,
　Some fatted beast to slay ;
But ah ! he smells the fresh spilt blood,
　And grimly stalks this way.

63.

He sees the lamb, and crouching low,
　He crawls along the ground,
Then like an arrow from a bow,
　With one tremendous bound

64.

He lights upon the carcasses ;
    But, in a moment more,
His throat is torn, and, from the wound,
    Ensanguin'd torrents pour.

65.

For Satan, fiercer far than he,
    Tears down the savage brute,
And turns the streaming arteries
    Upon the ugly root ;

66.

And soon with grim convulsive throes
    The monster breathes his last ;
And on the lamb and monkey then
    His lifeless corpse is cast.

67.

" Ah ! there's another link complete,
    That fellow's blood will tell ;
'Twill rouse men to pugnacious heat,
    And loose their passions fell ;

68.

For in the middle of the feast
    Hot quarrels shall arise,
And men shall scowl upon their friends,
    With fury in their eyes ;

69.

Their tongues shall loud and bitter taunts
    Against each other fling,
Till blood the insult shall atone,
    And loud the death-shriek ring.

70.

But now, O vine, another beast
    Must on thine altar bleed,
To perfect what I have begun,
    And fit you to my need."

71.

As thus speaks Satan to himself,
    A mud-bespattered pig
Is heard to grunt with glutton glee
    Above a fallen fig.

72.

Then gaily rooting in the ground,
  He revels on some yams ;
When he is clutch'd in Clootie's claws
  As if in some huge clams.

73.

Oh my ! the awful noise he makes,
  As Satan tears his throat!
Far more unearthly are his yells
  Than those of martyr'd goat.

74.

But as he squeals he bleeds amain ;
  This nearly drowns the vine,
And adds the last sad element
  Unto the future wine.

75.

For see, the braggart blusterer
  Has tippled deeper still,
Till like an overgorged pig,
  He can no longer swill

76.

The potent juice, but helplessly
  He grovels on the earth ;
Worse than a pig he senseless lies,
  A butt for ribald mirth ;

77.

Yet seeks again the fatal bowl
  To drown his sense of shame:
Till, by degrees, debased in soul,
  He loses goods and fame.

78.

His friends fall from him one by one
  As from a thing accurs'd:
While hunger, rags, and wretchedness,
  And ever-craving thirst

79.

Cling closely to him in their stead ;
  Till prematurely old,
He sinks, a scorned and blasted thing,
  Into his kindred mould.

M

80.

Then Satan laugh'd with wicked glee,
 And threw the pork away,
Exclaiming—" 'Tis a goodly spell!
 So, Vine, my care repay ;

81.

Take root and flourish,—bring forth fruit.—
 Let men its juice imbibe,
And they shall come to me, as slaves,
 From every race and tribe."

82.

E'en as he spoke he disappear'd
 In elemental war ;
Leaving, upon the rain-soak'd soil,
 Those bloodless bodies four.

83.

Old Noah wondered very much
 Next morning, when he came
To view his vine and cabbage plants,
 At seeing so much game.

84.

I should have said their skins and bones ;
 For, sometime in the night,
The jackalls had been there in packs,
 Above the prey to fight.

85.

Suspiciously he gazed around,
 And scratch'd his aged head,
Concluding it was just as well
 That he had been in bed.

86.

But if he then had some forecast
 Of what his vine would do
In future times, I do not know,
 And so I can't tell you.

MORAL.

87.

And now some small advice I'll give
 At this true tale's suggestion ;
Thus, first of all, enjoy good grapes,—
 They're easy of digestion.

88.

And then their juice, if you'd imbibe,
  Be sure 'tis well fermented,
And has a year or two of age,
  Or you may go demented.

89.

Indeed, instead of toping wine
  In this hot drouthy quarter,
When urged by thirst in summer time,
  Go in for tea, and water.

90.

Don't go to eating-matches, where
  To honour toasts, men guzzle,
And toady one another, till
  They stagger home to puzzle

91.

Their loving spouses, as to if
  They still are men or swine !
But if you do, 'twixt merriment
  And folly draw a line.

92.

Don't wink at other people's wives,—
  Don't knockers wrench from doors,—
Don't beat your friends, or you may find
  The law, like Nick, has claws.

93.

And any project you may try,
  And wish to carry through,
Be sure that Satan in the pie
  Has not a finger too.

TULIP.

1.

Tulip is dead ! a dusky, native flower
   That bloomed—(not scentless !)—in this desert place,
And blush'd unseen in Nature's simple bower
   All unadorn'd—although of ancient race,
That to old Adam and to Eve trace back
A lineage, perhaps not always black !

2.

Who knows ?   I don't—and so will not pursue
   The supposition further, but will state
That though no person ever thought her Jew,
   She ne'er would eat (what Pat would call) the " mate "
Of that queer quadruped with cloven feet,
Which Jews abhor, but Gentiles love to eat !

3.

'Twas rather odd,—this abstinence from bacon,—
   When coupled with a certain ancient rite
Her kin indulge in ; not to be mistaken
   For aught save that which Moses, that meek wight
Upon his son perform'd ;—for which, we're told,
From Zipporah some slight abuse then roll'd.

4.

Which plainly proves that e'en in olden times
   The " better halves " had tongues which glibly wagg'd
As they do still, in hot or frigid climes,
   Unless by fear, or force, unmanly gagg'd !
And Tulip,—well,—at consorts she possess'd,
Could hurl tongue-missiles sharply as the rest !

5.

And yet she was a cheery-hearted soul,
   With " perfect " English to express her mind
In plaintive cadence, or with vicious roll—
   A tidal-wave of phrases of a kind
The most expressive !—but of flavour queer,
Not to be properly repeated here.

6.

And so I'll leave them out, and say that she
   Who own'd the name of plant the Dutch love well,
A native belle, at one time used to be,

Sigh'd after greatly by each dusky swell ;
Till old Tanbelta, as her parent's choice,
Just took her home to grumble, or rejoice !

7.

And fight with Jenny,—who was there before her,
    At his most simple *menage* to preside,—
And who, with jealous rage oft beat and tore her,
    When she would slumber at Tanbelta's side.
But not one-sided was the warfare bitter,
For Tulip was a terrible hard-hitter !

8.

But how both managed to sustain the whacks
    Which flashing waddies rain'd upon each head,—
And left thereon, or rather in, deep cracks,
    Which, like stuck porkers, most profusely bled—
I'll leave you to imagine,—but will say
Their lord looked on quite placid at the fray,

9.

And would the slain have quietly interr'd
    Had an encounter come to fatal end ;
And, from his conduct, it may be inferr'd
    That he'd have got some simple friend to lend,
Or give an extra " rib " to cook his " bardoo,"
And pound her rival's head instead of " nardoo."*

10.

But both had skulls which, like a clout-head nail,
    Seem'd made especially for being hammer'd !
And so, when waddies were of no avail,
    They at each other like two fish-wives clamour'd ;
Until the " gin " of Tura Jemmy died,
Aud he sought Tulip for his second bride.

11.

That is, I, thinking old Tambelta greedy,
    Told Jemmy with the lady to levant ;
When he,—with promptness that was more than speedy,—
    Of Tulip made a very pretty plant !
Which so incensed her grizzled lord more lawful,
That his expressions were (I'm told) most awful !

12.

But as he'd not the very least idea
    Of courts of law, or spicy *crim. con.* cases,
He hunted like a demon for his dear

---

* Meal.   † The seed Burke and Wills lived on.

And her abductor, in all sorts of places.
But by good luck,—and on their part some dodging,—
He found them not in their rude sylvan lodging.

13.

Then, bye-and-bye, his wrath began to cool ;
   As did the love of Jemmy, that black rascal !
The former found he'd made himself a fool—
   The latter, that he'd lately had to task all
His amatory graces, to be pleasant
To his dark flame when no one else was present !

14.

So to society they both returned,
   And went to visit at Tanbelta's wurley.
(To leave their cards our friends had not yet learned,
   And cared not, whether they call'd late or early.)
But I have heard that Jemmy had the grace
To look uneasy when they reach'd the place.

15.

While old Tanbelta wore a sullen air,—
   (Which might mean mischief, Jemmy knew right well
So kept on him his optics !)—while the pair
   Of ladies told whate'er they had to tell ;
For both, quite satisfied with the transaction,
Felt just as loving as an Irish faction !

16.

And with sweet converse whiled the time away
   In gossip, light as that their fairer sisters
At home indulge in on small topics gay—
   Dress, lovers, children, and new social blisters ;—
Which last, although they touch dear friends most keenly,
They, with prim looks, enjoy, Sir, quite serenely.

17.

But as I did not happen to be there,
   And niggers are not gifted short-hand writers,
I cannot reproduce the fun most rare,
   Which then indulged in, those two whilom fighters.
And so I'll just suppose that they, like others,
Convers'd about—some other black gin's brothers !

18.

(Or white ones for that matter,—for they both
   Were not averse unto a fair-skinn'd lover ;
But liked his presents, being nothing loth

To take a blue shirt as a fancy cover,—
A pipe, tobacco, anything in fact,
Of such like luxuries that either lack'd.)

19.

And so that ruction ended ; though Tanbelta
   Would break out sometimes, and want Tulip back ;
When, like a lion lashed into a pelter,
   He roam'd about on Tura Jemmy's track ;
And had he caught him in a state unguarded,
That worthy's " caul " would soon his hide have larded !

20.

But Jemmy, like a weasel, kept one eye
   Wide open, while he with the other slumber'd ;
And though his enemy was very spry,
   His carcase has not this dry soil encumber'd ;
For he, the vagabond, lives to this day,
Although, like me, just slowly turning grey !

21.

And thus flow'd on their sluggish tide of life,
   With Jemmy's jealousy, its only ripples—
Which made him oft-times " pleasant " to his wife ;
   (A jealous man is just like one who tipples,—
He can't get over it when fairly started,
Until by death, from wife or tipple parted !)

22.

And yet 'tis strange how custom can enthrall us,—
   Black, white, or tawny, and of any nation !
Its beck imperative can always call us,
   Like wretched slaves unto their avocation !
And so it fell out that this tyrant haughty,
Led our dark friends to conduct we'd think naughty !

23.

That is, our Tulip by her *pro. tem.* lord,
   Was render'd to Tanbelta's arms and wurley ;
Who then, to show how well his mind was stored
   With notions liberal as well as surly,
Sent Wanna Jenny to the place vacated,
When, for a time, the couples were cross-mated !

24.

But in such action there was nothing strange,
   For all their friends and relatives were doing
The self-same thing along the Flinders Range,—

And which, I told them, they'd be likely rueing.
But they just laughed, and seemed to think me foolish,
And I thought them a great deal worse than mulish.

25.

But times are changeable, and fancies too,
   And so it was with Jemmy, and Tanbelta,
And all the rest of that free-thinking crew
   Who went into adultery helter skelter,—
For just as suddenly as they divided,
Each took his own, and to old grooves subsided.

26.

And then ?   Well then, for physic some enquired ;
   While others should have done, but came not near,
Who much an Esculapius required,
   And left this life for want of one, I fear.
Howe'er, it did but help to clear more quickly
This drought-scourged land, which ne'er was peopled
   thickly.

27.

And after that, I neither saw nor heard
   Of poor old Tulip till the other day.
And only then, that she had been interr'd
   In leafy tomb, as is their simple way.
And so methought I would her story tell,
Which having done, I say to her farewell !

ENVY.

1.

A DEMON dwells within the soul of man—
   A canker'd, mean, and most pernicious thing,
Which, thro' all time, hath been beneath the ban
   Of saint and preacher ; yet, with folded wing,
   Doth to his dwelling-place tenacious cling ;
And with right feeling wages constant strife,
   Instilling poison from his hidden sting,
Till he ascendance gains, and mars the life
Wherein, if not for him, contentment would be rife.

2.

Envy by name, and Protean in shape,
 He is all-present in the human race ;
From torrid zone to Arctic icy cape
 He stirs the soul, and agitates the face
 Of rich and poor, of highborn, and of base.
E'en saint and preacher, more than now and then,
 Feel him within them, wrestling hard with grace,
And hinting, plainly, that *less* pious men
More saintly are proclaim'd by Fame's loud tongue and pen.

3.

The square-jaw'd cracksman, hater of the light,
 (Save when he is not " wanted" by the force),
Is goaded mad by him, when in the night
 He to some city safe doth take his course,
 And finds the little lay a total loss,
Because some brother of the bar and key
 Hath been beforehand to the iron source
Of orgies wild, and many a drunken spree,—
The end and aim of life with wretches such as he.

4.

Unto the highborn beauty, proud and fair,
 He says at court, at opera, and ball,
" The Lady Lily has a skin more fair,
 A smaller hand, a finer Eastern shawl,
 Or nobler suitors at her beck and call,
That still more costly is her jewel case,
 That royal eyes on her more gracious fall,"
That Lord knows what about her form and face
Is more replete with style, with beauty, or with grace !

5.

The beggar-woman, with her pair of twins,
 Which she hath borrow'd for her daily round,
Incited by *his* whisper, soon begins
 To hate the rival who, perchance, has found
 A pair more sickly ! and whose voices sound
With weaker treble on the kindly ear
 Of soft Benevolence, which wanders round,
With hand in pocket, and with ready tear,
To give the starving bread,—which oft means gin and beer !

6.

The Queen upon her throne—but halt, my muse !
 If you are loyal, you had better stop,

And 'mongst some lower caste examples choose,
 Where you will find a quite sufficient crop
 To harvest from, e'er you the subject drop.
So take the cats'-meat man, whose piercing cry
 Lures cats from basement and from chimney top ;
And watch him well before the tripe-shop nigh,
And you will see the fiend run riot in his eye.

7.

The general, resistless in the field,
 Thank'd by his country, and with riches blest,
E'en *he* unto the demon oft doth yield,
 On seeing some gay soldier more caress'd,
 Though with no medal on his blithe young breast ;
But whom the eye of beauty loves to scan,
 As down life's stream he glides with youthful zest ;
Yet, with the strange perversity of man,
Longs for the other's state, e'en with his life's short span.

8.

The rich man envies honest Hodge his health,
 His sturdy offspring, and his appetite.
Hodge in return, begrudging him his wealth,
 Laughs in his sleeve at his sad gouty plight,
 And says, " The glutton oaf ! it serves him right !"
But why go on ?   No preaching e'er will stay
 The livid demon's ever active spite ;
Though, in conclusion, I, my friends, would say,
Scotch him whene'er you can, but to him ne'er give way.

9.

And if at times persistently he try
 To prove that God has been unjust to you,
Just search your own affairs with quiet eye,
 And all the fortunes of your life review,
 And you may find them of a brighter hue
Than you had thought.   Now, let the envied state
 Be analysed, and you will see how few
Its real blessings, though of gold its plate ;
For pomp and pride oft kill the pleasures of the great.

RICHES.

PHILOSOPHERS and Saints may sneer
At " filthy lucre" gathered here ;
 Just let them say their say.
But watch them well, and you *may* see
Them selfish to the last degree,
 In Life's parts each may play.
For saints and sinners clutch at pelf,
 And pouch it if they can,
For love of gain, and love of self
 Are wedded fast in man !
   O Money ! 'tis funny
   How love of thee can sway ;
    Till Death's dart, with fell smart
   Drives it, and Life away !

For Money, winsome maidens sell
Themselves to Age ; and often dwell
 In misery and sin.
And bosom friends, when interests clash,
Of enmity soon feel the lash,
 Their inmost souls within.
While gallant men, in aught beside,
 For it their honour fling !
For rough-shod o'er us it can ride,
 And conquer Conscience's sting.
   Tho' cash, sirs, is trash, sirs,
    How strong are golden chains,
   To gag us, and drag us
   To grovel in our gains !

Yet it is good, bright gold to win,
In Life's stern battle's press and din,
 As store to have at hand
To form a potent barricade
'Gainst fell Misfortune's force, array'd
 In haggard sullen band ;
And, as we march along through life,
 To have our mite to give,
And, shunning avaricious strife,
 To let our neighbour live.
   Then earn ye ! nor spurn ye
    The yellow shining store ;
   But air it, and share it,
    With Merit at your door !

THE AUSTRALIAN MAGPIE'S SONG.

LIST, list to my musical song with delight,
As I hail the bright advent of dawn,
When bashful Aurora comes robed in soft light,
And smiles on the day newly born;
While Echo, who lurks in each shadowy dell,
Repeats the sweet bars of my musical swell!

Or better, when Phœbe, the queen of the night,
Floods valleys and hill with her rays,
My vespers I warble from gum-tree's tall height,
And Nature seems sooth'd by my lays;
While Echo, who lurks in each shadowy dell,
Repeats the sweet bars of my musical swell!

No rival have I in this land of the free,
Whose music with mine can compare;
And lovers at eventide oft list to me,
When wattle-bloom scents the wild air;
While Echo, who lurks in each shadowy dell,
Repeats the sweet bars of my musical swell!

SELF-RELIANCE.

MARCH on! march on! thou mortal bold,
In the van of life be thou enroll'd,
And breathe thou, aye, defiance
To Fate—whose darts shall blunted be
On stubborn armour worn by thee,
Of sturdy " Self-Reliance."

March on! march on! with courage high,
With manful heart and stedfast eye,
And charge, with cheer like thunder,
Misfortune's legions! whose array,
With gloomy banners, bar thy way,
And fain would bear thee under.

March on! march on! with Hope to lead,
And Faith to aid in time of need,
And Fortune's steep rock clamber.
And should'st thou fall upon the way,
Like a man in harness, pass away
To Death's calm realms of slumber.

SONG OF THE DRINK DEMON.

Ha, ha! Ha, ha! with a loud guffaw,
  I laugh at my slaves as they throng to me.
'Tis little *I* care for right and law,
  'Tis *they* who go to the gallows-tree;
While, stalking forth in the glare of day,
I set my snares by the Queen's highway.

They come! They come! and they have no fears
  As I lure them on with my sparkling bait,
To the fatal bowl that they fancy cheers
  Their foolish hearts, as they tempt their fate;
For the yawning gulf of ruin lies
At their very feet,—but I blind their eyes.

They come! They come! and they sip and sip,
  Strong men with caution, fair women by stealth;
Soon laid aside—for the thirsty lip
  Heeds not in its greed fair fame or health.
Good angels seek to save in vain—
Oh, I herd them soon in my ghastly train!

They come! They come! and my fangs sink deep
  In their very souls, while my poison creeps
Through heart and brain, as they near the steep
  And treacherous brink; while Friendship weeps
The headlong, downward rush to see
Of my wretched serfs to their misery.

They come! They come! though wise men warn,—
  Though their parents beg, or their children weep.
"Drink! drink!" I cry;—and with stupid scorn
  They laugh at fate, as they downward leap,
To the dismal, dark, unfathomed slough,
Where reigns foul Want, with its sin-scarr'd brow.

Ha, ha! Ha, ha! could they know at first
  How a living death 'neath my tempting lies,
At Nature's fount would they quench their thirst,
  And turn from me with abhorrent eyes.
But no, they list to my jovial laugh.
And slay their souls as my bowls they quaff.

Ha, ha! Ha, ha! what a throng of ills,
  Like a jackall pack, on my steps attend
Their maws to sate, as my poison kills,
  And with countless pangs my dupes to rend,—
Till oft they rush, with a red right hand,
To the Judgment Seat, from my soul-stained band.

SISTERS OF MERCY.

In quiet village, busy town,
  Through our adopted land,
True women, garbed in russet brown,
Seek hopefully a heavenly crown
  At their Great Master's hand.

For sorrow and for misery
  They search with anxious care ;
No sinners vile they hurry by
With cruel scorn or frowning eye,
  But help their woes to bear.

With pleasant words, with loving hearts,
  They do their Master's will ;
With gentle hands they soothe the smarts
Of fell disease's rankling darts
  That but for them would kill.

With steady faith they onward go
  With wretchedness to cope ;
The orphan's pain, the widow's woe,
Are softened by their ready flow
  Of charity and hope.

No trumpet blast with flourish loud
  They sound to tell their worth ;
But quietly amidst the crowd
They meekly glide, with visage bowed
  To do His work on earth.

Then honour show them everywhere
  (Whate'er your creed or birth),
These gentle souls, whose kindly care
Both innocent and wicked share—
  Angels are they of earth.

SOUTH AUSTRALIA.

AIR—" THE ENGLISHMAN."

THERE's a land of fast-increasing fame,
    Though so lately a savage spot;
Its healthful clime the palm can claim,
    And who shall say it can not.
For the balmy winds through thickets blow,
    Where wattles shed perfume,
No grim Ice King, in his robe of snow,
    Its winter shrouds in gloom.
'Tis a bright sunny land, deny it who can,
And the home of a South Australian man!

There's waving wheat on hill and plain,
    Fair homesteads in each dell,
Where the husbandman can his living gain,
    And in peaceful comfort dwell.
For his children play beneath the vine
    And fig-tree's chequered shade,
When at noon he drinks his cup of wine
    From the grapes of his vineyard made.
'Tis a fair fruitful land, deny it who can,
And the home of a South Australian man!

There are countless flocks of world-fam'd sheep
    On her spreading inland plains;
And cattle roam o'er each hill-side steep,
    Where his steed the bold stockman reins.
And the squatter dwells by the winding creek,
    Which the grand old gum-trees shade.
O! never in vain need the stranger seek
    For a meal, but is welcome made.
For 'tis freedom's land, deny it who can,
And the home of a South Australian man!

There's gleaming gold in each torrent's bed,
    There are mines in the earth below,
Where the miner well may earn his bread
    If he works with a steady blow.
Then her shipping sails to every land,
    And rich products bear away;
While wealth flows back to the hardy band
    That has come to her shores to stay.
'Tis a prosperous land, deny it who can,
And the home of a South Australian man!

THE TALE OF A TERRIBLE TRAP.

1.

AWAY to the northward of famed Port Augusta—
For commerce, for beauty, and lastly for dust, a
Nice place, quite unequall'd ; and where merchants trust a
    Great deal to,—they don't care a fig who 'tis—
Stretch (ridged well with sandhills), the plains yclept
    " Western,"
From which, in the summer, the tourist had best turn,
Unless he would view a place (really at best, stern),
    When dry as a bald mummy's wig it is.

2.

They are girt to the westward by that immense cesspool
Call'd grandly " Lake Torrens," but which is a messpool
As black, when you're in it, as many a less pool
    Which oft has a pestilence started ;
Black, sticky as bird-lime, with saltest salt water,
Excell'd not, in that line, in any salt quarter ;
Not even by that where Eve's back-looking daughter
    In the shape of a salt-pillar parted

3.

From Lot, her good man, when he ran from Gomorrah
And Sodom.   But she, looking backward in sorrow,
Became a salt statue ! and he, on the morrow,
    Bewailed her—(I hope with sincerity).
Again to the eastward—a lofty range hinders
The outward-bound view, and is named after Flinders ;
(Some say not volcanic, although we find cinders
    Quite near it, and slag to a verity—

4.

And so my premises were 'gainst their geology,
For which I must humbly now tend an apology,
As no doubt my notion arose from parology—
    An old crater, " the Pound," to be thinking);
But 'tis not a nice place, for I've been to the top of it,
Where granite abounds,—yea, a very fine crop of it,—
But water, in summer, there is not a drop of it,
    Save quite at the bottom, for drinking.

5.

Yet not about there is the scene of my story,
But far in the sandhills, where, all in its glory,
A dense scrub is growing in rotten sand, pory
    And useless for ought except woolspoiling.

But where a few squatters, with trials unceasing,
Strove steadily on, some with fortunes increasing
Till '64's drought took, with runs they were leasing,
    The whole of the fruits of their long toiling.

6.

Then the plains, like the rest of the North, were deserted,
Which, as well as the squatters, their foes disconcerted—
In fact the most bitter, and those who most hurt did,
    Then went in for lessee encouraging.
The squatters brought back their few jumbucks remaining,
When they, in strange quarters, heard how it was raining
Upon that parched land, after years of refraining ;—
    They glad were, indeed, to leave foraging.

7.

Then they dug out the huts and the stockyards and wells again
From red glaring sand-drifts ; and working bulls' bells again
Tinkled at night on the hills and in dells again,
    While wild dogs the sheep again worried.
For though all the rodents, except the tall " Coodla,"*
And banded rock-wallabies, up on Nooroodla,†
Were all past recalling from long lack of food—*la*
    Dingo et fils, still their coats curried.

8.

And were, and are still, as jolly as sandboys
(Whatever that means—I expect though, not grand boys,
But tatterdemallion young organ or band boys,—
    And they are what dingoes are jolly as),
And as mischievous too—that I know to my sorrow ;
And so I invested (I don't care to borrow)
In sundry steel traps, which were set on the morrow
    To teach a few dingoes what folly was.

9.

But now come with me to Lake Torrens' border,—
A wild, lonely place, where thick scrub is the order
Dame Nature insists upon, much as disorder
    Like measles, she sows on man's cuticle !
Where soft, lofty sandhills run closely together,
And spines *will* intrude, till you scarcely know whether
You won't have to take to twin garments of leather,
    When prickles or mulga sticks, you tickle !

---

* Kangaroo.   † Native name for Mount Eyre.

N

10.

The sun is declining, but still brightly shining,
When, hark ! by that black oak, what can it be whining ?
(Or rather, what can *they*, for I am opining
    'Tis made by two singular creatures.)
But just as I'm speaking, a curious squeaking
Joins in like a chorus ; so let us be seeking
The gifted performers ! Ah ! see, 'tis two sneaking
    Sleek dingoes, with lupuline features.

11.

And there, on the sandy soil sprawling, quite handy,
A clutch of fine puppies crawl, blunt-nosed and bandy,
Around a large lizard, which once was a dandy!
    (Perhaps far too gay for a sauri 'n.)
But now 'tis affecting to see them dissecting
The poor defunct " Berdua," his scales not protecting
His inward format'on from those now inspecting
    It well, by the method Cæsarian.

12.

And the students themselves, loving brothers and sisters,
Sweet tempers are showing, as if they had blisters
On some tender places ; for though they're not fisters,
    They worry each other delightfully ;
But maybe 'tis only a thirsting for knowledge
Which makes them so eager in that sylvan college
To study minutely in this their " dog's doll-age,"
    The creature they fight for so spitefully.

13.

But there is another not happy,—the mother—
Who glares at her master, as though she could smother
Or finish his breathing by some means or other.
    What has he been doing, I wonder ?
From swift glances flying—not what they are saying—
I rather suspect that he well deserves flaying !
Most likely from virtue's stern path some slight straying
    Has happen'd, his mate's love to sunder !

14.

Or else, without reason, she's horribly jealous ;
But still, I don't think so, for he is too zealous
In that rural mansion, or rather rude dell-house,
    To get in, once more, her good graces.
Through pond he wants dragging ! for see how he's wagging—
His great bushy tail, while she's shrewishly nagging.
Why, he won't even hint that she well deserves gagging.
    Yes, guilt in his rascally face is !

15.

Yet somehow or other there's something about him
A deal to his credit, although we so doubt him.
He's keeping his temper, howe'er she may flout him,
    And then he's so jaunty and festive ;
Besides, he don't linger to glance once behind him,
But looks as if Lupie might not quickly find him ;
For off on his travels, with no one to mind him,
    He goes from his helpmate so restive.

16.

Who, dropping her tail and her bristles together,
Returns to her litter, in doubt as to whether
Her Frisky may ever come back to her tether ;
    Perhaps she was *just* a bit hasty !
But she, and her puppies, as *we* can't well drown them,
We'll leave with a longing that fortune may crown them
With gunshot or strychnine ere summer shall brown them !
    How Chang *would* enjoy them in pasty !

17.

The shrubs are all wet from a sunshiny shower,
And so he's avoiding each rain-laden bower,
For his fine yellow coat like a buttercup's flower,
    When driest, he thinks the most dandy.
So, over the sand-hills. quite merrily tripping,
Our dingo speeds on through the bushes all dripping,
Just thinking of lambkins, which ought to be skipping
    About on the tank-sides quite handy.

18.

But never a lambkin is there about playing,
Or anything else that our friend may be slaying ;
No weakly young calf or a nanny-goat straying ;
    The wild is a wilderness—silent !
But little that troubles our frolicsome dingo,
Who would, I believe, scarcely notice a pingo,*
For, ah ! by a fence there is something, by jingo !
    At which he gives what's for a smile meant.

19.

Yes, there, 'twixt the wires, two bright eyes are shining
Above a slim mouth, most delightfully whining,
(At least, to our masculine dingo's opining,
    And he is a judge of ability.)
Two velvetty ears, cocking forward quite knowingly,
A lithe slender body which wiggles quite flowingly,
At which our friend Frisky twists his about wooingly,
    And capers to show his agility.

*Ant-eater.

20.

But here I must say that, with sorrow and sadness,
I view the false Frisky's expressions of gladness.
His *sposa* at home ! why, it really is badness
    Quite counter to Honor's commanding !
But ears when not hearing, and eyes when not seeing
Are never offended,—and so in his spreeing,
With this soothing maxim is always agreeing
    Our dingo of fine understanding !

21.

And so his cold nose to the nose of the stranger
He lovingly thrusts, not imagining danger
In the shape of a trap, newly set by the ranger—
    Where his tail marks a circle's diameter !
A terrible trap, with a newly-oil'd trigger,
And terrible jaws, which would hold a wild nigger,
Or leave him at best but a one-legged figure,
    Or what my friend Pat calls " a lameter."

22.

A bold rakish leer, he just gives, and a wriggle,
To which I'm afraid she returns a light giggle,
Which makes our bad Frisky his thick brush to wiggle—
    A motion in prudence most wanting !
For just when it popped on the sand so delusive,
The trigger is sprung (an event not conducive
To poor Frisky's fun) and an ending conclusive
    Is put to his wild galavanting.

23.

With sharp yells resounding, whose echoes rebounding
Quick startle the parrots from Mulga's surround ng,
He bites at the vile trap his tail now impounding,
    And even would bite his Delilah !
But the terrible snap which the trap made when closing,
Gave her nerves such a shock, she required composing ;
And now a dim vista is rapidly closing,
    On the tail of that faithless young smiler.

24.

Oh ! why had his thoughts from his fair Lupulina
E'er wandered a moment ?—ah ! would that he'd been a
Poor exile like " Nap." on the famed St. Helena,
    So his tail were well out of its trouble !
But then 'tis a strong one, as well as a long one ;
And that terrible trap, why, it just is the wrong one
To let go its hold, even should it have wrong done ;
    And so there's an end to the bubble

25.

Of hope, which at first might poor Frisky be cheering !
Its teeth, tho' so strong, are too blunt to be tearing
His fine furry tail—and then, as for his clearing
Its great ruthless jaws now so firmly adhering—
    The springs are too strong for such action ;
So, howling and springing, and on the ground flinging
His sand-besoil'd body is nought towards bringing
Himself from the troublesome trap to him clinging ;
    Oh ! he is approaching distraction !

26.

And he tries to bolt off, but his tail gives due warning
His tether's length reach'd, which he cannot be scorning ;
Oh ! nought can he now do by scheming or fawning—
    The trap has a grip inexorable !
He raves and he swears in a dingo's wild fashion
When in a cold fright or a boiling hot passion ;
But the trap is of steel, *sans* all fear or compassion,
    And he's in a state most deplorable.

27.

But, ah ! there's a beaming of comfort still gleaming—
Not so hard is his fate as it look'd at first seeming,
And Frisk *may* escape yet, by means of some scheming,
    For of hide is his torment's tough tether ;
And his teeth—that the steel has left broken and bleeding—
Are still in condition for biting and feeding—
And now gnaw a spring which, by slipping, is leading
    Them down to the "makings of leather."

28.

But, then, how would leather and hide put together
Resist Frisky's grinders ?   Who thinks as to whether
He won't leave where his tail is exposed to the weather,
    Like Æsop's famed fox in the fable !
And soon his fierce snapping results not in gapping,
But severs the hide with its strong double lapping,
When gaining his freedom, at least from the strapping,
    He once more for running is able.

29.

He gives one lithe bound like fresh uncoupled hound,
And the trap—a vile incubus—springs from the ground,
While his shadow about there no longer is found,
    He is off like the hunt of St. Hubert.
Don't talk of a cur with an ending of *kettle !*
None ever ran yet with the half of Frisk's mettle,
For he is, no doubt, in a fine racing fettle,
    And could with a good coursing few spurt.

30.

A great greedy shark giving chase to a sailor—
A harpoon just stuck in a whale by a whaler—
A needle, point upward, sat down on by tailor—
    Are things to produce locomotion.
And so are fierce tigers let loose from menageries,
Or pompous policeman when after a cadger he's
Running like winking, till he, like a badger, is
    Quite blown out with wrath and swift motion.

31.

But what are they all to the trap on Frisk's narrative?
He flashes like light, or hot water through narrow sieve!
Oh! dear, what a pace! sure for long it can never live,
    Unless he's possessed of a devil!
O'er plain and o'er sandhill, how scrubby no matter,
He races top-speed, just as mad as a hatter;
The trap bounding after with bump, thump, and clatter.
    Nought could touch him at all on the level!

32.

But now, by sad chance, not at all of his seeking,
He makes a bee line for his puppies all squeaking,
Where poor Lupulina, who feels rather peeking,
    Is listlessly strolling quite near 'em.
And like a chain-shot through the startled air flashing,
Or typhoon of hardware thro' tulip-bed crashing,
The engine and Frisk of five pups made a hashing
    Ere Lupe from their passage can clear 'em!

33.

(A loss! by-the-bye, man! for no mutton-pie man
Is there to convert them to "pies" in his high can,
Or turn them to sausages—"German"—by sly plan.)
    Frisk now is *not* careful of trifles!
Lupe gives him one glance, full of anger and sorrow,
Then thinks of the wigging she'll give him to-morrow!
And wonders where he that fell fury could borrow!
    But he's off like pea-bullets from rifles!

34.

Oh, on, speeds poor Frisky, on errand so risky,
Demolishing bushes the Cornish call "kiskee,"*
And next knocking over a "boomer" quite frisky,
    But never delaying to worry him.
Through a large flock of sheep, and without even biting them,
And almost too fast to be even affrighting them,
He leaves them to wonder why he is thus slighting them,
    And to fancy that something *must* flurry him.

---

* Decayed.

35.

On, on, and still on, with a motion unceasing,
By night and by day and with haste still increasing,
Thro' sunshine and storm ; and e'en death there's no peace in,
    For he keeps up a gallop eternal.
Yea, on, and still on, tho' defunct, Frisk's careering,
His looks as time passes becoming less cheering ;
For bones thro' his once glossy skin are appearing,—
    He presents an appearance infernal.

36.

And I have no doubt that his skeleton ghastly
Will race on wild nights, and will frighten folk vastly—
The rusty trap clinging, of course, to his " lastly."
    Oh ! they'll think him a ghostly hyena !
And their fears his proportions will so magnify
As he hurtles along 'neath the thunder-vex'd sky,
That I fancy the more superstitious will fly
    From the wild woods of Wallelberdina !

37.
MORAL.

Now, Benedicts all, when you leave your fond spouses,
Don't visit queer friends at their shady town houses,
And where (ungrammatic'ly speaking) such rows is,
    Or you'll know what a *trap* is, that's certain !
And do not go leering at servant girls pretty.
Whatever their names be—Jane, Martha, or Kitty—
Unless you would find yourselves objects of pity,
    And also of lectures called " curtain !"

38.

And so from poor Frisky's sad story take warning,
And do not this fine moral lesson be scorning,
Or sometime or other you'll understand pawning—
    Or maybe, *too well*, do some writing—
For though Frisky's friend *did* so suddenly vanish,
You might attain some not so easy to banish,
Whose "clinging affection," far stronger than clanish,
    Your whole after-life might be blighting.

39.

Not to speak of the time when your dim earthly taper
Expires, and yourself on the Styx bank must vapour
(I mean your vex'd shade,) which with many a caper
    Will try to gain Charon's attention.
But he'll only pole on with his craft leaking badly
(In which, ne'ertheless, you would stow yourself gladly,)
And leave you behind him to think over sadly
    Those sins which I cannot here mention.

40.

And you, married ladies,—to men so superior,—
Don't make for your husbands too hot the interior
Of cottage or mansion if once they are beery, or
    But look at the fair who so try men ;
For though even-tempered they are when first starting,
And love you sincerely, if always they're smarting
'Neath nagging so senseless, some day they'll be parting
    The ties both of love and of Hymen !

41.

And, my readers, remember, each *pater* and *mater*
Such misgovern'd doings will, sooner or later
Incite to like action the cubs in your crater !
    (The children, I mean, in your nursery.)
So, both for the sake of yourselves and your darlings,
Just keep from their ears, if you can, all your snarlings ;
Or else, when they leave your hot nest, like young starlings,
    You'll look, and they'll look, when you meet awry !

THE GAMBLER'S LAST STAKE.

Another throw ! I'll try just one more throw !
  Double or quits ! No ? But I will, I say !
You do not want my cash ? Then why say "no,"
    And talk to me about " the breaking day ?"
    You only fear the notes will fly away
From your swoll'n pockets back to me again ;
  Or, should I lose it, that I cannot pay—
Just *one* more throw ! " Refusal gives you pain ?"
Then, give me one more chance my money to regain

The same old luck ! Damnation seize the dice !
  The devil of his children takes good care !—
Here is my I.O.U. And now a slice
    Of your good fortune I must claim to share.
    We'll try a dozen more—don't leave your chair !
You would not let *me* quit when I would go
  Home quietly last night, and I declare
You shan't go now, till we the dozen throw !
Follow your go, I say !—What ? do you still say no ?

" Some other time" you'll give me my revenge ?
   Then why not now ;   My luck is out, you say ?
What matters that to you ?   You feel no twinge
   Of sorrow for the losses that this day
   Will make me homeless !   But I will away
To those I've ruined !—How my temples throb !
   Curs'd be the cards, the fatal dice, and they
Who by their aid have just conspired to rob
   Me, and through me the helpless ones that pray
   In vain at home for him who thus can them betray !

     *   *   *   *   *   *

Upon my brow the morning's cold wind blows,
   But cools it not,—a fierce fire burns within
That sears my brain !—but here the river flows,
   And with a sullen murmur, tempts me in
   To hide 'neath its dark waters all my sin,
My shame, and vain regrets—yet I'm afraid
   Of *that* which I by this last cast may win—
Yes !—I *must* face the ruin I have made,
By folly hurried on,—which now I can't evade !

How shall I meet my wife and children dear,
   Who love me so ?   What story shall I tell
To break to them their future prospects drear ?
   While vain regrets within my breast must dwell,
   And form therein a gnawing, earthly hell
Unquenchable ! But ah ! here is my home.
   My home ?—which *was* and still might so remain
But for those tempters, and my passion fell
   For play's excitement,—that insidious bane
   Which has destroyed the peace I ne'er may know again !

FINIS.

CONTENTS.

No.		PAGE.
1.—THE LAST VOYAGE OF THE LONDON	... ...	4
2.—THE CALL OF DEATH	...	32
3.—THE BUSHMAN'S REVERIE...	...	35
4.—CHRISTMAS, 1876	...	39
5.—A BUSHMAN'S ADDRESS TO THE MORNING STAR	...	40
6.—THE DINGOES	...	42
7.—THE THUNDERSTORM	...	79
8.—A DINGOE HUNT	...	82
9.—BLOWING BUBBLES	...	91
10.—THE FLOOD	...	92
11.—NO FRIENDSHIP IN BUSINESS	...	98
12.—AN ECHO	...	98
13.—THE FOURTH OF JANUARY, 1864	...	99
14.—A DREAM OF THE DROUGHT, 1865 ...	...	102
15.—THE LIFE OF A WORKING BULLOCK ...	...	106
16.—THE DEATH-BLOW...	...	109
17.—A FISHY LEGEND OF DORSETSHIRE ...	...	110
18.—LYRES AND LIARS	...	112
19.—GOOD ADVICE	...	113
20.—SLOTH	...	114
21.—TO A BLOW-FLY	...	115
22.—"GO TO THE ANT, THOU SLUGGARD" ...	...	115
23.—THE NATURALIST AND ICHNEUMON FLY ...	...	116
24.—THE VILLAIN AND THE HERO	...	117
25.—STUPID PETER	...	117
26.—SONG OF THE FAR NORTH MAIL	...	118
27.—BURNING OF THE COSPATRICK	...	121
28.—MOODS OF THE OCEAN	...	131
29.—IN MEMORIAM	...	131
30.—LOST	...	132
31.—TIME	...	139

No.						PAGE.
32.—THE GUM-TREE	...	...	...	...	...	140
33.—110 DEGREES IN THE SHADE		...	...	...		141
34.—THE MYSTERY OF LIFE	...	...	...	...		143
35.—THE FLYING DUTCHMAN	...	...	...	...		145
36.—THE HUNT OF GOLD	...	...	...	...		153
37.—LEAP-YEAR		...	...	...	...	154
38.—TOT AND BESSIE	...	...	...	...		155
39.—LINES ON THE DEATH OF A MUCH RESPECTED LADY						156
40.—DEPARTED FRIENDS		...	...	...	...	156
41.—SONG OF THE NEWSPAPER	...		...	...	...	157
42.—THE POST-OFFICE	...	...	...	...	...	158
43.—SUSPENSE	...	...	...	...	...	159
44.—FAME	...	...	...	...	...	160
45.—THE SOD OF TURF	...	...	...	...	...	162
46.—THE MORTAL TO HIS SOUL		...	...	...		163
47.—THE GARDEN OF THE MIND		...	...	...		164
48.—THE STORM-WAVE	...	...	...	...	...	164
49.—LOVE IN A CHURCH		...	...	...	...	165
50.—GOLD	...	...	...	...	...	169
51.—MEDITATIONS IN A DUST-STORM	...		...	...		171
52.—PLANTING THE VINE		...	...	...	...	172
53.—TULIP	...	...	...	...	...	184
54.—ENVY	...	...	...	...	...	188
55.—RICHES	...	...	...	...	...	191
56.—THE AUSTRALIAN MAGPIE'S SONG			...	...		192
57.—SELF-RELIANCE	...	...	...	...		192
58.—SONG OF THE DRINK DEMON		...	...	...		193
59.—SISTERS OF MERCY		...	...	...	...	194
60.—SOUTH AUSTRALIA		...	...	...	...	195
61.—THE TALE OF A TERRIBLE TRAP	...		...	...		196
62.—THE GAMBLER'S LAST STAKE		...	...	...		204

FREARSON & BRO., PRINTERS AND PUBLISHERS, ADELAIDE.